To Les

interference

KAY HONEYMAN

ARTHUR A. LEVINE BOOKS
An Imprint of Scholastic Inc.

Library of Congress Cataloging-in-Publication Data

Names: Honeyman, Kay, author.
Title: Interference / Kay Honeyman.
Description: New York : Arthur A. Levine Books, an imprint of Scholastic
    Inc., 2016. | Summary: Kate Hamilton is a congressman's daughter, used to
    the world of Washington politics, but after some pictures of her cause a mild
    scandal, she finds herself exiled to her aunt's West Texas farm and animal
    shelter, in the district where her father is planning to run for office — and
    then she discovers that politics in a small town can be even nastier than
    Washington, especially when it involves the local high school football team.
Identifiers: LCCN 2016009345 | ISBN 9780545812320 (hardcover : alk. paper)
Subjects: LCSH: Photography — Juvenile fiction. | Political campaigns — Texas,
    West — Juvenile fiction. | School sports — Texas, West — Juvenile fiction. |
    High schools — Texas, West — Juvenile fiction. | Animal shelters — Juvenile
    fiction. | Families — Juvenile fiction. | Texas, West — Juvenile fiction. |
    CYAC: Photography — Fiction. | Politics, Practical — Fiction. |
    Elections — Fiction. | Football — Fiction. | High schools — Fiction. | Animal
    shelters — Fiction. | Family life — Fiction. | Texas — Fiction.
Classification: LCC PZ7.H7473 In 2016 | DDC 813.6 [Fic] — dc23 LC record
available at https://lccn.loc.gov/2016009345

10 9 8 7 6 5 4 3 2 1   16 17 18 19 20
Printed in the U.S.A. 23
First edition, October 2016
Book design by Yaffa Jaskoll

chapter one

I dropped three bottled waters and a bag of potato chips on the counter between the cashier and the girl who was yelling at him.

"Most boyfriends take their girlfriends out once in awhile."

The cashier picked up his phone and checked the screen. "We go out."

"I need to pay for these," I said.

"We've been dating three months, and we've gone out twice," the girl snapped.

"I don't have money," the cashier said.

"I have money. To pay for these." I pushed the bottles closer.

"You had enough money to go to Lubbock with your cousin last weekend."

I looked out the window. Mom was still in the passenger seat, digging through her purse. Dad was pumping gas. I didn't have much time. "I'm kind of in a hurry."

"It's not like I don't have options," she continued. "Gabe called the whole time you were out of town."

The cashier started scanning my items. "Next time, tell him I say hi."

The girl balled her fists. Her purse smacked against the candy rack, sending packages flying as she spun and stormed out the door.

The guy didn't flinch. "Anything else?" he asked me, pulling a plastic bag from under the counter.

"I need to use your phone."

"Sorry. No pay phone. There's one at the gas station two exits east."

I smiled. "No. I need to use *your* phone."

The guy tipped his chin to the right, an early sign that he was going to say no.

"It's an emergency," I added.

"You're calm for someone who is in the middle of an emergency."

"I'm very good in a crisis."

He crossed his arms over his chest. "You're not using my phone."

Refusals were tricky to undo, but not impossible. "Fine, we'll go a different direction." I leaned over the counter and locked my eyes with his. "You're going to let me use your phone because someday your girlfriend will be stranded in some nowhere town and need to tell you something life-changing." His eyes remained empty. "The test results came in." Nothing. "She found your dog."

"Tucker?" the cashier said.

Bingo. "She needs to call you to tell you that Tucker is okay. She wants you to know where to pick him up. Wouldn't you want someone to loan her a phone?"

"Is *your* dog in trouble?" the cashier asked.

I looked over my shoulder. I needed to move this along before I got caught. "My cheating ex-boyfriend posted humiliating pictures of me online. My school hates me. My parents blame me for Dad's nosedive in the polls. And my college future is in the toilet."

"Man, what a week. And now your dog." He slid his phone to me.

I skipped the gratitude and dialed Tasha's number.

"Hello?"

"Hey, it's Kate." I moved toward the back of the store.

"I've been trying to call you. Is your phone dead?" It sounded like Tasha was at the coffee shop just across from the school. I could hear the clatter of plates and the hiss of the espresso machine.

"No, just held hostage."

"So I guess you're still in trouble?"

"I'm in Texas," I said.

"Wow, when your parents punish you, they really go all out."

"It's not punishment. It's protection, according to them. We're lying low while the scandal blows over."

"That may be sooner than you think. The board and the principal made a decision yesterday."

"That was fast," I said.

"They're trying to get ahead of the bad press."

The cashier eyed me suspiciously. I turned my back on him and slipped behind a display of chips. "So we won?"

Tasha hesitated. "Kind of."

"What do you mean, kind of? Don't tell me there are more pictures on the website. My dad is going to lose it."

"No. Pictures are still down. The board decided that the principal will write three letters of recommendation. One for the most school service hours."

"That has to be you."

"Dances don't plan themselves," Tasha said. "The second letter goes to the student with the highest GPA."

"Fair," I said.

"And the third goes to the person with the most volunteer hours."

"To help the school with the bad press. Smart. This all sounds like a win."

"Well, you know that the student council secretary keeps up with everyone's volunteer hours."

"David Tressler, who has been in love with you since freshman year."

"Right. So I asked myself, what would Kate do?"

"I would try to get a peek at the hours," I said.

"Exactly. That's the kind-of part." I could hear the breath Tasha took before she broke the news. "Parker's in the lead."

My grip on the cashier's phone tightened. "He's never volunteered a day in his life! I should know. I dated him for a year. Well, almost a year. He was too busy to volunteer. You know, with all the lying and cheating."

"Apparently, before Parker moved to DC, he spent the summer building houses in Juárez."

"And they believe that?" My voice echoed through the store.

"You okay?" the clerk called.

I smiled and gave him a wave.

"It's still a win," Tasha said.

"It's not a win until he pays for what he did," I said.

"Remember why we did all this. The school news articles, the calls to the press, the research," Tasha said. "It wasn't for revenge. It was to make the system more fair."

The bell above the door rang. "Sure, but Parker already hacked the new system," I said.

4

"Kate," Dad called from the door of the store.

"Got to go." I hung up the phone and grabbed a giant bag of potato chips to hold in front of it. "Just getting a snack, Dad."

I put the bag and the phone on the counter. The guy started to scan in silence. Dad strolled over. "This your phone?" he said to the cashier.

I gave the guy a look and shook my head. For a moment, one sliver of time, I thought I had gotten away with it.

The cashier nodded. "She needed to make a call to save her dog."

"The empathy angle. Not bad." Dad picked up the phone and tapped the screen until he found the call history. "A DC number? Kate?"

"Your dog got all the way to Washington, DC?" the cashier said. "That is some dog."

"We don't have a dog," Dad said.

I bit my lip. "I was speaking metaphorically."

"So the dog is okay?"

"The dog is fine," Dad said. "Kate, you can go back to the car. I'll pay this gentleman and we'll be on our way."

When I walked into the dry air that choked West Texas, I spotted the cashier's girlfriend leaning against a stack of propane tanks. As I started past her, she wiped her hand across her eyes. I paused and walked over to her. "Look, it's none of my business, but I don't think he's worth crying over," I said.

The girl's shoulders dropped. "You don't know him."

"He doesn't take you on dates. He didn't take you to Lubbock. He's not worried you'll get lost and need to call someone. He'll probably just string you along until he cheats on you with some snotty ambassador's daughter." I leaned against the wall next to the girl.

"I don't think Jesse knows any ambassadors—"

"He certainly doesn't deserve a year of your life. Almost a year. And you know what he really doesn't deserve? An amazing college recommendation."

"Are we still talking about my boyfriend?"

"No, I guess not." I took a deep breath. "Still, that guy doesn't deserve the two minutes you gave him in there."

She hiked up her purse. "You're right. So, what do I do?"

"You said it yourself. You've got other options."

"Yeah." Her back straightened. "There's Gabe."

"At the same time," I said, "the idea of a boyfriend is usually a lot less trouble than the actual boyfriend."

The girl nodded slowly. "You're right."

The bell on the door rang as Dad pushed it open. "And don't forget to vote next Tuesday," he said into the shop. "Got to love democracy." He let the glass door close behind him.

I followed Dad.

The girl called after me, "Hey, I hope that guy you dated gets what he deserves."

"He will," I said.

"What was that?" Dad asked as we walked to the car.

"I was trying to help."

"Last time you tried to help—"

"I know. I almost got kicked out of school, the donors dried up, and you dropped ten points in the polls." I snatched the bag of chips from Dad's bag. "I don't see why we had to leave DC. I didn't do anything wrong."

Dad opened the door for me, then slid into the front seat, handing Mom a water bottle. "Appearance is reality," he said. "Besides, we're not running away from anything. We're running toward opportunity."

"I thought you said appearance is reality," I said.

"Very funny," Dad replied.

As we drove, I raised my camera to my eye and framed a graveyard, then a series of collapsing houses landscaped with tires and metal buckets making a final stop on their journey to the dump. Those melted into another line of houses, these with peeling paint but trimmed hedges, followed by a series of small churches painted white, with bell towers squatting over the broad doorways. The scenes were charming enough, in a conventional small-town sort of way.

"Dad, can you slow down?" I said, looking through the lens of my camera again.

He glanced in the rearview mirror. "Are you still working on that photography project?"

Portfolio. It was a photography *portfolio,* the kind I needed to get into a decent fine arts school. Especially now that Parker had stolen my recommendation. That's what I wanted to say. But I forced the corners of my mouth into a smile. "Yep."

Mom patted at the faint shadows under her eyes, then closed the mirror on the car's visor as Dad sped by a line of tumbleweeds pressed up against a fence. I had thought Texas would be prettier. In fact, I counted on it being prettier—large red barns, oversized flags whipping in the wind, fields of wildflowers, a few horses. I planned to spend the next two months diversifying a portfolio that "lacked soul," according to my art teacher, Ms. Prescott.

When she said this, I told her that soul was overrated. She assured me that admissions committees felt differently. I said that "soul" was subjective, that some people might see soul in my photographs. She said that some people see Jesus in potato chips, but those people aren't professors at top-tier art schools. I asked if she could be sure of that. Ms. Prescott said her office hours were over.

But if my pictures needed to sprout legs and dance when the admission committees opened my portfolio, I'd find a way to make it happen. That might be easier than uncovering some beauty in this landscape of spidery tree limbs and washed-out colors. An earthy smell gripped the air.

"Why does Texas stink?" I asked, leaning back against the seat.

Dad's eyes met mine. "Shall we review the talking points again?"

I shook my head. "No, I wasn't saying—"

His phone rang. Three pairs of eyes jerked to the cup holder where it rested. Dad's hand moved automatically to answer it before gripping the steering wheel again, his knuckles white.

"I've been doing this since I was five," I said. "I'm not actually going to tell people that Texas stinks." I turned to Mom. "Tell Dad that I would never say that."

"Your father is returning to his roots," Mom said.

Dad nodded. "The family is slowing down the pace of life and focusing on what's important."

I watched a cloud of dust dance at the base of a telephone pole. "Who is going to ask these questions? Isn't that the point of this extended vacation? To escape the questions?"

"Kate," Dad prompted. "What are the Hamiltons doing in Texas?"

The phone stopped ringing. The silence grew heavier. I used to be able to parrot what my parents said, but lately the words stuck in my throat.

"Having a ready answer keeps you from saying something you'll regret," Dad said.

Like the truth.

When it came to college recommendations, Principal Strickland's were legendary. One got Brian Lucas into Stanford despite that prank with the donkeys on his permanent record. Another got Amber McKinley into Columbia, even after an anxiety attack made her pass out during her interview.

But in a school full of the daughters of congressmen and sons of senators, people's agendas could easily get tangled. The most valuable commodity in DC is power, and I quickly figured out that only the best-connected students got the principal's recommendations. Tasha didn't have power like that—her dad owned a car service company—but she deserved a recommendation.

It would have been a perfect plan without the backlash. I made a quick call to the *Washington Post*. The resulting cover story turned into a round of headlines and talk-show punch lines, then a flurry of meetings at school and rewritten policies to make things right. Tasha would get the recommendation she deserved. Win.

But Camille lost her letter of recommendation, and Camille had never lost anything that her father's diplomatic immunity didn't cover. She barely had to bat her dark brown eyes at Parker to get him on her side. But instead of just breaking up with me, he cheated on me for most of October. I'm usually better at reading people, but Parker was really committed to the role of loyal boyfriend. I had pictures of him smiling behind the camera to prove it. I just didn't realize he was taking so many of *me*.

Then his photos started showing up on the school website. Most made me look drunk. Some made me look mean. But what pushed Mom and Dad into this three-day, five-state road trip was that the pictures made *them* look bad, like they were neglectful parents. Part of me wished that for once they'd spent some of their political capital to defend me. I imagined Dad storming into Principal Strickland's office to say that the system was wrong and the school was lucky to have someone like me who would fix it. I imagined Mom "accidentally" dumping tea on the woman in her book group who implied I was lucky to be with Parker. Instead, we packed up and drove to Texas.

There was another truth. Even before the pictures appeared, Dad was down fifteen points in his bid for reelection to North Carolina's Ninth Congressional District.

Dad always said that campaigns were like riding wild horses. You tried to control them but didn't expect to. A candidate's best bet was just to hold on for the ride. But in what should have been an easy trot back to the House seat he'd held for twelve years, Dad dropped the reins. He'd let quotes in the press go unanswered and missed opportunities to sling dirt on his opponent, a fresh-faced thirtysomething who had popped out of the political woodwork. He'd allowed emotions to leak onto his face and into his voice. One night in late October, just before the first pictures appeared on the website, I'd heard his campaign manager in our DC house, yelling words like "impossible" and "delusional." Dad had shouted his own two words back: "You're fired." Firing a campaign manager three weeks before the November general election when you were double digits behind an opponent . . . Dad didn't just drop the reins; he set fire to the horses.

Now he was stepping down to save face. "Family business," the press release said. Politics *was* our family business, so the excuse was truer than usual. We'd had an unspoken agreement since we'd left DC: I wouldn't bring up his mess and he wouldn't bring up mine.

"Okay, but there really is a smell," I said. "Something . . ." *Disgusting? Putrid?* ". . . strange." Outside my car window, gas stations crept by on one side of the road while railroad tracks lined the other. These gave way to one-story storefronts, their windows painted with foot-high red letters that proclaimed RED DIRT #1.

Dad took a deep breath. "That's the smell of money. Oil money. Welcome to Red Dirt."

We passed a one-story building picketed with bright political signs. Then Dad's phone started to ring again. He set his jaw, glanced at the campaign signs, applied the brakes, and started to turn into the parking lot.

"Why are we stopping?" I asked. "Aren't we almost to Aunt Celia's house?"

"I'm dropping off some paperwork." Dad shook his head. "And start referring to it as *our* house," he said. "We need to establish ourselves here."

"Why? We're only staying two months."

He pulled into a space. "And that two months can get us back on track or further off, depending on how we use it. We better get our feet on the ground."

I leaned forward between the seats. "This sounds like a campaign. I don't mean to bring up bad news, but we're not campaigning, remember? You're lying low for now."

"I'm lying low in North Carolina," Dad said. "This isn't North Carolina. I want to get a feel for the political waters." He stared at the brown building with a hungry look.

"Why would you care about the political waters?" I asked.

"I *always* care about the political waters. Especially in my hometown."

I reached for the door. Politics was probably like any other addiction—there would be relapses. It seemed harmless to let Dad get one last fix. The next round of congressional elections wouldn't be for two years, so unless he planned to run in a local election in Charlotte after the bad press died down, I was free from campaigning for the first time I could remember.

I stepped out of the car and stretched, giving Mom the opportunity to do a full scan of my outfit—a sweatshirt, sweatpants, and flip-flops. Her eyes lingered on the chipped polish somewhat covering my toenails. She looked at my father, and a whole conversation passed in their glance. "Why don't you just stay in the car, Kate?" Her voice dripped with her usual sweetness, which was a half pitch too high to be real.

"It's not like Dad is running for anything," I said.

"I don't think this is what you want people's first impressions of you to be."

"You people really have no idea how to take a break," I said.

"You heard your father. He's not taking a break. He's getting back on track. You could do with some of that yourself," Mom said.

Back on track? How was I supposed to get back on track when I was out in Texas while Parker pretended to be some do-gooder?

Wait. That was it. If I couldn't get good pictures in Texas, I could use the two months to volunteer. I spotted the red light blinking on my phone. If they left me in the car, I could call Tasha. "Okay, I'll stay in the car."

Dad raised an eyebrow. I'd made the shift too quickly. My mind searched for the right words. "You wanted me to be more cooperative," I said.

He nodded, pulled his jacket from the backseat, and closed the door. He fell for a classic Hamilton maneuver—people usually believe you when you're saying exactly what they want to hear.

I watched Mom and Dad disappear into the building before scrambling for my phone.

I called Tasha. "How many hours ahead of me is Parker?"

"About a hundred and twenty. Do you have a plan?"

"If Parker's hours transferred from Juárez, mine will transfer from Red Dirt. I'm going to rack up as many volunteer hours as I can over the next few months."

"How long are you in Texas?"

"Until Dad can show his face in DC again. Maybe two months."

"You're leaving me alone without a best friend for two months. What am I supposed to do?"

"Try to keep Parker away from children's hospitals and food banks."

The front door of the building opened, and I slumped down in my seat, letting the car door hide my phone. But instead of Mom and Dad, two people my age came out. The guy said something,

13

and the girl smiled and gently punched his arm. They looked like a good match. "You could go after that secret crush you won't tell me about," I said.

"I don't have a secret crush."

"You've been leaving lunch early for the past two weeks, which means you're trying to get to English class early. You're never early. Who is it? Derek Whittler?"

"No, I got over him months ago."

"Hudson Mann?"

"You know I'm not telling you."

"Adam Benson?"

"If I tell you—"

"It will never happen. I know. Your ridiculous superstition."

"It's not ridiculous. It's a fact. If I tell anyone who my crush is, it never works out."

"Fine. I'm just saying my absence will give you more time for Mystery Man."

"I do need someone to take me to the movies while you're out of town," Tasha said.

The girl's blonde ponytail swung behind her as she handed the guy a stack of books. *Books*. I sat up straighter and scanned the building for a sign.

RED DIRT LIBRARY. Just what I needed—an underfunded mecca of volunteer opportunities.

"I'm taking Mom's advice and getting back on track. I'll call you later." I jammed the phone into the front pocket of my sweat-shirt and stepped out of the car.

chapter two

I pushed through the double doors of the library. Dad's warm meet-and-greet voice floated from one direction, so I turned the other way.

Haphazard stacks of books lay around the room. The corners of posters peeled away from the walls, revealing lines of dried tape. Squares of faded construction paper dangled from bulletin boards. I smiled. There was plenty of work here. I just had to find the right person to ask.

Two men in black shirts and jeans sat with newspapers resting in their laps. Their eyes swept over me, then slid to a woman in an oversized floral top and cropped khakis. Wavy white hair billowed from her head. She pushed a pair of bright red glasses farther up the bridge of her nose and studied a stack of papers.

She would make an interesting portrait photograph, I thought—the lines on her face, the folds around her eyes. But I never took portraits, no matter how complex the light and shadows. As soon as people saw a camera, they leaned closer to the person next to them, tilted their chin forward and down, and settled their hair over their shoulders. And then there wasn't a hint of real left. I had dozens of pictures of Parker, and not one of them showed him as a heartless jerk. Pictures are about what the photographer sees. And I'd been blind when it came to Parker.

The woman passed books from a cart to the city of piles that littered the desk. I pasted a Hamilton campaign smile across my face and strolled toward her. "Hi, I'm Kate."

The woman looked up, her glasses slipping to the tip of her nose. "Can I help you?"

"I'm new in town and looking for ways to get involved."

"I'll just bet you are." The words dripped sticky sweet from her tongue.

I hesitated, then tried brightening my smile. Maybe getting to the point would help. "I'd like to talk to you about volunteering." I waited for a wave of gratitude to wash over her face. "There are a lot of ways I could help around here."

"Help, huh? Maybe make it a little nicer?"

Something in the exchange remained just out of my reach. "Absolutely." I nodded and widened my eyes.

"A little more like the library over in Junction."

I'd never seen the Junction library, but the best way to get people to trust you was to mirror their words and expressions. "Sure. There's no reason this place can't be just as nice as the library in Junction."

The librarian leaned forward and tapped her fingers on the counter. "If you *are* actually new here, you might be interested in last year's yearbook."

Actually new? "That would be great," I said, dialing the voltage on my smile up a notch.

She kept me pinned with her stare as she pulled a large, thin red-and-black book from behind the desk. As I reached for it, she picked up the phone and punched a few numbers. "Bo, it's Caroline Fisher. Can you come up here? . . . Yeah, I think I found the person we're looking for." That sounded promising. She hung up, put her hands on her hips, and let the full weight of her gaze hang over me. Her red lips pressed together. "With Red Dirt playing Junction this week, I'm going to have a parade of mischief-makers wiggling their way in here trying to stir up trouble."

A murmur of agreement came from the two men reading newspapers. We had an audience.

"I don't like hoodlums coming into my library."

"Right, no hoodlums," I said, nodding my head again.

The librarian yanked the yearbook from my hand and opened it to a page covered with pictures of guys in football jerseys. Someone had scratched "LOSER" over each face.

"Terrible," I said, hoping my face broadcasted sympathy and competence. "What do you need me to do?"

"What do I need *you* to do?" she asked incredulously.

Just as I was about to offer to research security cameras, a guy my age strolled in the door. He wore faded jeans and a gray T-shirt that pulled against the muscles across his chest. "Hey, Mrs. Fisher. You look nice today. You have those books?" He flashed her a grin, going the obvious route of mediocre charm and blatant flattery. "I'm in kind of a hurry."

"Trouble with your mom?"

The guy's head jerked slightly. "No, the doc's cow."

A warm smile spread reluctantly over the librarian's face. She put the yearbook down and turned to collect a stack of books on the back counter. "I got the financial aid books you needed, Hunter. I'm still looking for a couple of the test prep books."

"Actually, Hunter, I'm in a hurry too," I said. I needed to get back to the car before Mom and Dad returned. I turned back to

Mrs. Fisher. "If you just want to tell me when I can start, we can figure out the details later."

"Did you get that one I couldn't find?" Hunter asked Mrs. Fisher, stepping around me.

She pushed the stack of books toward him. "I called the librarian at College Station and they sent it over. I thought I put it with the others."

Hunter flipped through the books at a relaxed pace. "Do you mind if I check?"

"You make sure what you need is in there. I want you to have everything you need for your college applications," Mrs. Fisher said.

Mom and Dad would be back any minute. I put my hand on top of the stack, forcing Hunter to look at me. "Excuse me. We're having a conversation."

He raised an eyebrow. "This will just take a second."

"I'm trying to volunteer here."

"That's generous of you," he said. One side of his mouth twitched with what might be amusement.

"I'll deal with you in a moment," Mrs. Fisher said to me.

I buried my irritation behind a sympathetic smile. "You're clearly overworked. I'd love to help out."

She lifted her petite frame and put her hands on her hips. "I'll tell you what you can do for me," she said.

Finally.

"You can take your skinny butt back to Junction and tell that second-rate quarterback of yours with slow feet and a peashooter of an arm that he can't beat the Red Dirt Raiders by sending his girlfriend in here to mess with my books."

I took a step back. My mouth dropped open.

"You must think I'm an idiot," the woman said, pressing her lips together.

"Can I get my books now, or are you still talking?" Hunter asked innocently.

My face turned red as I struggled to unclench my jaw. Only the image of reviewing talking points again kept my lips zipped. Then a man wearing jeans, a plaid shirt, a tan cowboy hat, and black boots filled the doorframe. There was something very familiar about him. It wasn't his features; I had never seen his face before. It was the way he scraped his glance over the room, looking for who mattered. When he saw Hunter, a smug look of satisfaction took over his face. "So you're the vandal," the man said to him. "Can't say I'm surprised."

Hunter didn't flinch under his stare, but he didn't defend himself either.

"No, Bo. This is the girl," Mrs. Fisher said, pointing to me.

"Are you with the police?" I asked.

"Mr. Stone is the booster club president," Mrs. Fisher said. "And I think we all know who you are, Kate . . ."

My stomach dropped.

". . . Conner."

"Kate Conner? I'm Kate Hamilton."

If I had thought about it for a split second, I would have realized that this was not the best time to introduce myself. The corners of Mr. Stone's lips turned down. He and Mrs. Fisher exchanged glances. "Jeff Hamilton's daughter?" Mr. Stone asked.

I nodded.

A smile broke across Mrs. Fisher's face—a real smile. "Jeff Hamilton, quarterback of the 1987 Red Dirt Raiders state champs? Jeff Hamilton, who could drop a fifty-yard pass over the shoulder of a receiver who's triple covered?"

"It's nice that you remember me, Caroline," Dad said from the door. "I see you met my daughter."

"I thought you were staying in the car," Mom said, moving to stand beside me. Her cheeks twitched a little from the strain of smiling.

Bo Stone's face hardened. He took a step forward. "What are you doing here?"

"At the library?" Dad's smile stiffened. "Saying hi to some old friends."

Bo's chest rose and fell. I'd seen it thousands of times before—Dad's ease burning beneath the surface of an opponent's skin. "No, what are you doing in Red Dirt?"

"We're slowing things down to take care of a little family business," Dad said.

Mrs. Fisher scurried around the counter and wrapped Dad in an enthusiastic hug. "Well, it's great to have you home."

"You here to run for Haynes's seat?" Bo Stone demanded.

Dad broke his stare and glanced at the wall behind Bo. "Who's Haynes?" I asked.

Mom shook her head, but Mrs. Fisher was happy to share. "He represented the Red Dirt congressional district after your grandfather retired. He died three weeks ago."

That lined up eerily with Dad firing his campaign manager.

"It was a lovely funeral, even if it was in Nettleton," Mrs. Fisher continued.

"Now his seat's open," Bo said. "The governor called a special election to fill it before Congress is back in session at the beginning of the year." He frowned at Dad. "But I'm bettin' you already knew that."

"You can't be serious." I looked from Mom to Dad.

"It sure would be nice to have someone who knew the district and had Washington experience. Someone like that could hit the ground running," Dad said, the weight of his steady gaze returned to Bo.

My shoulders collapsed. "You are serious. All that talk about how I messed up, and we're not here because of me. You're here to campaign."

"You don't live here," Bo said.

"I've owned a house in this district for over a decade. I was raised here. My father and grandfather represented the district for over half a century." He looked at the chunky ring on Bo's finger. "I believe I brought a state championship back here once. Unless that doesn't matter to anyone anymore."

Bo poked his finger at Dad. "You're full of crap. Always were. Had to watch where I was stepping half the time in high school."

"Would have been safer if you weren't always hanging on my coattails." Dad's voice stayed cool.

Bo's face turned red. "I wasn't hanging on to your coattails; I was covering your ass."

Mrs. Fisher twisted her hands. "Now, Bo, that's no way to talk to an old friend."

Bo continued, "If you're thinking of taking that seat, you can just tow your hide back to DC. I'll meet you there once I'm elected."

"*You* are running?" Dad said, stuffing his fists into the pockets of his pants.

"I've been waiting for years to run," Bo said.

Dad took a step forward and glared at Bo. "You know that's my family seat. The Hamiltons have been in that seat for two generations."

This was it. The end of my break.

"I haven't seen anyone in your family around here for a while," Bo shot back.

"I've been in Congress. What have you been doing since high school?" Dad said coolly.

"I've been *here*."

Dad opened his mouth to reply, then shut it. He reached out to shake Mrs. Fisher's hand. "Nice to see you, Caroline. We'll catch up soon."

"Of course," Mrs. Fisher said, her hands fluttering with excitement. She pushed the yearbook into my hands. "Take this. It may help you get your bearings."

"I'm going to need more than a yearbook for that," I muttered.

chapter three

"Why didn't you tell me that we were here to campaign?" I asked once we were in the car.

"It wasn't supposed to be official yet," Dad said.

"It sounded official enough when you found out about the opponent," I said.

"I wanted to lie low until I got my staff organized. Your stunt ruined that." Dad rubbed his face, then stared out the front windshield. "Bo is going to make this look as bad as he can."

"It was thoughtless to leave the car, Kate," Mom said.

"And reckless," Dad added. "This is exactly what I was talking about, the same problem you had in DC. You've got to learn not to stick your nose where it doesn't belong. This is not the time for you to start acting like a teenager."

"Maybe your consultants didn't tell you this, but I *am* a teenager."

"No, you're the daughter of a congressman and a candidate." He looked at me over his shoulder. "This is my best shot at getting back my family's seat. We can't make stupid moves."

"How can you blame me for this? No one told me that we were campaigning."

"We're always campaigning," Dad said as we backed out of the parking lot. He kneaded the wheel and stared at the road.

That might have been the truest thing he'd said in a long time. "Why don't they just wait to fill the seat during the next round of local elections?" I asked.

"People deserve representation, Kate," Mom said.

I frowned. "What's the real reason?"

Dad sighed. "The party put pressure on the governor to call a special election and get someone there when the congressional session starts in January. The votes are tight in the House for a few key bills that party leaders want to push through. This is a locked seat, so they need a party voter sitting in it. Election in four weeks. Runoff in another three. Only a person with a lot of experience running and organizing campaigns has a shot. The field will be wide open because most people can't pull a campaign together this quickly. There will be challengers in two years, but that gives me plenty of time to establish myself and defend my seat."

"Your seat is in Charlotte," I pointed out.

"Not anymore." Mom put a hand on his shoulder.

"We didn't bring anything. Campaign staff? Clothes?"

"Most of the staff arrives in the next few days. I'm calling Frank tonight to send a manager. The rest of our things come tomorrow."

Dad pulled into a long driveway that stretched toward a two-story house and stopped. "We all want to go back to our lives in DC, agreed?" He turned and looked at me.

"Agreed," I said.

"So there's no reason to argue. No scenes, no blowups. No taking on causes or changing the system."

"Fine," I said, crossing my arms.

"What were you doing in the library?" Dad asked.

"Volunteering."

Dad's shoulders relaxed. "Great. I'll talk to Caroline tomorrow. It's a good way to integrate yourself into the community."

I tightened my hands into fists and pressed them into the seat next to me. "No thanks." I didn't want another piece of my life tied to Dad's campaign strategy, but I also didn't want Parker to get that recommendation. Not everything can be win-win.

We pulled up to the house. Wood planks lined the sides, their white paint covered in a layer of dust. A few blades of dry grass struggled to survive, but low shrubs with tangled limbs had taken over most of the yard.

A quiet sigh escaped Mom's throat. "Where's Celia?" she asked.

"She's probably at the shelter," Dad said.

"Shelter, like animal shelter?" I asked.

"Yeah, Celia inherited the back acreage while I got the house. She runs her animal shelter on it. It's one of the reasons I kept the property all these years. Who knew her halfway house for misfit animals would pay off one day?"

A shelter was also an opportunity to rack up volunteer hours day and night. For once, Dad and I were on the same page. "I'm going to check it out."

Mom and Dad looked at each other, then Mom turned to me. "Fine," she said. "Don't be gone too long. We have to unpack."

The land rolled out behind the house. A trailer sat under one of the sickly looking trees poking up from the horizon. Its door swung open and a figure strode down a dirt path toward a barn. I walked across the cracked earth toward it.

A haze of dust and animal fur softened the corners of the dilapidated fences and lean-tos that made up the shelter. Two goats milled along a path paved with white rocks, and a few small pigs curled around a plastic pool whose blue had faded to white. Horses munched oats from buckets tied to a fence.

I caught up to the person at the door of the barn. "Aunt Celia?" I said. She was a tall, thin woman with Dad's long legs, brown hair, and focused eyes. I tucked my hair behind my ears to keep it from flying into my mouth and pasted on my best smile.

Aunt Celia swept her eyes over me. "You got here quick. I wasn't expecting you for a couple of hours. Where are your parents?"

"Getting settled."

She leaned back, one hand resting on her hip. "I know I'm supposed to say things like 'Welcome' and 'Make yourself at home,' but I'm a little too busy for pleasantries." She turned and walked away.

I had to move fast. I knew nothing about Aunt Celia other than that she was Dad's sister. I had pale memories of awkward phone calls and scattered birthday and Christmas gifts. We'd come to Red Dirt a few times when my grandparents were alive, but my grandmother died when I was four, my grandfather two years later. The party line on the house and land in Red Dirt was always "Aunt Celia is taking care of it." That made it difficult to find something that would convince her to take me on as a volunteer. I decided I would start with flattery.

I caught up to her again when she stopped in front of a bale of hay. "This shelter is amazing, Aunt Celia. I can't believe you run this yourself."

"It's a dump. The whole place is falling apart," she said, kicking a bucket out of her path.

I veered another direction. "Maybe I could help out."

She didn't even glance at me.

I decided to try the family angle. "It will give us a chance to get to know each other."

Aunt Celia picked up an armful of hay and loaded it into a faded wheelbarrow. I followed her. I'd run out of political approaches, so I tried honesty. "I need community service hours to get a college recommendation."

"All right." Aunt Celia pulled a pair of yellow rubber gloves from her back pocket and held them out to me. "Can you start now?"

I took the gloves, feeling a burst of victory. Even in politics, the truth worked, when applied at the right time in the right way. "So, what do you need me to do? Sweep up, call a carpenter?"

"Birth a calf," she threw out.

I froze on the threshold to the barn. Had I heard her correctly? Was this some West Texas lingo? I turned the corner into a stall where Aunt Celia knelt next to a cow laying on her side. She patted her gently. My throat tightened and I swayed a little, until I put my hand on one of the worn beams holding up the roof.

The cow moaned and stumbled to her feet, only to fall again. Aunt Celia looked around the barn. "Sorry, Dolly. I wish you were in a cleaner stall."

"Or at the vet," I suggested. "I can make a call." I pulled out my phone.

"I am the vet," Aunt Celia said, moving to the backside of the cow.

My chest tightened. "Is this the *only* thing you have for me to do?"

"Bring some of the straw from that corner. Put it where the calf will fall, then lay a blanket over it." She pointed to a spot very close to the backside of the cow. We were definitely talking about an actual cow birth. I took a deep breath and looked over at the pile of hay. It seemed harmless enough. I gathered an armful of straw, trying to blink the dust out of my eye. When I looked at Aunt Celia again, she was sticking her hand in the backside of the cow!

"What are you doing?" I asked, horrified.

"Trying to figure out what's wrong." Her brows furrowed as she continued to grope around inside the cow. "He's facing forward, but something's stuck."

"Seems like you have everything under control," I said, taking three quick steps toward the door, the hay still in my arms.

"Kate, do you need the hours or not?" Aunt Celia looked over her shoulder at me, the challenge in every line of her pressed lips.

I needed the hours, so I dropped the hay behind the cow, pushed my sleeves up, and pulled on my gloves. They reached past my elbow. The smell of hay and blood and animal flesh made me dizzy. I took a breath and knelt beside her.

"I have to get some rope. I worked the legs forward as far as I could, but she's still not coming. Put your hands here, hold the legs, and don't move." She pulled one of my hands to where hers had been. There was a slimy film on the cow. I could feel its warmth under my gloves as I closed my fingers around what Aunt Celia said were the legs of the calf. My eyes started to water and my nose itched, but my hands were buried halfway to the elbow in cow. I turned my head away and held my breath.

"Kate, if you can't do it, just say so now. You let go of the legs and that hoof can do some real damage to the uterine walls. It was enough trouble getting the calf this far. I don't want to leave and have you quit on me."

I sat up straighter and shook my head, blinking away the water in my eyes. "I don't quit."

Aunt Celia gave me a small nod. "Fine. Don't move. Do you understand?"

The cow jerked and then settled again on her side. I set my mouth in a determined line and nodded.

Aunt Celia got up and walked out. I was alone in the barn, my hands inside a cow. Fluids pushed at the edges of the gloves. My stomach flipped and twisted. I leaned my torso back, turning away slightly. The muscles in my legs tensed and my foot started to wiggle. The cow moaned, and only the strictest self-control kept my hands rooted inside it.

This is just temporary, I told myself. *When I'm in a fabulous art school and Parker is pushing lattes at Starbucks, this will all be worth it.*

The cow moaned again and tried to raise her head. "Listen, don't die," I said to her in a shaky voice. "We want the same thing, you and me. We both want this to be over. Win-win." I closed my eyes and tried to ignore the soft push of flesh against my lower arms.

I heard footsteps behind me. Finally, Aunt Celia was back. But when I turned, careful not to move my hands, Hunter, the guy from the library, was strolling toward me. He pulled a pair of gloves from his pocket. "You need some help?"

"What are you doing here?"

He looked me up and down, one side of his mouth curled with amusement. "I don't think I'm the surprise. Can I take a look?" He nodded toward the cow.

I hesitated. "I'm not supposed to move." Against every instinct, I shifted closer to the cow.

"Then I guess we'll have to get to know each other," he said, sliding behind me. His arms wrapped around mine and stretched toward the cow.

"Get off me," I spat.

"You can move out of the way anytime." His hand pressed against mine, and the cow let out a long groan of pain. "You must want those volunteer hours pretty badly. Tryin' to fit in? Worried people will mistake you for some delinquent from Junction?"

"I fit in fine."

"Naw, you're not the type to fit in." He reached farther into the cow, pushing closer to me. "Probably 'cause of a guy."

I sucked in a horrified breath, but the stench was too much, and I ended up half gasping, half coughing. His laughter brushed against my neck.

"I would *not* do this for some guy," I sputtered. "Not the way you're thinking."

He leaned closer. "That must be some guy if . . ." His voice trailed off. Suddenly his profile got serious. His fingers moved around mine, feeling the legs I held.

"What?" I said.

He was up in a second. "Move," he said. The easy slide of his words was gone.

"No."

His eyebrows lowered. "This isn't a game."

"You don't think I know that?"

He stepped behind me, wrapped his arms around my waist, and dragged me three feet back across the floor.

"What are you doing?" I said as he settled into my spot, his hands already inside the cow. "I don't think you understand. Aunt Celia told me—"

"I don't think *you* understand that I don't give a crap about whatever you're trying to pull here or at the library."

"I'm not pulling anything. I'm trying to help." I stood, holding my arms out a foot from my sides and trying not to look at the cow fluid clinging to them.

Aunt Celia's boots clomped into the barn. "Hunter, thank God you're here. Dolly is having trouble. We'll have to get that calf out."

Hunter frowned. "Not calf. Calves."

Celia dropped some rope beside him. "That's why the calf was stuck. I was pulling on the legs from two different calves."

"I would have realized it sooner, but your new volunteer wouldn't get out of the way," he muttered.

"Kate isn't a volunteer. She's my niece." She said *niece* like you might say *skin disease*. She knelt beside Hunter. "Kate, I think you've done enough today."

"Can I come back tomorrow?" I asked.

"Leave the gloves," she said.

I peeled off the gloves and exited with as much of my dignity as possible. A few volunteer hours—that was all I needed.

I headed toward the house. A bench sat under a tree, just past the glow of the back porch light. I wasn't ready to go in and face tomorrow's campaign schedule, so I sat down and stared at the long horizon.

It was quiet, the first quiet I'd had since Parker's pictures of me turned up on the school website. I pulled up the website on my phone. Tasha was right. They were gone.

It was easy to get the pictures off a website. It was harder to scrub them out of my head. One showed me with eyes half closed, red cup in my hand. It was taken at the school dance last year. I wasn't drunk. I was imitating one of the bigger idiots in the senior class. (A guy who, incidentally, got a recommendation letter from our principal, thanks to the fact that his dad was the top civil defense attorney in DC.) In another picture, I had runny mascara, stringy hair, and a furious expression after a dunk-tank incident at the school carnival. The pictures were all out of context. Except for one.

I was at a rally in Charlotte in early October. Mom and Dad stood slightly in front of me. On my face was an irritated look—the one I got when we stayed at a fund-raiser too late, which broadcast to my parents that I had shaken too many hands and needed to be sent back to the hotel room. The event wasn't any worse than normal. But the photographer had captured the height of the look, the moment that my face was scrunched and my eyes narrowed. I looked frustrated, resentful, angry. But the real problem was that I had pointed that look, for a moment, at Dad. That picture was the most dangerous. It held the most truth.

The campaign kept the picture out of the newspapers, but I showed a print of it to Parker, thinking he might help me laugh about it. He was usually good at that. I guess I left the picture in his car. He was already cheating on me with Camille by then. I didn't see the photo again until it was on the website.

I pulled my knees up to my chin. Maybe it would hurt less if I wasn't so mad at myself—for letting my guard down at the event, for leaving the picture in Parker's car, for trusting him, for being so clueless and wrong about everything.

I didn't know how long I'd sat there when my phone rang.

"What kind of volunteer gig did you get?" Tasha asked.

I wiped a tear away and tried to shake the anger and disgust that itched inside my skin. When I beat Parker out of that recommendation, maybe it would fade away. "Nothing yet, but I'm working on it."

"You didn't get something you want?" Tasha was silent. "When's the last time that happened?"

"There was this guy, Hunter."

"Wait, a guy. Is he cute?" Tasha said.

"No."

"A little cute?"

"He pulled me out of a cow birth."

"Are you using some sort of local slang?" Tasha said.

"I wish." I explained how Hunter robbed me of both my volunteer jobs. "Besides, you know I've sworn off boys."

"You can't reject all guys just because one cheated on you."

"And posted a bunch of pictures that made me look drunk, stupid, mean, and disloyal."

I could hear the pops of Tasha's gum while she thought. "Okay, let's just pretend that Parker gets the recommendation."

"That can't happen."

"I know, but just in case. You are going to have an amazing portfolio. You won't even need that recommendation. Why don't you focus on taking pictures?"

"That's the other problem. I think I've landed on the hairy, dry big toe of the earth."

"It can't be that bad."

"I'm looking at beige ground under a slightly less beige sky." I scanned the rocky landscape stretching out from my feet to the horizon in all directions. Dust and sky. That was all I had to work with. "There is zero soul here. If you like pictures of clay or dirt or dead plants, I'm all set."

"The backlash at school is dying down. You've got no volunteer job, no photos. Why don't you just come back to DC?"

"Can't. Dad is running for Congress here."

"Whoa. Why didn't you tell me?"

"I just found out."

"What is with your life?"

"Tell me about it." I rubbed my forehead.

"So you have to move to Texas long-term?"

"No, we'll be back. Dad gets hives outside the Beltway."

I heard the crunch of footsteps behind me. It was Hunter, an easy smile tugging the corners of his lips. "We should use that 'big toe' line in the brochures," he said.

"I have to go, Tasha. I'll call you back." I clicked off the phone, stood, and started walking toward the back porch. "What are you doing here?"

"I was making sure you didn't get lost. There are rattlers out here," Hunter said.

"Rattlers?"

"Snakes."

Only my pride kept me from breaking into a run. "I'll be fine."

"You don't even know what a rattlesnake looks like," he said.

"I know what a jerk looks like," I said.

Hunter laughed again. "What are you so upset about?" he asked. "You didn't want to be there."

"You don't know what I want." I stepped onto the front porch and put my hand on the doorknob. Hunter's hand covered mine. "I got it," I said, jerking away from his touch.

"Don't worry. You'll find another way to impress what's-his-name."

"His name is Parker. I'm not trying to impress him. I'm trying to make sure he gets what he deserves."

"So you don't care about the animals *or* the library." If he was surprised, he hid it under a dusting of sarcasm.

"That's not what I meant."

"It's kind of what you said." He pulled the door open. "The birth went fine, but the mother is rejecting the calves, so it's going to be a long night. I knew you'd want to know, since you care so much." Hunter turned and strolled across the porch. "Oh, and in about ten minutes the sun will hit the underside of those clouds and turn them purplish-blue, with lines of pink, gold, and orange. Makes the place look less like a hairy toe."

chapter four

I found Mom in the kitchen chopping up carrots and adding them to a bowl of lettuce at her elbow. When she saw me, she did another scan of my outfit, no doubt noting the dirt now on the knees of my pants and my tangled hair. Exhaustion had deepened the creases around her eyes. I sat on a stool.

"What is Aunt Celia's shelter like?" she asked.

"Traumatizing." I picked out a few croutons and popped them into my mouth. "Has Dad been planning to run in Red Dirt this whole time?"

Mom put down her knife. "Kate, the election was announced. It seemed like a great opportunity. For all of us."

"How long have you been keeping this opportunity from me?" I asked.

"You needed to get out of DC."

"I was doing fine in DC. How long?"

"About two weeks." Mom stared at me.

Dad walked into the room, his phone pressed to his ear. "I need someone here yesterday, Frank." He paused for a few seconds. "They know me here. They love me. Stone is a wild card." His jaw tightened. "I didn't quit. I went home to a district that would benefit from my experience and expertise." Dad was the master of spin. He had a talent for shaping the story until he was the hero. "Good. Good. I knew you would come through for me." He hung up. "He'll send someone tomorrow. Staff will arrive the day after that. I'm still calling around for a media person, but I think we'll be up and running soon," he said to Mom. That's when he spotted me. "How was Aunt Celia?"

"I'm not sure she's thrilled we're here," I said. "I offered to volunteer at the shelter, but she didn't seem interested."

"She'll come around."

Aunt Celia appeared in the doorway. "Who'll come around?"

"Kate was just saying how much she was looking forward to spending time with you." Mom wasn't so bad at spin herself.

Aunt Celia opened the fridge.

Mom tried again. "I made some salad. You're welcome to it."

Celia looked at the bowl. "I'm more of a meat-and-potatoes gal."

"I moved some boxes into the fourth bedroom. I thought I'd use it for an office," Dad said.

"You're not running your campaign from here too?"

"It might take a few days to find a place," Dad said.

Aunt Celia stepped back from the refrigerator and pointed at Dad. "I get that technically it's your house, but you haven't acted much like you wanted it for a long time. I don't need half the county traipsing through here."

"We'll be out of your hair by January."

"You'll barely know we're here. Right, Kate?" Mom said.

Aunt Celia frowned at the salad. "I'm going back to the shelter." She left out the back door.

Mom looked at me. "You're right. She's not happy."

"What if we went back to the original plan, and you didn't campaign?" I said. "It would be easier on everyone. Aunt Celia would be happy. I would be happy. Win-win."

Dad gave me a single nod. "You're absolutely right. Your mom and I were just talking about that while you were at the shelter."

"You have made a lot of sacrifices," Mom said.

"And it was unfair not to tell you about the campaign," Dad said. "You probably need a break."

The bubble popped. "A break?" I said.

"This campaign is built on my past with the town and in the area. There will be appearances in a few of the larger cities in the district, but it will be won and lost in the smaller towns where turnout is higher." He pulled a carrot from the salad and tossed it in his mouth. "I know we put a lot of pressure on you. Take a break from campaigning. Be a teenager." Dad put his hand on my shoulder, a gesture designed to communicate compassion and control. "We don't really need you."

"This is still about the pictures. You're distancing yourself from me." I listened for what was behind the words—disappointment, anger. I didn't hear any of that. This was business. They really didn't want me campaigning.

"It's what you want. Win-win." Dad's phone rang. He checked the screen. "And when I say be a teenager, I mean one who doesn't get arrested or go on any reality TV shows." He walked out of the room.

"There. Everything worked out," Mom said. "I put your suitcase in the bedroom down the hall."

I walked down the hall, still a little dizzy from the argument that was yanked out from under me. I wouldn't miss the endless rounds of shaking hands and plastered smiles. I wouldn't miss hearing Dad give the same ten-word answers to the same questions. I poured every ounce of my persuasive powers into my gut, but it couldn't fill the hole there. Dad was getting back on track by dropping me. It was a little like being broken up with . . . again.

When I got to the doorway, I stopped. Apparently, I'd be living in Dad's old room, complete with football pictures, shelves of cassette tapes, and letter jackets in the closet. I knelt beside my suitcase and dug through the clothes for a brown folder. I opened the folder and held the glossy paper between my fingers. They were the last pictures I had developed in DC. One was a wide shot of construction in the city, with bright trucks crisscrossing the top left-hand corner of the frame. I had another shot of a hallway in the congressional wing. The architecture was sharp, but the people moved in ghostly blurs. How would I get pictures like this here?

I picked up the yearbook from the bed where Dad had tossed it and flipped through the pages. Girls posed with arms around each other's shoulders. The guys all lifted their chins slightly as the camera snapped. They were photos stuffed with stale life and false emotion.

I turned another page, and one picture caught my eye. It framed a man's back as he stood against the railing of the football stands. You couldn't see his face, but you could see the tight lines of his shoulders raised a fraction of an inch closer to his ears. As he pointed at the field, his arm reached outside the frame. A football player looked up at him from the sidelines. Lines of worry and hurt splashed across the player's face. In the background, a few players pumped fists in the air.

I brushed my hand over the picture. It was a shot of personal defeat in the midst of victory. It wasn't particularly beautiful. The composition was off and parts fell out of the frame. But it was real.

Someone who took a photograph like that knew photography, cared about photography. The person who took this picture knew how to slip into moments and capture them. My pictures were beautiful, but even I knew that whiffs of effort leaked onto the paper. This one was like a bubble of time. The person who took this picture was doing more than pressing a button. And that person might know where to find a darkroom. There might be hope for my photography plans after all.

chapter five

The next morning, Mom pulled up to a long rectangular two-story building lined with windows painted red and black. The clouds rested low in the sky, only a strip of blue separating them from the horizon. "Stop by the front office and get your schedule," she said.

"Fine," I said, pulling my bag onto my shoulder.

"Are you still pouting about the campaign?" She looked in the rearview mirror and adjusted her pearls. "Go easy on your dad. He's under a lot of stress right now."

"I know the drill. Lie low and don't embarrass him."

"Things will go back to normal once the election is over."

I knew she was trying. If anything, this campaign would be harder on her than on me. "Mom, this *is* our normal."

As I squeezed into the entryway, students milled around open doors, finishing bites of breakfast, their backpacks hanging from their shoulders. The slap of hands and clatter of slamming lockers pulsed over the hum of morning chatter. A few eyes shifted toward me, ponytails swung, and voices lowered.

My instincts told me to take a step back; my training pushed me forward. It was not the first time I'd walked into a room of people who looked at me with guarded curiosity. It usually led to enough fragile bubbles of fake friendliness to buoy me socially, but I didn't need to navigate the winding but predictable web of high school politics. I was here to collect volunteer hours and work on photography. I notched my chin up a little higher and sailed through the stares to the office.

The office smelled like a mix of scented lotion and brownies. The school secretary bustled from her desk to a waist-high counter that stretched the length of the room. "You must be Jeffrey's daughter. I'm Mrs. Perkins." She leaned forward. "Your father had the best arm this school's seen in almost thirty years. I still remember those passes that seemed to hang in the sky for days." Her vowels dripped off her tongue.

"I came to pick up my schedule," I said.

She fumbled around below the counter, pulled up a slip of paper, and slid it across to me. "We got your transcript from your school in DC. You're bright as a new penny." She flashed a toothy grin. "But we don't offer some of the classes you were taking. I had to put you in Spanish I."

"I was taking Chinese."

"We don't have a Chinese class. You took a class called Ethics of Science. I'm not really sure what that is, but since you had credit for biology, physics, and chemistry, I put you in Agricultural Sciences."

"Agricultural Sciences?"

"Honey, you'll love it," she said.

All the icing on her words didn't fool me. Agricultural Sciences sounded a lot like calf births. I needed a darkroom, and that meant I needed a schedule change.

When you spend almost a decade of your life inside a political machine, you figure out how to work the system. Any system. The first thing you have to do is find the button that starts people moving and push it. Then you just steer them where you want them to go. I softened my voice. "Listen. I am new here, and I'm a little nervous. If I could just have one familiar class . . ."

The woman frowned for a second. "We usually don't make any changes after the schedule prints."

"Could you make an exception?" I asked. "Since I'm new?"

She hesitated. I picked at the corners of the paper and held my breath.

A smile burst over her face. "Sure, why not. Anything for Jeff Hamilton's little girl." She tapped a few keys on her keyboard. "What were you thinking?"

Now we were rolling in the right direction. "Photography."

Her fingers stopped. "I can't do that."

"Why not? I can show samples of my work. I'm sure I can keep up."

"We don't have a photography class, sweetheart." She frowned at the screen. Her fingers danced along the keyboard again. "I do have something. If I just switch your first period with your fifth, and swap . . . Yep." She hit one more key and the printer started to whirl. "Now, I couldn't keep you in Ag Science, so I moved you to Biology II with Mr. Quincy."

"Fine."

"It's a senior class. You'll be the only junior."

"No problem. I like a challenge."

"Then you're all fixed up." She slid a candy dish filled with miniature candy bars across the desk. "You sure do remind me of your dad."

"Thanks." My voice was flat. She passed me my new schedule. I scanned it. "Yearbook. I don't think . . ."

"It's perfect, sweetie. They need a photographer. Joey Warner twisted his knee during practice two weeks ago."

"And he was the photographer?"

"No, he's our kicker. Now they had to move up Rick Tubbs. He was the photographer, but Coach has him practicing every waking minute. They could probably use a substitute through the playoffs."

"I usually take more artistic pictures."

"Oh, honey, don't worry. I'm sure you can handle it. Another kid on staff can show you the ropes."

I opened my mouth to say that of course I *could* take pictures for the yearbook. A monkey could take pictures for the yearbook. But then the door to the principal's office swung open and Bo Stone walked out, followed by a man in a suit and a boy close to my age. Bo turned and shook hands with the man, keeping a tight grip while he spoke. "We're glad we got that sorted out, Billy. Aren't we, Kyle?"

Kyle flashed a dazzling smile. "Thanks, Principal Walker. This will really help us out Friday night."

The principal put a hand on Kyle's shoulder. "Consider it done. You can take your speech class next semester."

"What am I going to take fifth period?"

"We'll move you here to be an office aide. You can watch game tape in the back and get yourself ready for that state championship."

"Mrs. Hendricks means well. I just don't think she understands what's on the line," Bo said, his eyebrows knitting with sympathy. "I'd hate to have a disaster like last year."

Mr. Walker turned to Kyle. "You think you're ready for Friday night? Junction's defense is tough."

Kyle opened his mouth, but before he could speak, Mr. Stone said, "Don't worry. He's ready."

Kyle's eyes narrowed at his dad.

Bo turned and spotted me. His jaw hardened for a split second; then the bottom half of his face broke into a smile. "Hi, Mr. Stone," I said.

"This is Jeff Hamilton's little girl," Bo said to Mr. Walker.

"Did you get your schedule sorted out?" Principal Walker asked. It was the opening I was hoping for.

"Yes, but Mrs. Perkins put me in yearbook, and—"

"Good, good. You're taking Tubbs's spot. I'm sure they need all the help they can get with the playoffs starting next week," he said, nodding toward Kyle.

"Actually, I don't think I'll be able to join the yearbook staff. I'll be busy adjusting to a new school." I held out the schedule. "So maybe I could just do a study hall that period. Or be an office aide. Then if I could just get access to—"

Mr. Walker shook his head. "Schedule's already printed."

I jerked my head toward Kyle. "Isn't he getting a schedule change?"

"It's a completely different situation," Mr. Walker said.

A smile played at Bo's lips. "Guess you better study your football plays." He turned to Kyle. "This is my son, Kyle. He's a senior here."

"Starting quarterback of the Red Dirt Raiders," Mr. Walker added.

Kyle smiled and nodded at me, a spark of curiosity in his eyes. Bo clapped him on the shoulder. "So, what do you think of Red Dirt so far, Kate? You can tell me . . . What do they say in DC? Off the record? Is that it?"

It was a good setup. It made me look like a political insider and assured his outsider status at the same time. "It's great," I said. "Everyone is so friendly. It feels like I've lived here all my life."

It was the perfect tone—enthusiastic, specific, with notes of sincerity. It wasn't technically campaigning. I just wanted to prove that I wasn't an amateur. Kyle let out a snort of laughter.

Bo's face flashed with anger. "That is a compliment, since you haven't been here in, what? Fifteen years."

"More like eleven," I muttered.

"I still have a few things to discuss with Principal Walker. Kyle, I'll see you at practice." Bo led the principal back into his office.

Kyle nodded, then turned to me. "Sorry about that. Between the playoffs and the elections, Dad is wound even tighter than normal."

"Campaigning does that to you. How is the election treating you?" I said, dancing the next few steps in the campaign-kid sizing-up routine.

He smiled. "I don't get all these politics. It seems like kind of a waste of time." Children of politicians always downplay the politics of their lives.

"Your dad seems to care."

"He cares a lot more since your dad showed up. What do you have first period?" He grabbed my schedule before I could answer. "Biology II with Quincy." His smile brightened. "Me too. I'll show you where to go." He started off down the hall and I jogged a few steps to keep up.

"So, really, what do you think of Red Dirt so far?" he asked once we turned the corner. Banners with thick black-and-red victory slogans lined the hallways.

"I've been here less than a day," I said diplomatically.

"So I'm the first person you've met?"

"Actually, I met a guy named Hunter yesterday," I said.

Kyle's eyes snapped toward me, his face suddenly hijacked by a mean hunger. "Hunter Price?"

"I guess."

He relaxed his face back into a smile. "Well, I'm the first football player you met. Here we are," he said, swinging open a door. A roomful of people pulled their gaze off the man standing stiffly at the front, his glasses perched halfway down his nose. Their looks went automatically to Kyle, then rolled toward me. I didn't mind standing in Kyle's glow for a moment. The looks of curiosity from this morning shifted toward approval.

Mr. Quincy looked at my schedule. "Miss Hamilton, welcome to Red Dirt."

"Thanks."

"Let's get you settled at your lab table."

"I'll work with Kate," Kyle said. "I'm supposed to show her around today."

Mr. Quincy ignored him. It looked like not everyone bowed to Kyle's status as quarterback. "Miss Hamilton, you can sit at the back table. If you have any questions, I'm sure Hunter can answer them."

"Hunter?" I said.

"Your lab partner," Mr. Quincy said. I glanced in the direction his finger pointed—straight to a familiar smirk.

I walked to the back of the room and dropped my bag at the foot of the metal lab stool.

"I thought a politician's daughter would be better at covering her disappointment," Hunter said.

"I'm covering a lot of it," I said.

He laughed. "I guess if Stone is your tour guide, you've already been warned to steer clear of me. Bad for your reputation."

"I didn't need a warning to know that," I said.

"So you and Kyle are buddies now?"

"He was in the office when I got my schedule."

Hunter shook his head. "Of course he was."

"What does that mean?"

"Kyle is always in there trying to get something," Hunter said.

Mr. Quincy swept his eyes over the room and everyone quieted.

"Today we're starting our unit on animal behavior, and I thought we'd begin with one of my favorite animals. Can anyone tell me what animal kills more meat per year than lions, tigers, and bears combined?"

Hunter leaned forward with interest. Kyle said something to the guy sitting next to him, who laughed, then looked over his shoulder at me.

"This same animal can carry four times his own weight the equivalent of one kilometer." Mr. Quincy rubbed his hands. "If he doesn't have to walk far, he can carry a hundred times his own weight along a surface as slick as glass. Some species can endure hurricane-force winds."

I looked around. No one's hand went up.

"It isn't like a dinosaur or some animal no one has heard of, is it?" Kyle asked.

"No, in fact, I think it's safe to say you see this animal regularly. Maybe every day," Mr. Quincy said. He pulled out a stack of plastic boxes. "Ants!"

There was a hum of surprise and a few groans.

"We are going to study these amazing creatures over the next few weeks."

"Like an ant farm?" Kyle asked. Two guys in red jerseys chuckled and leaned back in their chairs. Classic politics—if you aren't in power, stand close to it and laugh at its jokes.

"Yes, Mr. Stone. But since you aren't five, we will do a little more sophisticated research with these ants. Perhaps a demonstration."

Mr. Quincy waved us toward the center table, stools squeaking against the tiles as we gathered around. Kyle eased into a spot next to me. Mr. Quincy tapped two dozen ants into the end of a tray, opened a door on the side, and let one ant onto the table. He put a drop of liquid on the far side of the table, about five feet from the ant.

"What's that?" Hunter asked. As he leaned closer to the tray, his shoulder brushed mine.

"Sugar water. Ants love it, Mr. Price." Mr. Quincy nudged the ant gently toward the drop with the eraser end of a pencil. It skittered across the table, tapped its antennae on the drop of water, then dipped its head to drink.

"What's he doing?" a girl asked.

"Drinking the water. He's putting it all into his social stomach. Ants use it to feed each other." The ant turned and started back across the table toward the other ants.

"Why doesn't he keep it for himself?" Kyle asked.

"He needs to get others to the food source. He's going to use it to tell them what he found." Mr. Quincy stepped back. "He put down a chemical trail on the way there. Now he just has to follow the scent back."

Mr. Quincy opened the door on the tray and a few ants scurried to the other side. The returning ant fed the first ant he encountered. That ant headed straight for the water.

One ant stumbled against the drop. He backed up a few steps and then started to examine it with his antennae. He tapped the drop, drank a little, then returned to where he'd started. Then another ant followed. And another. In a couple of minutes, all the ants had found the sugar water. They formed an undulating braid of ants weaving up and down the table.

Mr. Quincy nodded. "Ants have spent centuries perfecting their social behaviors so that their instincts serve the whole colony. In this case, the first ant laid down a trail. Then another followed that trail, laying his own trail at the same time. Then another. Now the trail is easy to find. And it just gets stronger and stronger. It's only one of many ways that ants excel at cooperation, communication, and teamwork."

"Maybe you can pick up some tips on what it means to be on a team, Hunter," Kyle said in a low voice.

Hunter crossed his arms and stared forward.

"It's easy to lead when you're headed to sugar water," I said.

"You're wondering if ants follow one another to something less delicious, even dangerous." Mr. Quincy started to pass out boxes. "Maybe that can be your first experiment. Each of you will study your ants. Give them puzzles to solve, obstacles to overcome, stresses to deal with. Watch how they communicate. You are going to have to observe them in a variety of situations and see what you can learn. The rules for a society aren't in its actions, but in its reactions."

Mr. Quincy sent us back to our tables. Hunter carried our box of dirt and ants.

I took out a spiral notebook and a pen. "Just so you know, I care about my GPA." I had transferred in with hard-earned As, and I wasn't going to transfer back with Bs from Red Dirt High School.

Hunter looked at me with cool amusement, the same way he had last night in the barn. "You probably think I'm dumb as dirt."

"That's not what I said." I scowled. "Fine. What should our experiment be?"

"We could separate them, see if they find each other. If you separate hogs, they recognize each other years later."

For a second I thought that was a slam at Dad because he left Red Dirt. But when I looked at Hunter, he was peering at the ants. "How are we going to know if they recognize each other? Are they going to hug?"

"Okay, Einstein. What do you think we should do?"

"What I asked Mr. Quincy. We know they will get each other to follow if they're headed toward something they like. Let's see if they'll follow another ant into danger. We could put a predator in there. What eats ants?"

"Bears?" Hunter said.

"If you aren't going to help with this, then I'll just get my own box of ants."

Hunter didn't even try to hide how much he enjoyed my frustration. "How about crickets?"

"Perfect. Bring one in tomorrow and we'll write up the experiment," I said.

"I came up with the predator. I'm getting the predator. Seems like you're not doing a lot of work for someone who cares so much about her GPA."

"I just asked you to get a cricket. How hard can it be?" I said.

Hunter held his hands up. "I'm glad you think you can handle it. I thought for a second I was going to have to tell Quincy what a slacker you are." He grinned.

We filled out the hypothesis and steps of our experiment in silence until the bell rang. Hunter seemed to gather his belongings in slow motion. When he finally left, I made a beeline to Mr. Quincy's desk.

"I hope you found your first day enlightening, Miss Hamilton," he said.

"Oh, yes." I smiled. "We never did anything like this at my school in DC." My ability to hold a smile and dig compliments from below all the irritation always came in handy with teachers.

"Did you and Mr. Price come up with an experiment?"

"Yes, but that's what I wanted to talk to you about. Hunter and I are not seeing eye to eye on this project. I think I would learn more if I worked alone."

Mr. Quincy stared at me.

"I know it would be more work, but I am willing to do it."

"We'll keep you and Mr. Price together for now."

"With all due respect, I don't see why."

Mr. Quincy tilted his head to the side. "Really, a smart girl like you? I would have thought you could figure it out. First, I can't let you work alone because I can't let everyone work alone. I don't have enough ants. So that makes it unfair."

I was forming the early versions of a counterargument when Mr. Quincy continued, "Frankly, Miss Hamilton, even if I had an ant tray for every student, I would still require you to work together. It's part of the assignment."

"I don't need to work with Hunter to learn about ants."

"I have a feeling you will learn more than you think."

My smile faded. "Fine. One more question. Where would I get some live crickets?"

He returned his attention to his papers. "I think outside would be a good start."

chapter six

After science I muddled through English, US History, and pre-calc, where half of the teacher's examples used Red Dirt football statistics. This kept the buzz-cut defensive line in the back of the room engaged, but the combination of math and football had my head spinning.

I followed the stream of students to the cafeteria. The morning had not gone as planned, but I was determined to make it to yearbook and get myself into a darkroom. It would make everything else worth it.

Movies showed high school cafeterias as circuses of social rankings and norms that take the fearlessness of a lion-tamer and the flexibility of an acrobat to navigate. But really, it's just another room full of agendas. As I compared two potential lunch tables—a benign group of second-tier cheerleaders who were chattering over one another and another table who had their lunches arranged around opened books—a girl stepped into the space beside me. "Does this place suddenly look like a giant ant colony to you?"

She smiled at me, her eyes more kind than curious. I relaxed slightly. "I guess you take Bio II."

The girl nodded. "Third period. It's the best science class at Red Dirt."

"I'm Kate Hamilton," I said.

"I know," the girl said, not unfriendly. "You're the new girl."

"News travels fast around here," I said. "You know my name, my schedule. How long until my lunch order gets around?"

"Not long. I'm Ana Gomez." She nodded to the lines. "Go for the tortilla soup. It's the only edible thing on Wednesdays."

"Thanks." I started to feel the tug of stares surrounding me.

"Mrs. Perkins said she put you in the yearbook class."

"Yeah, that's where I'm going next."

"Me too. It's really going to help having another photographer."

A girl with long, slightly frizzy blonde hair pushed her tray in line between us. "So you're the new girl." Her blue eyes narrowed in a challenge.

I wasn't sure what the challenge was, but I stared steadily back at her. "My name is Kate."

"I know. I'm Missy. Kyle said he met you first period."

Ah, there it was. "Then you know the whole story," I said.

She tilted her head and smiled, a smile that barely inched up her cheeks. "He's good at turning on the charm when he has a new audience."

I shrugged. Dad taught me never to give up more information than I had to.

"Just some friendly advice, since you're new." Missy seemed about as friendly as the daggers in her eyes. "I'd be on my guard if I were you. You don't want to get a reputation. Right, Ana?"

Ana looked away. I wanted to say something, but it's hard to fight in the dark, so I let a corner of my mouth flash up for a second. "I can handle myself."

"See you upstairs," Missy said.

I watched her ponytail swing as she walked away. "Is she always that helpful?"

"That was Missy lite. You should see her when she doesn't get the pictures she wants for yearbook."

"I guess every school has to have a Missy." I picked up my tray.

"The good news is that she works on layouts, so she only talks to the photographers when she wants pictures of her friends. Our first deadline is in less than four weeks. The staff eats in the yearbook room to get work done."

A red jersey bumped into Ana. He gave her a look—not hostile, but designed to make her uncomfortable.

"Hey, watch where you're going," I called after him.

Ana crossed her arms over her chest and her petite frame shrank more, the brightness draining from her eyes.

"What was that about?"

"Nothing," Ana said.

I wanted to tell her to stand up straight, that she had to look more sure when she was attacked, not less. Then I remembered what Dad said about helping.

Ana turned toward the hall. "Ignore Missy. She's a little bitter. She and Kyle dated since freshman year. He broke up with her at the end of the summer."

"I can't imagine why," I said.

Inside the yearbook room, six kids stood and sat at tables, their heads bent over pages. Another three or four stared at computers, clicking with one hand and moving food to their mouths with the other. Missy stood over one of the guys, frowning at the pictures on his screen.

"If someone doesn't get me the spread for the volleyball pages in two minutes, I will change the theme to 'It's a Wonderful Life' and fill the yearbook with pictures of cute puppies," a woman yelled from behind a desk. Her words were quick and clipped at the end, like the click of high heels on tile floors. Her long hair spiraled in tight curls down her back.

"The printer stopped working," someone said.

"Are you waiting for the yearbook fairy to fix it?" the woman demanded. "Come on. You know how it works in here. If it's broken, we fix it."

"When are we getting a new printer?" a girl asked as she ran over with a large sheet of paper.

"When yearbook becomes eligible for the playoffs."

"That's Ms. Serrano, the yearbook sponsor," Ana said. We stopped in front of her desk.

"People, we're down to one photographer, so get your requests in early," Ms. Serrano called out without looking up. Missy stood and made a beeline toward Ana, but Ms. Serrano waved her back, the bracelets on her hand jangling. "Me first. Ana, can you cover the basketball game tomorrow?"

Ana swallowed and shifted from one foot to another. "Not until eight."

If Ms. Serrano had glanced at her, she would have known Ana was lying. But she just said, "That's perfect," making large red circles over the text on the page in front of her. "By that time they'll be twenty points behind, and there will be four people left in the stands. We can record *that* for posterity."

"The season just started."

"And it already feels endless." Ms. Serrano crossed her arms. "I want their pages done for the first deadline."

Ana nodded. "There's good news. Ms. Serrano, this is Kate. The new photographer Mrs. Perkins recruited this morning."

Ms. Serrano didn't acknowledge me. "We don't have a single decent band shot." She flipped through a few more oversized layouts.

"I am so thrilled to be part of the yearbook staff," I said. "You clearly run a first-class operation. But I have to say, I am more of an artist than a yearbook photographer."

Ms. Serrano lifted her head and looked around me to yell at a cluster of students at a corner table. "Why is the French Club's page full of pictures of the same three people in different poses?"

"There are only three people in the club," said a girl across the room.

"I have a two-page spread for a club with three people in it." Ms. Serrano threw the piece of paper on her desk and picked up another.

I tried to ease back into her line of sight. "I'd be happy to help file papers or proof captions. Oh, and I was wondering if you had a darkroom available, for once I'm done with my yearbook duties, or after school."

"Combine the French, Spanish, and German clubs on these pages. The extra pages can go to Theater. They always have good stuff."

Ms. Serrano wasn't paying attention. I decided to try another strategy. "I am planning to submit my portfolio to art schools next year."

Ms. Serrano's eyes fixed on me. "You have to be on staff to use the darkroom."

Great—she was one of those people who were listening when you thought they weren't. "Mrs. Perkins put me on staff."

"She put you in the *class*," Ms. Serrano said. "I can't do anything about that, but the rest of the people here tried out in the spring."

"I need a darkroom."

"And I need inspiring pictures of a basketball team that is oh and three, but my best photographer—correction, my *only* photographer—is mysteriously busy every night the basketball team plays. Sometimes life is one giant disappointment."

"Believe me, I tried to get my class changed, but Mrs. Perkins had already printed the schedule," I said.

"Then it looks like we're stuck with each other. Try to stay out of the way." She turned, rose, and pushed past me.

Ana flashed me a sympathetic look.

"What if I took pictures at the basketball game?" I called after her. "You can consider it my application."

Ms. Serrano shook her head. "Impossible. I don't have time to train you."

"I don't need any training," I said.

"She'll do a great job," Ana said, bouncing slightly on her toes.

"Fine, but it's your problem if we end up with nothing."

"If I take the pictures, can I use the darkroom?" I asked.

"If they're good enough, I *might* put you on staff. Then you *might* be able to use the darkroom." She pointed a finger at me. "But I don't want artsy pictures. I need cheesy memories dripping with sentimentality."

"I can do that," I said.

Ms. Serrano nodded, her bracelets jingling as she waved us away.

It was a win. A partial win, but at this point I would take it. Ana leaned over to me. "Have you ever taken basketball pictures before?"

"No, but how hard can it be?" I asked.

"The lighting is tricky in the gym. And the action moves pretty fast."

"I'll have what I need in ten minutes."

"Okay, if you're sure. I'll show you how to use the computer program where we do all the layouts." She sat me at a computer and entered a log-in. She opened a file with lines of pictures spilling off the page. "We all have access to certain pages. Last year Missy put pictures of Kyle on every other page, so Ms. Serrano limited everyone's accounts. The photographers upload the options to the pages, then the staff members arrange them and write the captions. It looks like we need pictures for the Student Life section."

"What goes in Student Life?" I clicked through a series of photos documenting the backs of students' heads.

"Pictures of normal high school life. People in the halls, in classes, groups of friends."

I scanned the rows of pictures for another ten minutes. "Ana, these pictures are all starting to look the same."

She reached for the mouse. "I would have thought you would like this, peering into people's lives." '

"Because my dad's in politics?" I asked.

"Because you're a photographer."

"I don't like faces in my pictures. Put a person in a photo-graph and their feelings take over the entire picture. People are unpredictable."

"Don't you think that makes them interesting?"

I shook my head. "It makes them dangerous. It creates mistakes and messes."

"You don't like messes?"

"I like plans."

Ana clicked on a picture. "This is what I'm looking for."

I leaned closer to the computer screen. "A slightly out-of-focus guy walking in the hall and smiling at the camera. There are dozens of others," I said.

"Not the person walking." Ana clicked a few keys and the screen zoomed to the bottom left-hand corner of the photo, where a student was hunched against the wall, running a finger across an open copy of *The Catcher in the Rye*. She wore a tank top and a long skirt that billowed around her as her chin rested on her knees. Her eyes had widened slightly and her fingers were pressed to her lips. It captured a moment. It even brushed against art.

"How did you see that?" I asked.

"I just looked."

Missy walked over to peer at the screen. "You can't use that picture."

"Why not?" I asked.

"It's boring. Yearbooks are about memories. There's nothing memorable about this picture. Change it."

Ana reached for the mouse. I put my hand over hers and fixed my eyes on Missy. "Keep it."

"You're not even on staff," Missy said. "What do you know?"

I tilted my head and let a small smile play on my lips. "I know that if you had your way, you'd splash Kyle Stone across the center of every page to get his attention. I know that Ana found the only fraction of this photograph worth printing. I also know that if we ask Ms. Serrano, she'll side with Ana."

Missy stood there another beat, struggling to come up with something to say. When nothing came to her, she turned on the heel of her ballet flat and stormed back to her seat.

"That was amazing," Ana said, putting a hand on my shoulder. "We're definitely getting you on the staff."

In a political family, campaigning trumps everything else. It trumps piano recitals (unless there are some major potential donors attending) and birthdays (unless you can use them to swing the last few committee votes you need). It trumps holidays and minor surgery. So I wasn't surprised that it trumped picking up your daughter on her first day at a new school. When the after-school crowd dwindled into clusters of kids by the parking lot, I sat down on the curb and called Mom. "School's over. Do you think you could pick me up?"

"Give me twenty minutes," Mom said. "I ran into half the town at the grocery store, and if I don't manage to buy a few things, we'll be eating something called an enchilada casserole that Mrs. Fisher brought over."

"Is that bad?"

"It's swimming in cream and grease," Mom said.

"I'll just call Dad," I said.

"No, don't. He's finishing a round of fund-raising calls before the new consultant comes over."

A truck pulled to a stop beside me. Hunter leaned out the window. "Do you need a ride? I'm going to the shelter."

"Is that the kid who helps Aunt Celia?" Mom asked.

I sighed. I knew what was coming. "Yeah," I said.

"Perfect. Get a ride with him. I have a few more stops to make." She hung up.

Hunter pushed the passenger-side door open. I climbed in with a muttered "Thanks." Pile spilled from some worn spots in the seat upholstery, but other than that, the truck was pristine. We drove a few minutes in silence.

"Tough first day?"

"It was great," I said, staring forward. "People are friendly, the teachers are nice." My voice trailed off at the end. I was starting to sound like Dad.

"Do you always work so hard to find the right thing to say?" Hunter asked.

My face reddened. "Do you always work so hard to get on people's nerves?"

He shrugged. "It doesn't take that much effort."

I glanced at his profile. He leaned one elbow out of the window. It was infuriating how my jabs melted against him.

"I heard you got under Missy Carver's skin," Hunter said.

I rolled my eyes. "That girl is just looking for something she can poke her nose into. She's like the whip of high school."

"The what?"

"The whip. You know, in Congress."

"I don't know if you've noticed, but you're not in DC anymore," Hunter said. "We use whips to train horses. Or get hogs and cows ready for show."

63

"Maybe it's not that different. The whip makes sure the party has the votes it needs in Congress. They're always in everyone's business. And sometimes they flat-out bully people into behaving as expected."

"Yeah, that sounds like Missy."

"She even has a problem with Ana. The only person who actually made this day easier."

A flash of concern crossed Hunter's face. I might not have noticed except that it rippled the blasé expression that he wore. "What did she say to Ana?"

"Oh, you know, nothing. Something. It wasn't what she said. It was the way she looked at Ana, like she was scum."

"Can I give you a piece of advice?" Hunter asked.

"I got plenty of advice from Missy."

Hunter continued anyway. "Around here, it's easier to let people think what they want to think."

"What if they're wrong?"

"Let them be wrong. Just because they say something doesn't make it true."

I turned to face him. "That's terrible advice. If people lie about you, you confront them."

"Who cares what people think?" He pulled into the driveway.

"In my experience? Everyone." I climbed out of the truck and slammed the door.

"Don't forget to get that cricket, Hamilton," he said.

chapter seven

When I opened the front door, I could hear Dad yelling into the phone. "You can't treat me like I'm some local councilman who decided to run yesterday. I should have Atchison or Lewis . . . I'll call myself." His words trailed off.

As I shut the door behind me, I caught a glimpse of a woman sitting in the overstuffed chair in the living room. She saw me too, and stood to walk down the short hallway to the front door.

"This is a locked-up seat, but I can't win with a wide-eyed poli-sci dropout," Dad said in the kitchen.

The woman held out her hand to me. "India Truss. I actually got my degree in psychology, not poli-sci, but don't mention that to your dad."

India didn't look like any of the campaign consultants I had seen. Her red curls tumbled over her shoulders, and freckles dotted her nose and cheeks. She wore a dress whose color bordered on electric blue. Consultants normally like to blend into the background, camouflaged in gray suits and rumpled shirts, their faces half hidden behind cell phones. She also looked very well-rested for someone who worked in politics. Well-rested and available a week before the general election meant one of two things: You weren't working, or you weren't winning.

I shook her hand while Dad's yelling continued to pound the walls. I had to admit, if she could stay poised under this kind of fire, she couldn't possibly be as incompetent as he thought.

"You must be Kate. How was your first day in Red Dirt?" India asked.

From the sound of things, India wouldn't be around long. I said the only thing I could think of that would bring this conversation to a screeching halt. "I have to catch a cricket for homework."

I got ready to escape to my room, but she nodded thoughtfully. "Have you caught a cricket before?"

"No." I missed a lot of childhood experiences growing up in politics.

"Cricket hunting works better in the morning, but you could probably find a couple at dusk. You need a box and some paper to put over the opening. Drop the box on the cricket, slide the paper underneath the opening, and you should be good."

"How did you know that?"

"I interned for a gubernatorial campaign in Tennessee. And by interned, I mean I babysat the congressman's seven-year-old son. The guy could balance the state budget but didn't have a single parental instinct. He got the kid a briefcase for his seventh birthday. So I told the kid it was an insect collector."

"Nice spin. What campaigns have you run?"

"None," India said.

"And the party sent you to run Dad's campaign?" I asked.

"It could be a sign of faith."

I raised an eyebrow. "Sure, politics is known for its faith in people."

"I heard you were the funny one in the family." India smiled. "Any advice for when I meet your dad?"

"Most of *his* faith goes into polling results, not people. He likes practical solutions, and he loves to win."

India nodded.

"Oh, and he doesn't give people a lot of chances."

Dad appeared in the doorway. "Sorry you went to all the trouble to come out here." He headed down the hall to the living room.

India didn't flinch. She followed him. "You can send me away, but you'll still need a campaign manager."

Dad stopped and faced her. "I need a campaign manager, not some castoff."

I hated the way politics cooled Dad's natural warmth. "Dad—" I said.

"No, it's the truth," India said. "I'm a nobody in the party, which makes you wonder why they sent me to you. It couldn't be your disappearance ten days before the upcoming election, or the fact that your enemies are questioning your sanity and your friends are questioning your commitment. But the real question is—if you send me away, who are you going to get? You'd have to talk someone into coming down for a four-week special election, seven weeks if there's a runoff, with no lead time. Even if you do manage to track down a top-tier consultant in the remote cabins they all retreat to after campaigning, it will take days for anyone to get here. And you don't even have hours."

Dad swallowed.

I silently rooted for her.

"So maybe you should look at this as a gift. I'm hungry to prove myself. I know the party underestimated me, so I can only assume that they have grossly underestimated you."

Dad rubbed his chin. "I have to win," he said.

India met the intensity in his eyes with her own. "So do I."

It's rare to hear someone say the perfect thing. People in politics spend weeks, *months*, dial-testing language to dig it out of the vast terrain of words politicians have to navigate. India just let the words roll off her tongue, and they cast a spell.

Dad was silent for a moment, working his jaw. "I'll need a stump speech, talking points, research on the area, voting history."

India fished a stack of papers from her bag and held it out to Dad. "Here is a first draft of a speech and a breakdown of the district's voting trends in the last three congressional elections."

"It's a special election. We might want to target some micro-trends."

"Look at page eleven," India said.

Dad flipped through the pages, then stopped to read. "This is smart," he muttered.

"Your record matches voting preferences in the district. There's not much your opponents can do with that. Mr. Stone has connections, but you have better name recognition. If we can get enough votes to force a runoff, it will be about working the difference between the two of you." India reached into her bag and pulled out a laptop. "We'll recruit volunteers and start reaching out to community leaders. We need a nonstop schedule. I'll start making calls today. I'll get you, your wife, and Kate booked in every meeting, church, and VFW hall."

Dad looked up from the pages India had given him. "Kate is not available during the election."

"Why not?" India asked.

"She's focusing on her studies." He looked at me. "Right, Kate?"

India tilted her head and lifted her chin. "Is that the real answer or the answer we're giving?"

"You can consider it both," Dad said.

"If this is about that admissions thing, I think taking down the elite at a snobby prep school could play well here."

"You know about that?" I said.

India gave a single nod. "It's my job."

"Now your job is to run this campaign without Kate," Dad said.

She opened her mouth to argue, then snapped it shut. "Fine. Get me a list of other campaign surrogates, and we'll go from there."

"Kate, you probably have homework," Dad said.

"Yep, I've got to catch a cricket."

"Good, good," he said, already buried in the briefing book.

I flinched at the dismissal before I could catch myself. India's brow wrinkled for a second. "Good luck," she said to me.

I rummaged around my room and found a small box and a piece of paper. When my hand brushed my camera sitting on my desk, I picked it up and slung it around my neck. The weight grounded me.

Thirty minutes later, the wind had knotted my hair. Dust clung to my teeth and tickled the inside of my nose. The only thing that kept me going was the smug satisfaction I could imagine on Hunter's face if I showed up without a cricket the next day. I was so tired of people who thought I couldn't do things—Dad didn't think I could campaign, Aunt Celia didn't think I could help at the shelter, Hunter didn't think I could catch a cricket. I would love to prove one of them wrong.

I heard the crickets' song in the grass, but as soon as I inched up on one, it skipped away. "There is a meal of tasty ants for the next cricket who jumps in the box and comes to school with me," I announced.

The crickets went silent for a moment. Then one took a small leap onto a patch of dry grass. I held my breath and started to lower the box to the ground. The cricket jumped a few times, just out of reach. I took one step, then another. I eased the box down over him; then he took a flying leap. I lunged forward, but my shirtsleeve caught on a loose piece of rusted barbed wire hanging from a post. I tugged it free, tearing my shirt. Finally, I just hurled the box toward the horizon.

"You have a good arm. It must run in the family."

I turned around. Kyle Stone was watching me from two posts away.

"What are you doing out here?" I said.

"We're neighbors. I saw you from the back window. I decided to see what you were up to. Dad's got a bunch of potential donors talking campaign finance."

"My dad is meeting his new campaign manager. He's probably telling her what a disaster I am."

"Dad's probably telling his donors all my stats from this season." He stepped on a line of barbed wire with his boot, bent under another, and strolled over.

"You're lucky. Your dad's proud of you."

"Naw, he'll find a way to take credit for all of it. I thought you might be practicing taking pictures before the big game Friday."

I looked down at my camera and shook my head. "I don't need practice."

"Are you sure? You could take my picture." He brought his hand to his chin and struck a pose, looking thoughtfully into the distance.

I laughed. "I don't usually take pictures of people, but I'll keep you in mind. I'm trying to catch a cricket."

"Is this for your science project?"

"Yes."

"Why don't you get Hunter to catch it?"

"There was a dare involved." I tried to blink the dust from my eyes. "It's kind of a blur."

"Do you want me to catch you a cricket?" Kyle asked. "I don't like to brag, but I am pretty amazing at catching the little guys."

"It would be better if you could coach me through it. That way I could say I did it myself. I can't stand one more of Hunter's superior looks."

Kyle threw his head back and laughed. "I knew I liked you, Hamilton. How about we make a deal? I help you catch a cricket, and you take a picture of me."

"Deal." I smiled at him and brushed a strand of hair out of my eyes.

"You're better off getting settled and waiting for them to come to you." He crouched down and peered into the shade of a spiky bush about ten feet away. He was still for a few seconds; then, in one smooth movement, he cupped his hands over a spot of dry grass. He slid his hands together, leaving a bubble of space between the palms.

"You got one!" I said.

"Move fast enough and they won't know what happened until it's too late. I told you I was good."

"I thought you didn't like to brag," I pointed out.

"When you're this good, you have to get used to it. Your turn. Just settle in, and when it's in your reach, put the box over it."

I ran to get the box. I moved through the brush until I spotted a cricket under a tangle of brush. I waited. The cricket chirped, then hopped closer. It chirped again. A few hops later, it moved into the perfect patch of dry ground. I held my breath and slammed the box over the spot where the cricket sat. I could feel it bump against the box as it tried to get out. "I got one!"

"You're a fast learner." Kyle pushed the paper under the box. "And I'm an amazing teacher. Don't forget your side of the bargain."

I found a spot to set down the box and adjusted a few settings on my camera. I pointed to one of the fence posts. "Lean against it, like you were when I walked up." I raised the camera to my eye. Kyle crossed his arms, flexed his biceps, and lifted his chest. "Try to relax."

"I'm relaxed."

Kyle had the same confidence he was special that Parker had. He didn't have the deviousness, but that arrogance was enough to put the lid on any flirtation, as cute as Tasha would say he was. I snapped the picture.

"Can I see it?"

"It's a film camera. You'll have to wait until I develop it."

"You use actual film?"

"Yep."

Kyle winked. "Too bad. I was looking forward to showing my dad."

"You always looking for ways to drive your dad crazy?"

"Gotta have some fun." He waved a hand. "I guess I'll just have to trust you. I better get back."

"There's one more thing." I looked at the box, then up at Kyle. "I would love it if Hunter thought I handled this by myself."

"You don't have to worry. It will be our secret," Kyle said.

After he strolled away, I turned toward the shelter. If Hunter was there, I could hand him the box, enjoy my first victory in Red Dirt, and avoid worrying about keeping a cricket alive overnight.

His truck was parked in the driveway, so I headed to the barn to find him. As soon as I stepped on the worn floor planks, the animals pushed their heads over the stall doors. I walked with slow, hesitant steps down the center aisle.

"Hunter?" I called. No answer. I peered into the second stall, where the cow had been last night.

Two calves lay with their heads side by side, sleeping. I folded my arms on the door and rested my chin on them. Those had to be the new calves. Their dark fur was spotted with bright white. Long eyelashes rested against the fur around their eyes. Their thin legs curled under them. They were fragile and beautiful. I raised my camera and snapped a few shots.

The barn door swung open. "What are you doing in here?" Aunt Celia called.

I took a step back from the stall. "I had something for Hunter."

She eyed me as she walked over.

"We're science partners. I was supposed to get a cricket, and I just thought I'd deliver it before I killed it," I said.

"I sent him in my truck to pick up some feed for the chickens."

I nodded to the calves. "Did you name them yet?"

She rubbed her face. "Tip and Ty." She pointed to each.

I reached down and touched the top of Ty's head. "Where'd you get those names?" I asked.

" 'Tippecanoe and Tyler, Too'—the slogan for William Henry Harrison and John Tyler's 1840 campaign." Aunt Celia shrugged. "I would have thought someone with your background would know that."

"You named them after politicians?"

"All the animals are named after politicians."

I laughed, but the sound faded into the silence between us. Aunt Celia's face didn't crack. "It's just surprising," I said. "Surprising and perfect."

She walked to the corner, picked up a bucket, and started to fill it with water from a hose that threaded across the floor. "Don't you have something teenagery to do—rage against authority, roll your eyes, mooch off your parents?"

"I already filled my eye-rolling quota." I knelt down to get a closer look at the calves. "I'm waiting for Mom to get home. I'm hoping she'll drive me to the library. Dad thinks Mrs. Fisher will let me volunteer there."

"Caroline? That busybody could talk the feathers off a chicken. You'll waste half your time listening to town gossip." Aunt Celia crossed her arms. "Why don't you tell me exactly why you need these volunteer hours?"

74

I stood and faced Aunt Celia. "I need hours so that the principal will write me a college recommendation."

"I'm sure your dad can get you plenty of recommendations."

I looked at the floor. "Not to art school."

She whistled low. "Does your dad know?"

I shook my head.

"Your mom?"

I lifted my eyes and met her gaze. "What do you think?"

"Is this why you aren't doing anything with the campaign?"

"Dad said he didn't need me. Which is a relief, because I was getting tired of faking it all the time."

Aunt Celia put on her gloves and turned to leave. "It seems like you're doing as much faking as before."

The truth sometimes feels like a punch to the gut. I stiffened. "I'm just waiting for the right time to tell them," I said.

Aunt Celia looked around the barn, then back at me. "I could use some help Saturday if you have time." She jerked a thumb at the calves. "The mother is rejecting them, so Hunter has to spend half his time on feedings."

"Really?" I thought of Parker, bragging about getting the recommendation. "Do you think I could start earlier? I can come by tomorrow after school if—"

"Don't push it. We start at seven a.m. Wear something that can get dirty. You're not shelving books."

"Thanks, Aunt Celia," I said, fighting back a grin.

"Soak a cotton ball in water and put it in the box with the cricket. That should keep him alive until tomorrow," she said as she walked away.

chapter eight

As I reached for Mr. Quincy's door the next day, Kyle broke away from a pack of red jerseys and came toward me. Missy leaned against a line of lockers, her eyes following him possessively. Kyle ignored her while simultaneously placing his back squarely in her line of vision.

"Hey, did the cricket survive the night?" he said.

I patted my bag. "He was alive when I put him in this morning." I felt the weight of more curious stares. "Thanks for your help."

"Anytime," Kyle said, pushing open the classroom door. He stared down Hunter, then moved to his seat at the center of the room.

Hunter raised an eyebrow when I dropped my bag on the tile next to his boots. "What was that about?"

"What?"

"You and Kyle."

"You worried he might dazzle me with his science knowledge and steal me away to be his lab partner?"

Hunter snorted. "Naw, he's not the guy you came to the shelter to see last night." One side of his mouth turned up.

"I came by to give you the cricket."

He nodded. "Did it take you long to come up with that excuse?"

I reached down to the front pocket of my bag, pulled out the box, and set it on the table.

"You look pleased with yourself," Hunter said.

"Just trying to make a point." I leaned back in my chair. "I don't back down."

"I knew that when you refused to take your hands out of a cow," he said, laughing. He set the tray of ants next to the cricket. "Are you sure you want to do this? It could destroy our entire ant society."

I took a deep breath. "No guts, no glory," I said, nodding for him to open up the box.

He eased the lid off the container, dumped the cricket into the tray, and closed the top. The cricket's back legs twitched. The ants didn't react at first. They wove in and out of each other. Then one ant approached the cricket. The cricket slung his thin legs at the ant, so it scurried away, then circled to the other side. After a few seconds, another ant joined him. They almost seemed to be taunting the cricket. Soon a swarm of ants surrounded the cricket, tumbling over him. The cricket struggled, but the blanket of tiny bugs overwhelmed him and he fell to his side. The ants moved in waves over him until his legs were still.

Hunter and I exchanged looks.

"An interesting experiment," Mr. Quincy said, leaning over Hunter's shoulder. "Any observations?"

"It looked a lot like the experiment with the sugar yesterday," Hunter said, watching the swarm continue to roll across the cricket.

"Similar principle. Whether it's food or danger, they lead each other to it," Mr. Quincy said.

"Why would they lead each other into danger?" I asked.

He faced me, his eyes twinkling with that light teachers get when they see an opportunity to dispense knowledge. "Ants are more powerful as a group than individually. They create whole empires with collective will."

"Even if the collective will kills them?" I asked.

"Their strength lies in society, not individualism. Ants know that all you have to do is outnumber an enemy by enough and you can conquer anything."

"How did they know what to do?" I asked.

"Easy. They do whatever everybody else is doing," Hunter said.

Mr. Quincy tapped his nose and moved on to the next table.

Kyle strolled over and looked in the tray. "Nice cricket."

"Appreciate that, Kyle," Hunter said.

Kyle frowned. "I heard you weren't man enough to get one."

"So you stepped in," Hunter said.

He tilted his head and grinned. "I might have helped."

I winced. But I couldn't be too angry. It's part of existing in a campaign cycle—you get in the habit of grabbing any win you can. I didn't know if I could have resisted it either.

"I knew you could fill in. There's no shame in being the backup, is there, Kyle?" Hunter said.

Kyle's face tightened. "I wouldn't know."

"Good luck Friday against Junction. You shouldn't be worried. Even if you throw a couple . . . three interceptions, like you did against Stanton, the defense can pick you up. Good thing you don't have the weight of the entire team on your shoulders."

"At least I don't quit," Kyle growled, his hands gripping the end of the lab table. "Only losers quit."

Hunter slid his hands into his pockets. "No, you definitely don't quit. You just skip right to the losing."

"I heard your mom's back in town," Kyle said.

"Don't, Stone." Hunter stood.

"How long do you think she'll stick around?"

Kyle lifted his chest as Hunter took a step toward him. I put a hand on Hunter's arm. "Okay, boys. Relax." I waved a piece of paper in front of Hunter's face. "Let's get the experiment written up."

Before Kyle could say another word, Mr. Quincy called him back to his table.

"What's the deal between you and Kyle?" I asked Hunter as he sat down.

He took a breath. "Isn't it obvious?" He pulled out a spiral notebook and started writing. "We don't like each other."

"Is that it?"

"It's pretty simple, Hamilton. Most things are."

"It seems like there's history."

"Kyle and I have been in the same class since kindergarten. Of course there's history. Everyone in Red Dirt has history." He tapped the notebook with his pen. "Are we going to start working or what?"

I dug in my backpack for a pen. "You know, if you guys were ants, you would have to play on the same team," I said.

"We'd also live sixty days and spend most of them moving larvae. A lot to be grateful for."

I frowned and started writing.

After school, Ms. Serrano handed me the official yearbook camera.

"It's digital," I said.

"Is that a problem?"

"I could probably get better pictures with my camera."

Lines formed between her eyes. "You'll use our camera." She opened up the cabinet and reached for a lens. "You'll probably need this. And you'll need a flash to even out the gym's lighting."

Lines of black-and-white eight-by-ten pictures covered the insides of the cabinet doors. Some were portraits. A close-up of a grandmother rolling out dough with wrinkled hands caught my eye. "Those don't look digital."

Ms. Serrano slammed the cabinet door closed. "You'll get the pictures I want with the camera I want. Understood?"

I took a step back from the desk.

She closed her eyes for a second. When she opened them, they were softer. "Look, I get that you have far more artistic integrity than the average seventeen-year-old, but I need these pictures. We don't have many more basketball games before these layouts are due."

"I am going to take the best basketball pictures you've ever seen."

Ms. Serrano put her hand on her hip. "Because I'll have you copyediting the index if you don't?"

"Because I need that darkroom even more than you need a photographer."

She tilted her head, one of her giant silver-and-turquoise earrings swinging beside her face. "So what are you standing here for?"

I headed to the gym and tried to find a good spot to set up while the teams stretched. My plan was to take a few pictures and head back to the yearbook room.

Then the game started.

I had watched basketball before, but I didn't realize what a chaotic mess it was. Arms flew in front of faces. Players twisted and spun out of the frame. As soon as I found a decent shot of one player reaching around another, complete with gritted teeth, the player would rotate and shoot, and the shot disappeared. Most of the time, I caught part of the shot, or a slice of a blurry jersey or a segment of leg. By the middle of the second half, that's all I had—pictures of arms and legs.

When the second buzzer sounded, I collapsed onto the bleacher and scrolled through the shots. Great. This was going to be another thing I couldn't do.

"Do you have a few good ones?" I turned to see Ana peering over my shoulder.

"I think something is wrong with the shutter speed. This is why I don't like digital."

"It's not the camera. It's a tough sport to shoot," Ana said.

"It's impossible," I said. "How am I supposed to get anything in focus? At this rate people will think the basketball team is a bunch of blurry disembodied limbs."

"That would explain their season." She nudged me with her shoulder. "I can help you. First, get your easy shots on the sidelines so that you have something," she said.

"What do you mean?"

"You don't have to have the camera focused on the ball all the time." Ana pointed to the stands. "Watch the coach, the crowd, the other players on the bench. They don't move as much. And it gives you a chance to get the lighting right."

I framed the coach, his finger pointed at the chest of another player. I got the shot set up, then clicked, and the first decent picture of the night appeared in the viewfinder.

"Try the fans."

"All eight of them?"

Ana smiled. "Basketball games take a hit when the football team is doing well. They also lost two of their best players when grades came out."

"Grades?"

"No pass, no play. The Dirt Devil basketball team isn't exactly a bunch of brainiacs. Last year they lost so many players they had to pull from the JV team to finish the season. Fortunately, it's not about what you see. It's about what the lens sees." She took the camera. "You have to use your angles." She snapped a picture of the bleachers, then leaned the camera toward me.

"It's all about the context," I said. She'd framed a cluster of four faces but zoomed in on one, letting the others blur and fill in the background, making it look like the stands were packed. "You're brilliant."

"Now for the action. I think you're waiting for the perfect shot. Take a lot of pictures." She reached over and switched it to multi-shot mode. "Most of them are going to be terrible, but one or two will be good. That's all you need."

I clicked through dozens of frames in the last ten minutes of the game. I got a shot of two players battling over the ball. Even on the small screen, the intensity of their eyes popped. I caught a couple of players stretching to block shots. I even captured one shot of a line of players, wrestling to catch the rebound off a free throw. The game got worse as the minutes on the scoreboard ticked down, but with tight frames and constant shooting, the pictures got better.

I was surprised when the buzzer rang, ending the torture for the Red Dirt team with a 26 to 60 loss. Ana and I sat down on the bleachers and scrolled through the pictures. She pointed out the ones Ms. Serrano would like.

"Do you think it will be enough for her to put me on staff?"

"Hard to say." Ana handed the camera back to me. "Why do you need the darkroom so badly? Can't you just use digital?"

I shook my head. "It's not the same. You've never developed film before?"

"Some of us aren't stuck in the last century."

"Talk to me after you've watched a picture dissolve onto a blank sheet of paper."

Ana laughed.

"So you're only using digital in your portfolio?" I asked.

"What portfolio?"

"For art school. You haven't started one? London McCarthy didn't start hers until senior year and she ended up in some tiny program in Idaho," I said, packing up the camera. "What programs do you want to apply to?"

"I'm not applying to any art program," Ana said.

I looked up from the bag. "But you're amazing. I know you took that picture in the yearbook. The one with the player looking up at the stands while everyone celebrates behind him."

Ana nodded. "That was Kyle and his dad. I got in trouble for that. Well, not exactly me. Ms. Serrano took the brunt of it."

"Why?"

"I guess it wasn't the way they wanted to remember that game."

"But it was real. More than that—it was art."

She shook her head. "I don't see my pictures as art."

"What do you see when you look at your pictures?"

"Stories," Ana said. She twisted a strand of long brown hair between her fingers. "If I could ever get out of this town, I'd be a photojournalist. Travel the world taking pictures that tell people's stories."

The door to the locker room opened and a basketball player started across the gym. The guy's mouth turned down at the corners. A layer of sweat still clung to his forehead. Ana dipped her head and let a curtain of hair cover the side of her face.

The guy's nose wrinkled when he saw her. "Coach said there was some trash left in the bleachers."

Red rushed into Ana's cheeks. She rose. Two girls who had lingered in the stands giggled. "Let's go," Ana muttered to me.

I looked from her to the basketball player. "Okay, I can't stand by and watch you shrivel up when someone attacks you." I stood and raised my voice as loud as his. "Is he talking about you?" I asked Ana. "Are you talking about her?" I called to the guy's back.

Ana's eyes pleaded with me. But the guy's words had hardened a knot of determination inside me. There are rules. You don't attack when you aren't being attacked, and you don't hit below the belt. I nudged her side. "Say something like 'That's tough talk for someone who didn't put a single point on the board.' Or maybe you should just point to the scoreboard. It's subtle but has a bite."

Ana shook her head. The gym door slammed shut.

"You need a ride?" Ana asked, twisting her hair.

I took her wrist and pulled her hand away from her hair. "You're seriously going to pretend he didn't call you trash?"

"People say a lot of stuff. It's no big deal."

"It is a big deal if it keeps you from going to the basketball games."

She sighed. "Could you not tell Ms. Serrano?"

She looked so sad, so defeated. All the outrage inside me softened. "No problem. I owe you for helping me with the pictures." I nudged her shoulder again. "Who's the idiot?"

"His name is Hank. He's an ex-boyfriend."

"You dated that guy?"

Ana pressed her lips together and stared straight ahead.

"Was it a head injury?"

She smiled.

I looped my arm through hers and fell in step beside her. "You're not the first girl to date pond scum masquerading as a boy. I'll tell you about my ex sometime. What you need is some damage control with a touch of revenge. I guarantee I got a picture of him in a really awkward pose."

A tiny giggle escaped Ana, and her shoulders relaxed.

"Pictures can do a lot of damage. Trust me."

"Ms. Serrano is pretty strict about what goes in and what doesn't," Ana said.

I swung the camera strap over my shoulder. "I'd still be nice to the people printing the pictures in a book that I'll show my children."

chapter nine

Friday after fourth period, I bypassed the cafeteria and headed straight for the yearbook room. I'd printed the few basketball pictures that Ana helped me get at home. I didn't need the journalism department's perpetually broken or jammed printer to cause another delay. My stomach twisted as I walked to Ms. Serrano's desk and laid the stack of photos on top of a pile of other papers.

"Are these from last night's basketball game?" Ms. Serrano asked. Her face settled into stony stillness.

"Yes, ma'am," I said.

"Kate did an amazing job," Ana said next to me.

I tried to keep my breath steady and my posture confident while Ms. Serrano studied a picture of one of the players on the bench. He leaned forward, his elbows on his knees, his face chiseled into intense concentration. Then she held up a picture of a player knocking his shoulder into another player, the ball mid-dribble. "They're better than nothing." She threw the last two down on the desk in front of me. "Give them to Jessica. She edits the sports section. And make sure you take a camera down to the pep rally next period."

"Does that mean I'm on staff?"

Ms. Serrano pointed a red fingernail at me. "We lie low, we take pictures, we make a yearbook, got it?"

I nodded.

She yanked her drawer open and handed over a key. "This unlocks the darkroom. Knock yourself out."

Ana pulled me into a side hug. My stomach did flips of excitement.

Ana led me to a door in the back corner of the room. The darkroom at my old school had been my sanctuary. It was easy to control. You timed every step. There were no politics, no power plays. Everything was black and white, light and dark. Just me and the photographs.

"I've always wanted to see inside this room," Ana said.

"Wait, you mean you haven't been in there?" I said, sliding the key in the lock.

"Kate, no one goes in there."

I turned the key and pushed the door open. This was it. I caught the faint smell of chemicals before the door slammed to a halt a foot from the frame.

I peered in. The room was stacked with boxes from floor to ceiling. I squeezed inside.

"What's in the boxes?" Ana asked from the doorway.

I peeled open the flaps on the closest box. "Yearbooks." A puff of dust drifted into my nose. "Old yearbooks."

Ms. Serrano walked by and glanced in. "Oh yeah, I meant to move those last summer. Don't worry. I have the shelves for them. You just have to take them out, unbox them, and arrange them chronologically along the back wall."

I put my hands on my hips and stepped back. "Classic bait and switch."

Ms. Serrano stopped and turned. "Classic supply and demand. I supply the darkroom, but I demand that you move those yearbooks."

"I was hoping to get some pictures developed today. Maybe make a contact sheet, you know, with all the negatives—"

"I know what a contact sheet is," Ms. Serrano said as she marched back toward her desk. "And if you want to get anything developed, you should spend less time teaching me Photography 101 and more time unpacking boxes."

After twenty minutes pushing boxes, I had made a path to the sink and found a cabinet full of chemicals and trays. The room was well stocked and the chemicals weren't more than a few years old. It was perfect, even worth all the effort.

I went to get my camera. I hadn't finished a single roll, but I could at least get the chemicals organized and see what I had so far. Ms. Serrano looked up from her desk. "Are you two going to take your behinds down to the pep rally, or should I have some freshman text me some pictures from his phone?"

"Can I bring my camera? I need to finish a roll."

"Is it digital?"

"No, but I'll develop the pictures."

"Great. Then we can *burro* them to the publisher."

"She can scan them in," Ana said.

Ms. Serrano shook her head. "You two are trying to send me to the loony bin." She threw her arms up and walked away rattling off a string of Spanish words, none of which we'd covered in my week of Spanish I.

"That was a yes, right?" I asked.

"I think she's starting to like you," Ana said, picking up a camera.

Cameras slung around our necks, we followed the bass of the drums down the hall to the gym. Students squeezed between columns of balloons to reach the bleachers. Women tugging the hands of toddlers sat beside men with deep wrinkles cutting across their faces. Red-and-black banners wrapped the gym in slogans. The football players filed to their places in lines of silver folding chairs.

"You think it's a little much?" Ana said.

"It's impressive. Is the whole town here?" I asked.

"Yep. Junction is our big rival. Red Dirt is in the playoffs, but beating Junction means bragging rights for another year."

It was too many potential voters for Dad to resist. I scanned the crowd. The entire band joined the rhythm of the drums.

"What do you take pictures of?" I yelled in her ear.

"Anything that screams victory."

I raised my camera and snapped a few shots. I was framing a picture of a line of students pouring through the double doors when Dad stepped into the frame. He came over and pulled me into an obligatory half hug. "What's with the camera?"

"I'm taking pictures for the yearbook."

"Great. Nice to see you fitting in."

"Why does everyone think I have a problem fitting in?"

Dad took a step back. "Don't get defensive. I was just—"

Mom slid beside Dad. "Loaded mike, twelve o'clock."

India led a reporter to where we stood, a cameraman trailing a few steps behind them.

Dad's face broke into his campaign smile as he stepped in front of me slightly. He shook the hand of the reporter. "Jenkins! How's my favorite offensive lineman?"

"Doin' well," the man said. "Got myself a spot on the local news for the Midland/Odessa station, so when your campaign manager called and said that the prodigal son had returned just before the big game with Junction, I thought I might as well stop by and see if I can get a quote. Miss Truss can be very persuasive."

"I'm happy to answer a few questions," Dad said.

"Who's this pretty lady?" He nodded toward me.

Hesitation flashed over Dad's face. I wouldn't have noticed if I didn't know that Dad planned all his moves two or three steps before the moment came to make them. If he'd wanted to introduce me, he'd have had his arm over my shoulder, easing me toward the man before he finished his first sentence.

"This is my daughter. Kate, this is Mr. Jenkins, one of the best linebackers in the history of Red Dirt. If your quarterback is the heart of the team, the linemen are the guts." Mr. Jenkins grinned. Kyle might have a glow, but I had to hand it to Dad: He gave other people a glow.

"Let's go in the hall," Dad said.

"By the trophy case," India added.

Dad, India, and Mom took a step toward the gym doors.

"You comin', Kate?" Mr. Jenkins asked.

"Kate is taking yearbook photos."

I held up my camera.

Mr. Jenkins grinned. "Good idea. Can't come all the way out here and not get some footage of the pep rally. It will come in handy when the playoffs start next week." He leaned over to give a few directions to his cameraman and then turned back to us. "We'll meet you by the door in fifteen minutes."

The pep rally was decent as events go. Not a lot of emotional impact, but certainly attention-getting. Work in a few military veterans and some talking points and they would have had a respectable campaign stop. The cheerleaders lined up on the floor along the front row, and Kyle rose and moved to the microphone. A wave of cheers swept the gym.

Dad and India wandered toward the bleachers. I took a breath and looked at Kyle through the viewfinder. He stood at the center of the gym, microphone in hand. "WHO ARE WE?"

"RAIDERS!" the crowd called back.

"WHAT DO WE WANT?"

"VICTORY!"

Kyle was Hercules, larger than life. At the same time, he was predictable, almost a stereotype, and easy to digest. Just the kind of kid the media loved. I finally saw what Dad must have known the moment he found out Bo Stone was running: Kyle held the role of town hero. If I campaigned, it would give people the opportunity to compare me to Kyle, and I wouldn't measure up. This defeat burned inside me. I snapped the last pictures on the roll and lowered my camera. I spotted India by the door, waving me toward her, and I walked over while Kyle continued his speech. "Dad doesn't want me at his interview," I said.

"But he needs you there." She grabbed my hand and pulled me into the hallway. We crossed to where Mr. Jenkins stood. He handed lapel mikes to me, Mom, and Dad.

"Kate is not——" Dad started, but the band began playing full force, drowning him out. I looked at India, who grabbed the mike and clipped it to my shirt.

Mr. Jenkins pulled on a suit jacket as he strolled down the hall. "What do you think of our chances in the playoffs?"

"They look good," Dad said. "Stone has a cannon. We'll beat Junction tonight, then the first round next week will be against Sugar Elm. Their corners can't cover, and their safeties are lost."

"They have a mean pass rush," Mr. Jenkins said.

We turned the corner that led to the front hallway and almost ran into Bo Stone. His eyes scanned the group as he stuck out his hand. "Jenkins, good to see you. Did you come to get footage of the pep rally?"

"Yes, sir."

"You better get down there. It's already started," Dad said.

Bo Stone crossed his arms. "I've seen every Red Dirt pep rally for the past forty years. I think I can miss a few more minutes." His eyes fixed on me. "You probably don't know much about football, do you, honey?"

The image of how people saw me crystallized more. Kyle could bring home a state championship. I could hit all my talking points and smile for hours.

Mr. Stone softened his voice like he was talking to a child, still addressing me. "See, Sugar Elm has two defensive ends who are going D-1 next year."

I squeezed my lips shut and wondered how long this conversation could possibly go on. Across the hallway, Hunter pushed open the library door.

"Defensive ends are defensive players," Mr. Stone said slowly. "They are good at tackling the quarterback, the guy who throws the ball. That's Kyle's job."

The skin on my arms prickled with irritation.

Hunter approached. "Are we talking about Sugar Elm's pass rush?" he asked.

Mr. Stone's jaw tightened. "Not your concern anymore, is it, son?"

Something about Bo Stone's arrogance, the way he dismissed everyone else, twisted inside me. I dug out some information I'd picked up from eavesdropping and precalc word problems and said, "I don't think you have to worry about the defense. Kyle threw twenty-six touchdowns and only four interceptions this season, completing"—I thought for a second—"seventy-six percent of his passes, which is fairly impressive, considering how pass-heavy your offense is. And really, Coach Watkins should take advantage of that next weekend, because the Sugar Elm cornerbacks can't handle your receivers in press coverage. If Kyle gets it anywhere near his target, the game will be over mid-first quarter."

I enjoyed the moment. Bo Stone scratched his jaw. Dad frowned in my direction. If there was one thing I had been trained to do since birth, it was fake it. It actually came in handy sometimes.

"You really know your stuff," Hunter said. "So, what are you going to do if the Junction coach rolls his corners back into a cover three?"

My mouth went dry. I glared at Hunter. His eyes danced with amusement. "I don't know, I guess . . ." I tried to think of something that sounded like it would fit, but I was too furious. I had said the perfect thing, and Hunter had ruined it.

"You'd probably have your receivers break off their routes and sit down in their zones," Hunter offered.

I turned to Dad. A single line of worry creased his forehead. I spotted the red light on the camera. The mike was on and the camera was rolling. I'd done it again.

"Yeah, that's it," I said, my voice stretched tight with irritation.

"Don't sweat it. You can't know everything," Hunter said, strolling down the hall.

"If you're here to talk to someone about Red Dirt Raiders football, maybe you should talk to Kyle," Bo said.

Dad stepped forward. "But we aren't. As much as we all love football, why don't we talk about something that people in this district struggle with off the field—the Farm Bill. Work on the bill starts two years before the vote. Someone with experience could step into a seat and get benefits for small farms from day one."

And just like that, Dad had whisked me away from controversy again.

chapter ten

I stormed up to the yearbook room, which was unlocked. I fished the key to the darkroom from my pocket, slipped inside, and slammed the door behind me.

I knew I made mistakes. I'd even accepted that those mistakes got broadcast to a slightly larger audience than your average teenager's. But when a consultant or manager damaged the campaign, Dad fired them. When an issue caused problems, Dad spun it. I was a problem he couldn't fire or fix.

I shut off the lights and wound the film onto the developing reel in darkness. Then I turned on the red light and started to wash the film in a series of chemicals. The precise times and temperatures that it took to bring the negatives to life crowded out my disappointment, anger, and humiliation.

While the film dried, I adjusted the enlarger. Then I lined up the negatives in a sleeve, exposed them onto a sheet, and dropped the paper into the chemicals. This was the moment I loved, when a white sheet of paper became a picture. Nothing turned into something. Already my head had cleared, organized itself into lines of negatives, f-stops, and exposure times.

I decided to print a few pictures. I enlarged Kyle at the pep rally for Ms. Serrano. His body filled the frame, leaving just enough room to see that he stood in a gym surrounded by teammates, cheerleaders, and fans. I printed the picture of Kyle after he helped me catch the cricket, and a couple more of the pep rally, including the one I shot of Dad as he spotted me. Finally, I printed a picture of the calves.

I hung the photographs to dry on a line I'd strung between the bookcases in the hall. I pulled the photo of Dad out of the last wash and laid it on a tray. It wasn't the best picture I'd taken, and Dad would hate it. His hand rubbed a path through his hair. The edges of his eyes turned down and his brow wrinkled. But I had to admit, he looked . . . real.

I ripped it in two and tossed it in the trash by Ms. Serrano's desk.

The sun kissed the horizon when I pushed through the front doors. The pep rally was long over, and I didn't have a ride home. I didn't want to call Mom and Dad. I lifted my head, hiked my book bag higher on my shoulder, and started down the concrete road. It wasn't that far. I walked places all the time in DC.

Ten minutes later, dust coated my face, my backpack felt like I'd packed it with Dad's strategy notebooks, and my hair flew in a tangled mass. A truck pulled up beside me, kicking rocks against my ankles.

"What are you doing, Hamilton?" Hunter called over the passenger seat.

"Walking," I said, hoping he would drive on.

He eased the truck slowly down the road, keeping pace with me. "Do you want a ride?"

"No," I said.

"I'm going to the shelter."

I shook my head.

The truck crawled beside me.

"I said I didn't need a ride."

"And I said I was going to the shelter. We don't have to rush everywhere like you city folk do." Hunter drove a few more feet, then turned on the radio. A deep, gravelly voice accompanied the guitar chords from the speakers.

"You just want to get under my skin."

He turned down the radio. "Did you say something?"

"What do you have against me?"

"It's a free country, Hamilton. I can drive on this road if I want to."

"Not this. I mean you're always there, waiting for me to fall on my face. I don't know if you've noticed, but I have enough people watching for that."

"You don't know the first thing about falling on your face. Why do you try so hard to win?"

"I don't have to win." I brushed the beginnings of tears from my eyes and tightened the grip on the emotions spinning inside my chest. "I just hate losing."

Hunter's voice turned serious. "Get in, Kate. I don't want you to have to walk home. It's about four miles and the wind is picking up."

I stopped walking and looked at him.

"I'm sorry about earlier. I didn't know it would matter this much. I was just trying to mess with you."

"On TV."

"I didn't think about that. You're right." He looked down. When he looked at me again, his eyes held an intensity that made my heart skip. "I'm really sorry, Kate. I get so used to ignoring everyone's opinions, sometimes I forget how they feel."

I wrenched my gaze away from his and stared into the distance.

"Now get in the truck. Do I have to remind you about the snakes?"

I pulled open the door and slid onto the seat.

"Why don't you have a car?" Hunter asked, starting to accelerate.

"It wouldn't matter. I don't know how to drive."

He slammed on the brakes. "You're kidding, right?"

"My parents just never had time to teach me. We're always busy campaigning. And in DC we have this thing called public transportation."

Hunter put the truck in park and got out.

"What are you doing?" I yelled through the open back window. "We're in the middle of the road. Get back in the car."

He strolled to my door and pulled it open. "Move over."

"Why?"

"I'm teaching you how to drive."

I shook my head. "I can't."

"Come on, you have to let me make up for being such an idiot," he said.

I slumped against the seat and stared out the window. "No, you still don't get it. I'll hit something," I said. "Then people will find out that I hit something, and my dad will get furious, not because the car is wrecked, not because his insurance goes up, but because the talk shows will start asking him questions about teenage drivers. He'll be asked if texting on the road should be illegal, and as a father, does he support a curfew for teens. They won't ask about me, but it will be a barrage of questions that surround me, and he'll have to field every one. Then they'll start looking at Kyle Stone's driving record, which is probably perfect, and Dad will come home at the end of the day, and I'll get that look. The look you saw today."

Hunter pointed out the front window to the empty desert. "What are you going to hit?"

I looked at the horizon. The sky stretched for miles in front of me. It felt more part of the landscape than the sky in DC, like you could touch it. It was an irrefutable argument, elegant and simple.

"And if it helps," Hunter said, "Kyle drives like a blind monkey."

"Fine." I slid over and Hunter climbed into the passenger seat. "But this is your dumbest idea yet."

"Oh, good. As long as you aren't going to thank me. The pedal on the left is the brake. Put your foot on it and press down as far as you can."

I did what Hunter said, pressing the pedal.

"Now pull the gear toward you and down two clicks until it moves into drive." I did that, and he put his hand on the wheel and turned it gently. "Ease your foot off the brake and move into the road."

The car jerked forward as I switched from the brake to the accelerator to the brake.

"Don't worry. It's normal to make the passenger nauseous," Hunter said.

I gripped the steering wheel, sweat making it slippery. "Your idea."

"You should probably blink."

"Not if you don't want me ramming into something."

The roads were flat and straight. Hunter had me move slowly down the road at first. Then he let me push down on the accelerator. After a couple of miles, my hands were still sweaty, but the pounding of my heart had quieted slightly.

"What were you doing at the school so late?"

"Developing some pictures," I said. I glanced in the rearview mirror. "There's a truck behind me. What do I do?"

Hunter looked over his shoulder. "Nothing. Can I see your photos?"

"There wasn't anything worth keeping." I looked in the rearview mirror again. "Is there any way to make it go around me? I don't want it so close."

"It's fifteen feet back."

I tightened my grip.

"Fine, turn right at the next road," Hunter said.

"Turn? I'm going too fast. He's too close," I said, panic sending drips of sweat down the back of my neck.

Hunter put his hand on mine. "Ease down on the brake and start to turn the wheel." I managed to do it, and the truck rumbled down a gravel road. The road ended in the middle of a field. I brought the truck to a stop and put it in park. "Did you at least have a little fun?"

I had to admit, there was something exciting about moving a hunk of metal through space. I looked out over the dry pasture that we'd pulled into. It stretched beyond a wooden fence that had aged gray. "Is this where you take all the girls? Part of your tragic bad boy persona?"

Hunter laughed. "You think you have everyone figured out, don't you?"

"What's to figure out? You're the rebel without a cause. Kyle is the alpha-male jock. You can't stand each other because in the high school social order, he is at the top and you are on the outside. He threatens your alternative worldview, and you threaten his status quo. In politics, he's the incumbent and you're the challenger railing against the system."

"You have some interesting theories," Hunter said, putting his hands behind his head.

"Is that your way of saying I'm right?"

"It's my way of saying you've been here three days."

"Yeah, but I've been in politics for most of my life."

Hunter opened the door and stepped out of the truck.

"Where are you going?" I asked.

"Come on. We're getting a picture."

"Where?"

"Wait for it," he said, hopping up on the front of the truck. I climbed next to him. "Does that guy in DC you're obsessed with take pictures?"

"I'm not obsessed with—"

"I know. You just make it so easy to get a rise out of you."

I leaned back on my elbows. "I guess you could say Parker takes pictures. But not the artistic kind. The sadistic kind. And I'm not obsessed with him. I'm—"

"Hey, are you going to look at the sunset I've found for you or what?"

I gazed toward the horizon and realized how enormous the sky was. The bellies of clouds closest to the horizon shone with a gentle gold. The edges of the clouds popped with crisp outlines. The blue had a dusting of pink, and the horizon glowed.

"You know what this is, right?" I asked.

"A sky? A really big sky."

"A picture with soul." I grabbed my camera and snapped a series of shots.

Hunter sighed. "You don't know how to enjoy anything, do you?"

chapter eleven

Hunter pulled into the driveway just as India pushed open the front door.

"There you are!" she called. "Get in the car." She waved Hunter out of the way.

"Why? Where are we going?"

"The football game."

"I'm not supposed to—"

"Be campaigning. I know. But this game decides if Red Dirt gets in the playoffs."

"And it's easier to convince voters that you care about their issues than to make them care about yours," I said.

"Especially in a four-week election. I'm not having anyone associated with Hamilton for Congress skipping." She hustled me out of the truck and into her car.

"Did you run this by Dad?" I asked. Gravel hit the under-carriage of the car as we pulled past Hunter.

"Is there any way I can get you to start referring to him as Congressman Hamilton?" India asked.

"Absolutely not."

"What if I said it reminds people of his many years of experience and service to this country?"

I shook my head.

"Would bribery work?"

"Depends on the bribe," I said.

"It's in my purse."

I dug around and pulled out a plastic bag. Inside was a Red Dirt sweatshirt complete with the cartoon figure of a short man in a spinning cloud of dust.

"This is your idea of a bribe?"

"Put it on."

I stared at the shirt.

"Come on, get in the spirit." India glanced at my face. "You're going to feel left out."

"Peer pressure. You're going to use peer pressure to get me to do something?"

India shrugged. "Fine, don't wear it. Your mom said you'd never cooperate."

I hesitated. If Mom had actually said that, this was a golden opportunity to prove her wrong, and I rarely passed up those opportunities. But there was also the chance that India was manipulating me. I decided I'd rather be manipulated by India than underestimated by Mom, so I pulled on the shirt. When my head poked through the neck, India was drumming her fingers on the steering wheel.

"How mad was Dad?" I asked.

"Mad?"

"You don't have to lie to me."

India looked at me. "I may not be very good at reading your dad yet, but I don't think he's mad at you."

"He's worried people will compare me to Kyle, isn't he?"

"If he is, he hasn't mentioned it to me."

"Do you know Dad's history with Bo Stone?"

"I know they went to high school together. I know they both played quarterback, but all the stories people tell are about your dad. So either your dad played a lot more or he played a lot better."

"Or both."

"Or both. I also know that Bo grew up on a house on the wrong side of the railroad tracks. Apparently you can take that literally in a small town. He bought the big house he's in now about fifteen years ago. He worked his way up in a construction company, then started his own."

"And now he's running for Congress."

"He's done everything he can to build up his résumé—city council, local party leadership. Everything but get along with people. I don't know what kind of bad blood he and Jeff have had in the past, but I can see why he's mad now. Your dad is probably the one person who could beat him."

"Seems like Bo's been asking for a fight like this," I said.

"Maybe, but he only wants it if he can win." India pulled into a parking lot, sped to the front row, and parked beside a pair of Dumpsters.

"I don't think this is a parking spot," I called, but India was halfway to the entrance.

I caught up to her at the bleachers. "You want to sit with us?" she asked me.

I followed India's eyes to where Dad sat, surrounded by a cluster of men in faded jeans. Mom smiled and nodded as one of the men talked. Dad was in full-blown campaign mode—he was leaning forward, a hand on a man's shoulders, his eyes crinkled slightly. He was the personification of the perfect cocktail for politicians: leadership, sympathy, and optimism. You always had to have the optimism.

"I'll sit in the student section," I said.

"Meet me by the car when the game is over. Have fun."

I walked to the student section. Groups of freshmen gathered in the top bleachers. The middle school students took over the center. Everyone was in red and black, most of them in team gear. I was glad India had made me wear the Red Dirt shirt. I was about to head past the bleachers and wait out the rest of the game by the concession stand when Ana spotted me from the sidelines and waved me over.

"Where are you sitting?" she asked.

"I just got here."

"You can sit with my cousin, Theresa." She pointed to a girl with the same dark hair as hers. "That's her best friend, Theo, next to her. Don't let them drive you too crazy. I'll be there as soon as I get enough shots of the defense."

People peered around me as I made my way through a line of blanketed knees to where Ana's cousin sat.

"Hi, I'm—"

A sudden groan from the crowds swallowed the rest of my introduction.

"They need to run," Theresa said.

"Are you kidding me? They need to pass," Theo said.

"The run will set up the pass. They have two all-state pass rushers."

"That's the dumbest thing I ever heard. The pass will pass rush upfield and set up the run. That'll open up the dig routes in front of the dropping linebackers."

"Exactly! But you can't hit a dig route if you can't throw the ball."

I slid into an empty seat next to them. Theo registered my presence. "Hey, Kate, right?"

"Yeah, Ana said I could join you?"

Theo nodded, then returned his attention to the field. The intensity of the pep rally had not prepared me for the actual game. Thousands of cheering fans in their red-and-black shirts acted as a single unit, calling out instructions, moaning about missed opportunities. The girls pressed their hands to their mouths. The boys tapped their feet on the metal bleachers, their knees bouncing in the air. While the players lined up, the parents shouted accusation and threats, and then a hush fell as the ball went into motion for a few seconds of movement. The clock's numbers shifted slightly. The crowd reacted and the cycle started again.

It was easy to pick out Kyle, calling the numbers before the snap and scrambling as the line held a wave of defensive players back. Theo and Theresa's bickering became part of the background noise, woven into the drumbeats, cheers, and gasps.

After halftime, the score was tied. Kyle was struggling. I didn't have to understand football to see that. It was as plain as the frustration in his balled fists when he threw a ball out of bounds. Groans swelled from the stands. One man stood, his hands cupped to his mouth, and yelled down to the field, "Get your head in the game, Stone."

I had never played football in front of a crowd like this or stood on a field with opponents while fans on the sidelines demanded victory. But I had survived negative campaigns, trumped-up scandals, and jerky ex-boyfriends. It helped me understand why Kyle pulled a thick, glossy coat of confidence over all his actions.

"I'm going to get something to eat," I said. "Do you want anything?"

"A Frito pie," Theo said, fishing a ten-dollar bill from his pocket.

"Me too." Theresa kept her eyes on the field.

"Be right back." I grabbed the money.

The smell of grease and processed cheese led me to a concession stand. Chips lined the back wall. A big grease fryer sat in the corner. I scanned the menu. There wasn't a single thing on it that Mom would let touch her lips.

I ordered two Frito pies. A woman with large blonde curls hair-sprayed on top of her head and a bedazzled Red Dirt T-shirt sliced open two bags of Fritos and piled in mounds of chili and cheese. "You want onions and peppers?"

"Sure." It wasn't until I felt the warmth of the bag and the smell of chili pepper hit my nose that my mouth started to water. She gave me a fork, and I took a bite. A string of melted cheese stuck to my chin. "Can I get one more?"

The woman grinned. "You're Jeff Hamilton's girl, aren't you?"

I nodded, my mouth full of my second bite of Frito pie. I pulled out a couple of crumpled bills, but the woman shook her head. "It's on the house. I used to serve those to your dad when he came to the games in middle school." A cheer echoed from the far side of the field.

Ana met me on the way back. "There you are. I think I got what I need. You want to take a look?"

I nodded and followed her to where Theo and Theresa sat. Hunter had joined them. Red Dirt was down three points after a Junction field goal. Theresa made room for Ana by her and I was left to squeeze in next to Hunter. I passed out the Frito pies. "I didn't know you were coming," I said to Hunter.

"Can't miss the last district game."

"You too? I thought for sure you wouldn't buy into this football craze."

Theo laughed. "Hunter's got the best football brains in this stadium, which makes you wonder—"

Hunter elbowed Theo in the ribs, cutting off the rest. Then he turned to me. "I take it you aren't enjoying the game?"

"I've sat here for the last two hours, and I still don't get the magic of it."

"There is no magic. That's the greatness of football. It's eleven players trying to push a ball down a field yard by yard, and another eleven players trying to stop them." He looked at the field. "Sometimes it's skill, other times it's dumb luck."

"Mostly it's brutal and senseless."

"Sure, the best parts," Hunter said.

Theo asked Hunter to weigh in on the pass versus run debate. They talked until the last seconds ticked down on the scoreboard, when Kyle managed to throw a pass into the hands of a receiver in the end zone. Final score: Red Dirt 28; Junction 17.

Feet pounded on metal bleachers. Ana, Theo, and Theresa hugged. Even Hunter leaned back and looked with satisfaction at the field bathed in lights, where half the players pumped their fists in the air, and the other half lumbered into the darkness.

"Do you need a ride home?" Hunter asked me.

I shook my head. "Aren't you going to stay and celebrate?"

"I've always liked the game better than the winning."

"That would make you a terrible politician."

Hunter put his hands in the pockets of his jacket and shrugged. "I work better with animals than people anyway." He walked toward his truck.

Ana hurried into the swarm of football players, clicking pictures of their helmets raised over their heads. The crowd's electricity buzzed through me. I spotted Kyle talking to his dad. It was a reenactment of that first picture I'd seen in the yearbook. Bo Stone shook his head as he lectured Kyle. Kyle's head bent under the criticism, but tonight his eyes were like black stones. Principal Walker stepped onto the field and clapped Mr. Stone and Kyle on their backs. Kyle switched on his smile before breaking away from the crowd. He headed over to me, helmet in his gloved hand.

"Great game, huh?"

"I guess so. Everyone seems happy." I looked over the crowd.

Kyle chuckled. "You're not easily impressed, Kate. I like that."

I looked over my shoulder at Bo Stone. "Is your dad watching us?"

"Gotta have some fun with all this, right? I'm in for a whole week of Saturday-morning quarterbacking. What do you pull to get under your dad's skin?"

"Oh, I don't have to try that hard," I said.

He shifted his helmet to the other hand and moved closer. "Are you going to the party at the pit? Most of us are going to shower and change, then head over there. You can wait here, and I'll give you a ride."

"I'm getting a ride home with Ana."

"Perfect. You and Ana can head to the party. I'll meet you there." He scanned the crowd. "Ana! Ana!" I watched as Ana looked hesitantly at Kyle. It was the same wariness she'd shown when Hank walked into the gym after the basketball game. He gestured her over. "You want to come to the pit party?" Kyle said.

Missy walked up and stood as close to Kyle as possible. "Ana doesn't go to football parties. You're more of a basketball fan, aren't you?"

Ana shrank, pulling the camera to her chest. Missy's satisfaction pinched at my insides. "Hey, I still owe you a picture. I printed the one I took, but the lighting was off," I said to Kyle. Sometimes a flexible vision of the truth is convenient.

"All right, then you do owe me."

"I'll take it now." I held my hand out for the camera slung around Ana's neck. "You and Ana. Maybe it will even end up in the yearbook. Right, Missy?"

Missy frowned as Kyle put his arm over Ana's shoulder, tilted his chin up, and pointed a finger at the camera. Ana gave a weak smile. I clicked the shutter. "Ana can send it to you." I handed the camera back to Ana. "We'd love to go to the party."

I said it loud enough to make sure that Missy heard it as she walked away.

chapter twelve

When I told the adults about the party, India looked delighted. Mom looked surprised. Dad looked concerned.

"Stay out of trouble," he said.

"I will."

Ana, Theresa, and I squeezed into the cab of Theo's truck and drove past the scattered lights of town. When he pulled off the main road, we bumped along gravel for a minute or two.

"Are you sure you know where you're going?" I asked, craning my neck to search the darkness outside the window.

"You want to go to the pit, right?" Theresa said.

"Yeah, but—"

Theo turned the wheel and the truck plunged down an incline. I gripped Ana's hand and squeezed my eyes shut, bracing for the impact of the crash.

The truck slowed to a stop. "We're here," Ana said, pulling her hand from my grip.

When I peeled my eyes open, we were parked on the flattened bottom of a giant ditch. "This is the pit?"

We climbed out of the truck. "When are you going to learn that things are pretty literal around here?" Ana said.

"It's actually a caliche quarry," Theo said. Trucks and cars were parked haphazardly all over the pit. People sat in clusters on folding chairs, their feet resting on coolers.

"I don't get it. Why is this such a great place to party?"

Theresa wandered away. Theo lowered the gate of his truck bed and hopped up. "If we went anywhere else, the cops could see the car lights from miles away. Where do you party in DC?"

"I don't." I half climbed, half fell onto the tailgate of Theo's truck and let my legs dangle off the side next to Ana's.

"You guys don't party?"

"No, *I* don't party." Ironic because no one in DC would believe that after Parker's pictures. "There are a lot of rules in politics, but the most important: Always assume there's a camera and a loaded mike."

"What does that mean?" Theo asked.

"Someone's always watching and listening," I said.

"Same rule in a small town. Doesn't stop people from acting like idiots." Theo slid from the tailgate and walked toward a crowd of guys next to another truck.

"I would give up pit parties in a heartbeat to live in a big city like DC," Ana said.

"So why not go away to college?" I asked.

"You don't give up, do you?" Ana frowned and pressed her lips together. "I can't just leave. My whole family is here."

"It would give you a fresh start."

"People in Red Dirt don't get fresh starts," Ana said. Theo returned with two red cups. I shook my head. Ana took the one he held out to her.

"My dad left," I said.

"And now he's back," Ana said. "In Red Dirt, people either never want to leave, so they don't . . ." She pointed to a couple leaning against each other, one of the boy's arms wrapped around her waist. "Or they want to leave, but they can't . . ." She pointed to a boy in a plastic chair, playing a guitar. "Or they'll leave, but come back." She looked at Theo, who shrugged.

"Kyle will leave, right?"

"His dad's doing his best to get him recruited, but there hasn't been a lot of interest. He'll probably go to Tech, then move back and work for his dad," Theo said.

"Is it so bad here?"

"Only if you can't get out," Ana said.

Theo nodded, then strolled to join Theresa. "So what will you do in Red Dirt?" I asked.

"I'll finish up high school, then work in my uncle's restaurant. Maybe take a couple of community college classes in Midland. There will probably be a few times I almost get to leave, but then a cousin will get sick or my *abuela* will have another stroke." Ana stared over the quarry.

"Why can't you just tell your family that you want to go away to college?"

She shrugged. "My family doesn't make enough money to pay someone to waitress if I leave, much less send me to college. Even if they did, I'm not like you. I can't just tell people what I think."

I looked at the party. "The truth is, I haven't told my parents that I want to go to art school either."

"What do they want you to do?"

"Probably go to law school and practice with a big firm in a metropolitan area, preferably in the Northeast. Then after a decade or so, start running for office. If I wanted to, I could work through a city council or state legislature. Eventually I end up in Congress and continue the Hamilton legacy."

"It sounds exciting. Better than waiting tables," Ana said.

"Well, that may be what I end up doing if I can't get a decent portfolio and a letter of recommendation."

"That won't be hard."

I pulled my knees to my chest and rested my chin on them. "Maybe harder than you think. I stirred up a little trouble back in DC."

"Spill."

"You can't tell anyone. I'm supposed to be on my best behavior." I described what happened with the recommendation system. "So I don't think anyone there is going to write me a recommenda-tion." I sighed. "And I don't know if my photographs are good enough without it."

"I can help you with the photographs if you want."

"That would be great. I'd owe you. Again."

Ana and I watched the party in silence. After an hour, people's voices got louder and the words started to slur. Cups spilled; couples disappeared into the darkness. A Jeep flew down the side of the quarry and ground to a halt twenty feet from us. Kyle stepped out of it and navigated a maze of high fives and slaps on the back.

He scanned the crowd. When he spotted Ana and me, he gave us a wave and strolled over. A sophomore girl flanked by two friends stepped in front of him just a few feet from us. "Great game," she said, giggling.

He grinned. "Thanks," he said as he moved around the group.

"Are you always such a hero?" I asked when he joined us.

Kyle hopped on the back of the truck next to Ana. Perfect. She could use a little of his glow of victory. "Sure. Unless we lose."

"Hey, man!" a guy called to Kyle. "You comin'?"

"In a minute," Kyle called back, giving the guy the ambiguous chin-jerk. He turned to us. "Are you guys staying for a while?"

I looked at Ana, who shrugged. "Probably," I said.

Kyle wandered away. I followed Ana's eyes to Hank. He wore his button-down plaid shirt untucked and his hair neatly combed. His arm rested around the shoulder of a redhead, his head tipped back and laughter rolling out. It was the kind of overly amplified laughter that people did when they were hoping for an audience, so I wasn't surprised when his eyes swept the party. When he saw Ana, he whispered something in the girl's ear, nodded toward us, and started laughing again. Ana slumped.

"Don't do that." I elbowed her side.

"Do what?"

"Make yourself smaller. You have to straighten your back and lift your head, especially when someone is attacking. Try a small smile, comfortable but not superior." Hank laughed again. "Maybe a little superior."

Ana sat up a little straighter. "Is this some political trick?"

"Yeah, but the politicians got it from bears." I jerked my head toward Hank. "What does he have on you?"

"Nothing."

"You're going to have to tell me if you want me to come up with a plan to destroy him."

"I don't want to destroy him."

I narrowed my eyes at Hank. "Well, I do. I've got a chip on my shoulder and some extra time, so tell me what I've got to work with."

Ana rubbed her face. "It's nothing. We dated most of freshman year. He broke up with me. I got my heart broken."

"There's more to it."

"He spread a bunch of rumors about me."

"What kind of rumors?"

"Mostly about how far I was willing to go with a guy."

My face must have betrayed my surprise. Of all the things I suspected, this wasn't even on the list.

"We never did anything. I have six aunts, two grandmothers, and one great-grandmother, all with kitchens full of rolling pins and knives. I'd be skinned and served at Sunday night supper. But you don't have to believe me."

"If anyone knows about ex-boyfriends spreading lies, it's me. I've got the search history to prove it."

"I smell another story."

"People believe what they see. Right now they see you shrinking under Hank's accusations. It makes you look guilty. You have to go over there."

Ana shook her head. "No way."

"Why? You can't let him get away with that. If someone lies about you, you call him a liar."

Ana gripped the side of the truck. "Let people think what they want."

Another round of laughter swept across the quarry.

"That's Hunter's strategy, and it's a terrible one." I jumped down from the truck. "Be right back."

I eased my way between the groups to Hank's cluster. I knew this guy's type. He used his confidence to make other people feel smaller. He was Parker without the ironed shirts and hair gel.

"Hey," I said, squeezing into the group of Hank's buddies. I smiled and looked around the circle slowly. "I just came over to see what was so funny." I kept my voice breezy and let just a whiff of malice seep through.

Everyone looked at Hank, who shifted from one foot to another. "Oh, look. It's the new girl," he said. "It's an inside joke. You probably wouldn't get it."

"I saw your basketball game last week. I got how hilarious that was," I said.

That got a few chuckles from behind beer cans. A side of Hank's mouth lifted, but his eyes hardened.

"Maybe it's the kind of jokes you told after you broke up with Ana," I continued. "The ones about how far you got with her. Those *are* funny, because there's no way she felt that sorry for a loser like you."

Hank moved forward a step, his eyes thick with beer and challenge. "You want to know the joke? Come talk in my truck. I can explain it to you," he said.

The other guys laughed. Heat rushed to my face. I felt someone behind me.

"I like inside jokes," Kyle said. He stepped up beside me and widened his stance.

Hank shrank back. "It's no big deal, Stone."

"Ana wanted me to come get you," Kyle said to me.

I opened my mouth to protest, but I had to consider the end game. I didn't just want Hank mad, I wanted him a little scared.

Kyle had a couple of inches on Hank and cool anger in his eyes. He was the perfect person to fix this with Hank. I took a step out of the circle. "Thanks, Kyle. I'm losing brain cells talking to this guy anyway."

When I got back to the truck, Theo was opening the door for Ana. "You don't have to leave. I'm sure Kyle would take you home," Ana said to me, her voice small.

I climbed into the truck. "I'm going with you."

The truck rumbled down the road. Ana pressed her forehead against the window. "Are you mad?" I said. "I was just trying to—"

"Not mad. I just get tired of it all sometimes."

"Why do you let that guy get to you? You're so much better than him."

Ana lifted her head. "You don't ever use his name."

"What?"

"When you talk about people you don't like, you never use their names."

I shook my head. "It's political. You never mention your opponent's name. You define who they are in your speech. It's like taking a picture. You put some images in the frame, and you leave others out." I pointed at her. "That's it! You know what you need?"

"Chocolate chip cookie dough ice cream and a chick flick." She wiped away a tear.

"Sure, but long-term. You need a new image."

She turned back to the window. "Like a makeover? I don't think—"

I tugged at her shoulder, forcing her to face me. "No, you

actually don't have to change anything; we just change how people look at you. Shift the narrative. Someone ruined your reputation. Now we fix it. Politicians do it all the time."

"I don't know, Kate."

"I'll handle everything. Remember, I owe you."

chapter thirteen

When I got home, the media arm of Dad's campaign had arrived and was huddled in a circle, the glow of computer screens reflected in their eyes. India came into the kitchen and plunked her laptop on the counter while she started a pot of coffee.

"You're home early for a postgame party."

"My friend Ana was ready to leave, and I have to get some sleep. I'm helping Aunt Celia at the shelter tomorrow."

"Volunteering on Saturday. You're a campaign manager's dream." India leaned over the counter. "Or you're after something."

I shrugged. "Just staying out of the way."

Dad walked through the double doors and over to the fridge. "Good, you're home."

"We still need to go over your talking points for the Rotary Club tomorrow morning," India said to him. "Then you're having lunch at that senior center before you head to Stanton."

"What's in Stanton?" Dad asked, reaching into the fridge.

"A couple of meet-and-greets and a potluck."

"Did Mom go to bed?" I asked.

"Yep." I heard a familiar crinkle and turned to see Dad taking a big bite of Frito pie. "Don't tell your mom. I told her I brought it home for Celia." He winked. I didn't know if it was the jeans and boots or the lack of a phone in his hand, but Dad looked . . . different.

I started toward the door, then paused. "Can I ask you guys something?"

"If it's about the polling results, you know they don't mean anything this early," India said.

"It's not about the polling results," I said, wrinkling my forehead. "If someone wanted to change their image, how would they do that?"

"It depends," Dad said, his voice muffled by a full bite of chili.

"On what?" I asked.

"What they were and what they want to be," he said. "If it's an oil tycoon who wants to be perceived as an environmentalist, he has to put a lot of money and effort into green projects. If it's a billionaire who wants people to think he's common folk, he needs to change the way he dresses, probably the way he talks, maybe his hobbies. It's as much about who they were as who they want to be."

"What if it's a high school girl who has a questionable reputation?"

Dad put down his Frito pie, his smile gone. "Who are we talking about?"

I held up both hands and shook my head. "It's not me. You would know. It would already be on the news."

"True," India said.

"Completely hypothetically, what if it was me? What would you do if I did have a bad reputation and you needed to fix it for the election?"

"I don't like this, even as a hypothetical," Dad said.

India put her pen down and closed her laptop. "I would pull a Kim Jong Il."

"You would find a small country and make it Communist?" I asked.

"No, I would put you next to people who offer legitimacy," India said. "For decades, every time an American was arrested in North Korea, a former president or another high-up went over there to negotiate for their release, and Kim Jong Il got a picture standing next to a leader of the world's current superpower."

"I don't think I'm going to be able to get a sit-down with a world leader."

"You don't need a leader," Dad said. "The commodity in high school isn't power, it's popularity. Or just perceived popularity. Put her next to other people who are popular."

"That's smart. Thanks." I started to go.

"Be careful," India said, picking up her phone. "You're walking into shaky territory."

"It's just high school."

"High school politics can be the trickiest," Dad said.

This called for research. When I got to my bedroom, I pulled the yearbook Mrs. Fisher had loaned Dad off the shelf. After three days, I had a feel for where everyone fell in the social hierarchy, but I didn't want to make any mistakes. I had to find the person who would force Hank to crawl back into the pond scum he'd somehow escaped. I flipped through the different activities, jotting down lists of potential boyfriends to cross-reference. The social hierarchy of Red Dirt High School wasn't that different from my high school if you bumped all the sports teams up, added a layer for Future Farmers of America, and moved the band higher in the ranking.

Tasha texted me to see if I was still up. A few seconds after I sent a reply, the phone rang.

"What are you doing?" Tasha asked.

"Research. I want to find a boyfriend for the girl I told you about—Ana."

"Who are the candidates?"

"I don't have a lot." I flipped a few pages. "Someone in student government would work—high status, high visibility."

"Try the class president."

I cross-checked the junior class president with the homecoming page and Student Life section. "It looks like he has a steady girlfriend. I'm still checking a couple of drummers for the band and the captain of the soccer team."

"Aren't you ignoring the obvious—a football player? You said they were like gods there."

I turned to the football pages. It was hard to see faces under the "LOSER" written across them. "I don't want Ana to end up with another sweaty, hormone driven jock." I found the page with the picture of Kyle and his dad. On the next page lay a picture of Kyle, ball poised, ready to throw. Between the helmet and the mouth guard, you could only see his eyes, focused on the distance with the same intensity I saw in them tonight. His shoulders looked relaxed, while the muscles in his arms pushed at the jersey.

"Wait, it's perfect. Ana should date Kyle."

"The quarterback?"

"He's not dating anyone. He already defended her. He has the popularity to shoot Ana so far out of her ex's league that people would forget they went to the same school." Ana could smooth Kyle's rough edges, give him some dimension, make sure he wasn't doomed to be the high school quarterback his whole life. As a bonus, it would knock Missy down a notch or two. Win-win.

"Taking out another ex? Don't you have your own to deal with?" Tasha said. "Speaking of Parker, you aren't the only one questioning those hours that he got."

"Really."

"Yeah, I was waiting outside Principal Strickland's office and I overheard him in a meeting with a parent. Since the volunteer hours recommendation is the only one up for grabs, there's a lot of clamoring for it."

"So we're right back where we started."

"I thought you'd be happy. It's a win, right? As long as Parker doesn't get the recommendation?"

"It's not really a win unless I take it. Can you keep an eye on the hours?"

"No problem."

"How is Operation Secret Crush going?"

"Step one starts tomorrow. He'll be at the coffee shop for some open mike thing tomorrow afternoon."

"A musician? Dylan Parsons?"

"You're not going to guess this time."

I picked at a loose string on Dad's worn bedspread. "Well, good luck."

"I don't need luck. I've got new boots." Tasha hung up, and I went back to studying the football pages.

I looked at a smaller picture in the corner. It was a better photograph. It should have been the center spread. A player clutched the ball as his torso stretched across the thick out-of-bounds line. I could see his profile, sharp against the brightness of the stadium lights. I grabbed the book and looked closer. That wasn't Kyle. I moved my finger to the caption to confirm what I already knew.

Hunter played on the Red Dirt football team last year. Not only that, he was the quarterback. I turned to the page of "LOSER"-scratched pictures and found Hunter Price in the list of names. My head buzzed, trying to make sense of this new piece of information.

The next morning as light hit the eastern horizon, I pulled on an old pair of jeans and a T-shirt and headed for the back door.

When I got to the shelter, Celia was filling the plastic pools with fresh water. "I need you to rake the pigpen and lay down some new straw." She nodded to the shovel and wheelbarrow.

"Did you know Hunter was the quarterback for the football team last year?" I asked.

"Is this going to be a long conversation? Because the pigpen isn't going to smell any better afterward."

I picked up a rake. "It's just interesting. In a town so focused on football, I would think someone would mention it."

Aunt Celia turned off the water and wrapped the hose in a coil around her arm. "You can get started here, then move through the other seven pens."

"Did he quit because of Kyle?"

"Not my business," Aunt Celia said.

"But he did quit. That's why Kyle keeps giving him a hard time."

"I think it's weird that we're still talking about this. If you want to chat, get yourself a cushy volunteer job with Caroline at the library," Aunt Celia said. "If you want to work, start with the Taft pen and move down to Grant's."

"Taft?"

"William Howard Taft." She pointed to a group of five pigs. "There's Nellie, his wife, and Robby, Charlie, and Helen, named after the Taft children."

I looked in the pens, where five pigs were strolling next to the fence. "Do I just go in there with them?"

"Yeah, you should be fine."

"So I run the rake over the dirt?" It sounded simple.

"And pick up the manure." She turned the hose off and dragged it to the next pool. "Just be careful not to fall."

That was a piece of solid advice if ever I heard one.

After an hour of raking, the dust started to make my eyes water and my nose itch. My sweat made it stick in my hair, which the wind then blew into my face. That was when Hunter showed up.

"You missed a spot," he said, leaning on the boards that formed the fence, work gloves covering his hands.

"I'll get to it. Why don't you do your job and I'll do mine?"

Hunter didn't leave. "How'd you like the game?"

"Fine. You should have stayed. Kyle invited Ana and me to the pit party."

Hunter's lips tightened into a line. "I heard."

"And I heard a rumor about you." I leaned against the shovel.

"There are plenty of those."

"This one is confirmed. You used to be the quarterback for the Raiders." I watched for his reaction.

Hunter sucked in a quick breath, but he shrugged. "I know Kyle didn't tell you. You're been digging around in that yearbook you got from the library."

"I'm starting to think you're jealous of Kyle," I said.

A corner of his mouth curled up in a semi-smile. "You couldn't be more wrong."

"Then why don't you like him? Don't tell me it's because he took your position on the team."

"Nope."

"He stole a girlfriend? Punched your best friend in the face? Kicked your dog?"

Hunter frowned. "I'm going to get back to work. Don't forget that pile in the middle."

I spun on my heel and dug the shovel deep below the giant pile of manure. I lifted it, but I must have used extra force, because the shovel went flying up, sending the manure into the air and me tumbling to the ground. I had only a split second to register that this was exactly what Celia said not to do before I felt Hunter's hand on my elbow, lifting me up.

"Get up," he said as I struggled to my feet. "Hurry." He stomped his boot at an approaching pig. "Don't you know anything? *Never* get on the level of the pigs!" he yelled.

It was only the second time I'd seen him lose his cool. Before I could tell if it was from fear or anger, he looked down and focused on brushing off the knees of his jeans. "They'll bite you. Whatever they can get at," he said.

The pounding of my heart resonated through my head and gut. "Okay, I'll be careful."

"You need to start being smart." Hunter rubbed a hand through his hair.

"I'm plenty smart. Just because I don't know how to birth a cow or play football doesn't mean I don't know things."

Hunter pointed his finger at me. "Hear that? That's it exactly. You're so busy trying to prove what you do know, you ignore all the things you don't."

He stalked away, but his words settled deep inside me. I carried them around for the rest of the day. They wouldn't have been so heavy if they weren't true.

I cleaned the rest of the pens without any incidents. By then, the sun was high in the sky. I dragged myself to the trailer at the center of the property to see if Aunt Celia had any other chores for me to do.

When I walked in, she took one look at me and burst into laughter.

"You probably didn't even think I'd make it through the morning," I said.

"Through the first hour. I bet Hunter ten bucks."

"I'm glad someone had faith in me."

"He bet you wouldn't show up."

I winced. "Is there anything else you need, or should I hose off?"

"Hunter could probably use some help with the second calf feeding. He'll show you the drill."

I groaned.

"Let me guess—you two aren't getting along."

"I just get sick of his arrogance."

"Look, Hunter has enough to deal with. Don't you make trouble for him." She waved a hand at me. "Go make nice. Unless you're giving up on those hours already."

I walked on aching legs to the barn.

Hunter was bent over one of the calves, looking at his ears. "You cleaned all the pens?"

"Yeah, and I heard about the bet."

"I should have known you'd stick it out."

I crossed my arms over my chest. "Aunt Celia said you might need help."

Hunter handed me a bottle. "Feed Ty. Hold it in front of and above his head."

The calf stumbled toward me on unsteady feet and put his mouth to the bottle. It vibrated with the sucking. He took another step toward me. I could feel the warmth of his breath on my hand. I was so mesmerized that I didn't sense the weight of Hunter's eyes on me until a few moments later.

"Good job," he said.

"Thanks." I brushed back a strand of hair.

"Kate, I don't want to fight with you. I want us to get along."

"Why? It's not like you care what people think."

Hunter raised an eyebrow. "Apparently, I care a little." He gave me a half smile that melted my remaining frustration. "What if I resist the temptation to prove you wrong for the rest of the day?"

"And I stop trying so hard to be right? Deal." I nodded. "Did you already feed Tip?"

"I haven't even started. Tip doesn't drink well from the bottle."

"How do you feed her if she doesn't take the bottle?"

"I stick a tube down her throat into her stomach."

I cringed and instinctively ducked my chin.

"It's not pretty, but if I don't, she'll starve." He straddled the calf and grabbed for a grip around her nose and mouth. Tip started to jerk and twist.

"That's your plan?"

"You have a better idea?"

I held out my hand. "Trade with me. You take Ty and I'll take Tip."

Hunter hesitated.

"I thought we were trying not to argue," I said.

He placed the bottle in my free hand. "You have to give her the idea, then let her take the last step," I said. I held the bottle in front of Tip's face. She turned away. I eased closer. "Are you hungry?" I asked her.

Tip was still. We stood there together, her breaths coming in quick puffs at first, then smoothing out and quieting. I shifted another couple of inches.

"What are you doing?"

"Gaining her trust," I whispered.

I eased the bottle forward and put a drop in front of Tip. She jerked away, but I kept the bottle still and steady and took a breath. "Listen. All you have to do is take a few sips." She didn't move. "You're hungry. Don't be stubborn." I put it right under her nose. "You eat, no tube, win-win." I held my breath and eased the bottle between her lips. Then the bottle started to move back and forth as Tip sucked the formula.

Hunter leaned against the wall of the stall. "*That* was amazing," he said.

"I'm sorry about what I said earlier. I know you're not jealous of Kyle."

He shrugged. "It's no big deal. Sorry I snapped at you." He smiled, and before I knew it, a smile broke across my face too. "And I'm really sorry I bet against you. I could have ten bucks in my pocket right now."

"Never bet against a Hamilton. We always find a way."

Hunter laughed. "I'll keep that in mind." He rose and dusted off his jeans. "I told Celia I'd pick up some feed for the horses. You wanna come when you finish?"

I nodded.

When I was done feeding Tip, Hunter cleaned the bottles and passed me the keys. "You can drive. I owe you another lesson."

I pulled out of the shelter and onto one of the two-lane roads that crisscrossed the landscape. Hunter talked me through the first few turns, then leaned back and stuck his elbow out the window.

"So you really just quit the football team?" I asked. "Your senior year?"

"Yep."

"Why?"

Hunter sighed. "Does there have to be a reason?"

"There usually is."

"It just wasn't for me."

The wind carried the smell of burning leaves from far away. "Quarterback doesn't seem like the worst job to have in high school."

"You're welcome to it. All you'd have to do is hit wide-open receivers consistently, and you could probably beat out Kyle for the spot. Turn left up there."

I eased my way onto a narrow road. "I don't believe for a second that you are as much of an outsider as you want everyone to believe."

A flicker of surprise crossed his face. "What do you mean?"

"You act like you're on the outside, laughing at the rest of us, but I see Kyle watching you the way Missy watches me. You must have something he wants."

"Can't imagine what it is."

"So if you heard about me going to the party, I guess you heard about Ana and that idiot she dated."

"Hank." Hunter pressed his lips together. "Yeah, and I heard Kyle stuck his nose in that."

"Are you saying he shouldn't have defended Ana?"

"I'm saying the more attention you give a guy like Hank, the more dangerous he gets. Hank is like a mosquito bite. Ignore it and it goes away."

I sat up straighter. "You can't ignore people like that. You need to stand up to them."

"If that's true, *Ana* needs to stand up to Hank."

I glanced to him. "With a little help."

I looked back at the road, but I could still feel Hunter's eyes on me. "Did Ana ask for your help?"

"She didn't have to."

"Pull in here." Hunter pointed to a low, bright red building. "Like I said, I don't want to fight with you, but I'd stay out of it."

"Not everyone wants to be a complete loner in high school. Most of us want friends."

"You're not trying to get her friends. You're trying to get her popularity."

"That can lead to friendship."

Hunter snorted his reply. "Back up to that loading dock on the side." He opened the door, strolled around the side of the building, and started tossing bags of feed into the back.

My phone rang. I looked at the screen to find Tasha's name flashing. I walked toward the road and answered.

"I need your help," Tasha said.

"I was just telling Hunter how useful I can be."

"Great, now's your chance to prove it. I didn't get anywhere at the coffee shop."

"If you told me who it was, I might be able to give better advice. It's not Nathan Reed, is it?"

"Seriously, Nathan Reed? He wore luau shorts to junior prom."

"You know you are going to tell me eventually. You always do."

"This is different. I really like this guy."

"What have you tried?"

"The usual. I smiled and flirted."

"And?"

"He didn't even invite me to sit with him."

I nodded. "You oversold it."

"No, I didn't."

"I promise you did. I've seen you flirt. What you need to do is stand close but don't touch. Shift the beam of your attention just off of him, close, but not on. I've seen it work a million times at fund-raisers."

"I'll try anything."

Hunter climbed into the passenger seat.

"I have to go. Good luck." I walked back to the truck and started it. "I'm not trying to be right," I said to Hunter, "but don't you think a person should help others if they can?"

He sighed. "We're going to need more practice with this not-fighting thing."

"Ah, see, I agree with that," I said.

Halfway back to the shelter, Hunter's phone dinged. He looked at the screen. "Turn right at the next street."

"Aren't we going to the shelter?"

"I have to make a quick stop to check on something."

He directed me to a large lot next to the railroad tracks. We drove down a bumpy driveway that started off gravel, then turned to dirt, and stopped outside a small white house with peeling paint and a drooping porch. "Just wait here. I'll be right back."

Hunter disappeared into the house. It didn't take long before he slammed back through the screen door. "Mom!" he called to the vast horizon. He looked small and helpless.

I got out of the truck. "Is everything okay?"

"Mom!" he called again.

"Hunter, what's wrong?"

He shadowed his eyes with his hand and stared at the horizon. "It's probably nothing. Mrs. Fisher just texted that someone came in, saying he saw my mom walking along the road."

"And that's strange, right? Because in DC people walk all the time."

Hunter rubbed his face. "It's just . . . she's . . ." He paced in a circle, looking across the land. "Last time she wandered off, I didn't see her for three months. That's when I started living with my grandfather."

"Let's go look."

"Where?" He spread his arms. "This is just like her. She's probably fine, but she's got everyone spun up. She could be anywhere."

"Maybe she left a note?"

"There won't be a note."

"Then maybe she left a clue. Take the truck and drive around. Someone saw her less than ten minutes ago. If she's on foot, she's not far. Give me your number. I'll check the house, and I'll call you if I find anything. Come back in thirty minutes if you don't find her."

He looked at the truck, then back at the house.

"Go. You know it's a good plan."

Hunter nodded. I got his number, handed him the keys, and watched him drive off before I climbed the steps to the house and opened the door. The front room was dark, but the sun was low enough to illuminate the room. It was a disaster. Half-eaten plates of food on tables and chairs. Newspapers and mail scattered in piles on the floor. Evidence of half-completed chores, like a broom resting in a pile of glass in the corner and a full laundry basket by the back door. People littered places with clues about themselves. The trick was to know what was important.

I moved through the living room and into the kitchen—an even bigger mess. It was hard to imagine Hunter with his careful ways living in this house. There were more dishes, a mason jar of dirty silverware, and a bowl of dog food.

Dog food. I looked around for a leash. I didn't see one, so I called Hunter.

"I don't think she's running away. I think she's walking a dog."

"She doesn't have a dog."

"You didn't see the bag of dog food and the water bowl in the kitchen?"

"No. Why wouldn't Mrs. Fisher tell me about the dog?"

"She got the information secondhand. She probably didn't

know to ask. So your mom will be be on a road, but not a major one, and probably one that loops back to the house."

"I know exactly where she is."

Hunter's truck rumbled to the house a few minutes later with a woman in the passenger seat, small and frail, in jeans and a sweatshirt with frayed sleeves. Strands of hair hung around her face. A large dog with brown eyes and matted fur paced the truck bed. "I don't see why you raced out here. I was just taking a walk," she said as they got out of the cab.

"Mom, do you really think a dog is a good idea?"

The woman reached into the back of the truck and patted the dog. "I don't see why it's a bad idea." The dog licked her face. "What exactly are you saying?"

I knew a loaded question when I heard it. "Hi, I'm Kate."

Hunter's mom looked at me like she couldn't comprehend where I'd come from and what I was doing there.

"I'm a friend of Hunter's."

Her head started to nod slowly.

"He was giving me a driving lesson," I said, trying to explain my presence. "What's the dog's name?"

"Lucy," she said.

"Does she have her shots? Because you could probably have Hunter bring her to the shelter sometime. Aunt Celia could take a look at her."

"You're Jeff Hamilton's daughter?" She put her hand on her hip.

"Yes, ma'am."

"That's a good idea. Aren't you a smart girl?"

"That's what I keep telling him." I jerked my head toward Hunter.

He opened the passenger door of the truck. "I've got to get Kate back to the shelter. We'll talk about this later."

"That's fine, but I'm keeping the dog." She walked to the porch.

We rumbled back to the main road. After a few minutes, he broke the silence. "How did you know about the dog?"

"Research."

"One of your many talents."

"Why don't you want her to have the dog?" I asked. Hunter didn't answer. I watched the landscape pass. "I actually know that this is none of my business."

"You're right. It's none of your business," he muttered. A few seconds later, his jaw was still stiff, but his voice was softer. "She can barely take care of herself. You saw the house."

"A dog might be good for her. Maybe she gets lonely."

"I can't fix this situation, Kate. If I could have, I would have done it a long time ago and saved myself a lot of trouble."

"Fine, don't fix it. But that doesn't mean you can't help out a little."

"What do you mean?"

"Take the dog to Celia. Train it. Do the things you're good at."

"Why? So when she leaves, I'll already be used to taking care of her dog?" Hunter said.

"I'd do it. I'd probably be better at dog training than you anyway."

He drove a few more minutes in silence. "Okay, okay. You win. I'll think about it."

"But I still win. You said I win."

Hunter laughed. "Game's not over, Hamilton. But you do have points on the board."

chapter fourteen

The rest of the weekend, I stayed in my room, planning how to ease Kyle and Ana together. I went over it again and again, deciding on a gradual series of casual meetings that moved them quickly through acquaintance to interest to dating to my rubbing it in Hunter's face. I was really looking forward to that.

I was walking toward Mr. Quincy's room on Monday when Kyle fell in step beside me. I couldn't have planned it better. "I didn't get a chance to see you much at the party," he said.

"Ana wanted to leave after what happened with Hank."

"You're a good friend," he said, opening Mr. Quincy's door. Before I could go in, Kyle grabbed my elbow, pulled me to a stop, and leaned toward me. I caught a light smell of sweat and maybe some bacon. It took all my self-control and a reminder that he'd helped Ana to not step back. "That Hank is an idiot. I don't think he'll be talking about Ana anymore."

I loved the protective attitude. "Yeah, I think that's why she eats lunch in the yearbook room."

I waited a few beats while Kyle thought. It was just like feeding Tip. I wanted this to be his idea.

"It doesn't seem fair," I said.

He nodded twice.

"If only I knew a safe place to sit, but being new . . ."

Kyle's eyes lit. "Why don't you and Ana sit with me and the other football players? We spend a lot of the time going over plays, but he won't even look at her there."

Finally. "What a great idea, Kyle." I smiled up at him. "See you at lunch."

I wove my way to the lab table.

"What are you so happy about?" Hunter said.

"Just the satisfaction of a plan falling into place."

Kyle made his way through a pack of guys, giving high fives and fist bumps. Hunter groaned. "Please don't tell me that Kyle is part of your plan."

"What if he was?" I said, opening my science book.

"Don't get Ana mixed up with Kyle," Hunter said.

"What happened to not fighting?" I threw up my hands. "Of course, you think I'm an idiot."

Hunter pulled his book out and slammed it on the desk. "You're *not* an idiot, which makes it even more infuriating that you can't see what he's like." The hum of voices paused for a moment. Kyle looked over his shoulder.

I lowered my voice, but my words stayed clipped. "I know what he's like. Sure, he's a little too into himself, but he's pretty harmless. Why shouldn't I encourage him to ask Ana out?"

Hunter locked eyes with me. "First, Kyle is perfectly capable of tricking his own girl into dating him. Second, Kyle doesn't date girls like Ana. He dates cheerleaders, the dumb ones at that. You do remember his longest relationship was with Missy."

"Sometimes it takes a nudge in the right direction," I said.

"Third, Kyle isn't going to let you use him. I guarantee he has plans of his own."

I flipped through the science book, feigning deep interest in a picture of a shark's circulation system. Hunter opened his own book. After a few minutes, I couldn't stand it anymore. "I don't understand. Once again, you are so sure that you are right and I'm wrong."

Hunter continued to read. "Maybe it's the years of locker room talk I got to hear from that guy."

"People change. Not everyone is determined to be a complete jerk their entire life."

"I think you underestimate Kyle's commitment."

We spent the rest of the period in an uncomfortable silence. I piled up arguments in my head. The bell rang and I reached down to get my bag. When I looked up, Hunter had already left.

Hunter's lack of faith in my plan made it even sweeter when I saw Kyle making a beeline for Ana in the cafeteria.

"You're sitting with us, right?" He looked at me, then Ana. It was less a question than a statement said by someone used to getting what he wants.

"We usually—" Ana started.

"Come on. Follow me." He took Ana's tray and started toward a table.

Ana leaned over. "I need to get those pictures from last week's game downloaded," she said to me.

"I'll help you. It won't kill you to eat one lunch down here."

She frowned and looked around the cafeteria.

"Trust me. It's for your own good, and who's going to bother you when you're sitting with the star quarterback of the Red Dirt Raiders?"

Kyle waved at us from his table. I grabbed my overprocessed chicken nuggets, and we squeezed in between the football players.

"Ana got some amazing pictures at the game last Friday," I said.

Ana blushed, but didn't open her mouth.

"Really? I would love to see them," Kyle said, smiling at her.

"I bet you got his pass in the fourth quarter," I said to her.

"I tried," Ana said, warming to the topic. "We'll see when I get on the computer today."

"I liked the one Kate took of me and you." Kyle's eyes sparkled. I beamed at both of them. My plan was working even better than I thought.

Kyle chatted with Ana about the game while I studied them. He definitely smiled more than necessary. He also ignored everyone else at the table. When one of Ana's french fries dropped onto the floor, he handed her one of his. As usual, Hunter didn't know what he was talking about.

"Not many girls can talk football like you," Kyle said through a bite of burger.

"I guess I learned a lot taking pictures for yearbook. You have to know a little about the game to know where the right shot will be."

"I like a girl who can talk sports."

"Is that your type?" I asked.

Kyle played it cool. "Type?"

"Yeah, like your type of girl."

He grinned and leaned closer. His eyes shot quickly to Ana, then back to me. "I guess I like a girl who is unique. Someone who's original and not a carbon copy of every other high school girl."

A smile crept over my face. Ana was one of a kind. If Kyle wanted special, he'd found it.

Kyle stacked Ana's tray on his; then he grabbed mine. "I have to go see Principal Walker. Quincy is killing me with this ant project. I can't believe he expects us to do it during playoffs."

I didn't see any problem with the timing. Then again, Hunter pulled his weight as a lab partner. Maybe Kyle's partner stuck him with everything. "It's not that much work once you get started. What can Principal Walker do?" I asked.

"He just talks to the teachers. Makes sure they understand the demands that football players are under. Maybe he can get Quincy to push back the deadline."

"I don't know," I said. "Quincy doesn't seem like the type that bends the rules."

Kyle shrugged. "Principal Walker will get it done. Red Dirt can't make it to the state championship game without their quarterback." He stood up.

I nodded and waved good-bye, then kicked Ana's leg. She gave a halfhearted good-bye.

"I think he likes you," I told Ana in the hall.

"Who? Kyle? I don't think so."

"He's paying a lot of attention to you," I said. "He practically said you were his type." I opened the door of the yearbook room.

"Oh, great. You two found time to join us," Ms. Serrano said. "Ana, I need those pictures from the game in ten minutes. Kate, don't you have yearbooks to shelve?"

Ana fidgeted with the straps of her backpack.

"Don't worry. I can fix this. I'll download while you crop and print," I said.

Some of the color returned to Ana's face. "Then I'll help you finish unpacking the books." She followed me to the computer. "I'm glad you're here, Kate. We make a good team."

My heart gave a jump. A team. I might like being on a team.

Later that afternoon, we sat in the hallway buried in dusty yearbooks. Ana pulled another from the box. "They had a lot of dress-up days in the seventies and eighties."

"I think those are their actual clothes," I said.

"Look at this. Is that your dad with Mr. Stone? I didn't know they were friends."

She showed me the book. A picture of Dad lay across the center of the spread. His face was smooth and thin, his hair longer. His eyes stared straight at the camera. He wore a button-down shirt tucked into a pair of jeans. Bo Stone stood next to him, grinning, his arm slung over my father's shoulder in casual friendship. Dad had the same easy smile, but Bo's eyes had a hungry look.

"Me either." I slipped the yearbook and a few from the years around it into my backpack.

Ana dropped me off after school. I found India in the kitchen trying to wrangle a table of volunteers into completing a mailing. Dad always set up hasty offices in larger cities: teams of well-oiled volunteers who probably had worked dozens of campaigns before. But he never moved his main headquarters out of the house.

"These need to go out by five, people." India looked at her watch. "If we don't cut the chitchat and focus on getting these envelopes stuffed, we are going to be hand-delivering them across the district."

"Do you want help?" I asked, dropping my bag at the doorway to the kitchen.

India put her hand to her head. "I think it's a lost cause at this point." She pushed through the swinging door.

I looked around at the ladies. They were practical, from the tips of their reading glasses perched in their hair to the worn soles of the boots on their feet. "I guess Dad will have to hire out his mailing to that firm in Midland," I said.

"That's throwing away good money," one of the ladies said.

I sat down next to Mrs. Fisher, the librarian. I may not have known how to catch a cricket, but I had a foolproof method for completing mailings quickly. "You can get all of these done. The trick is to fold both sides of the paper at once." I brought the edges into a tri-fold and smoothed the folds with both thumbs.

The conversations trickled to a stop as everyone's eyes turned to me.

"And once they're stuffed, you can stack about five to lick them." I stacked a few envelopes with the gummy side showing and licked them all in one smooth movement. "Now, there's no reason to pay some high school dropout fifteen dollars an hour to do this, right?"

The women around the table nodded.

"Okay, ladies," Mrs. Fisher said. "Hold your tongues for the next half hour, and we'll have it."

The table worked in silence. After twenty minutes, the table was stacked high with envelopes ready to mail. When India came back, her mouth dropped open.

"You don't have to stand there lookin' like you've seen the second coming," one lady said. "Kate was nice enough to show us a few tricks."

"I'm impressed, but I still can't get these to the post office until tomorrow, which means they get to people on Thursday and Friday. I might as well throw them in the trash myself," India said.

"We only have a few more to go," one of the women said.

"Post office closes at five," India pointed out.

"I'll call. Herb will usually stay open a couple of minutes if he knows you're coming," one of the women said.

"He won't tonight, Pat," another woman added. "He has his poker game."

"We'll see," Pat said. "Keep stuffing." She pulled out her cell phone. "Herb, this is Pat. Can you stay open a few minutes?" She listened for a minute, then reached for the plate of brownies at the center of the table. "That's a shame. I had some treats to drop off, but I'll just take them to the sheriff instead." A smile flickered across her face. "See you in a minute."

"If only that trick would work with Congress," India said. She collected most of the envelopes and packed them into boxes while the rest of us stuffed the few remaining.

Mrs. Fisher went into the kitchen and returned with the coffeepot. "Who knew you were such an efficient volunteer, Kate? I should have snatched you up when I had the chance," she said.

The women around the table laughed. It was a warm laughter that told me they'd heard the story.

"This will make Thursday nights go faster," one of the women said.

"Are you stuffing more envelopes for Dad on Thursday?" I asked.

"No, sweetheart. We go volunteer at the Stone headquarters downtown on Thursday and Saturday, and we come here on Mondays and Wednesdays."

"You volunteer for both campaigns?"

"Of course," Mrs. Fisher said.

I shook my head. "I don't think I'll ever get used to it here."

"I bet it's been an adjustment moving from DC to Red Dirt," one of the women said, pushing a napkin with a lemon bar on it toward me.

I took a bite. "It's different."

"I say it's about time your father brought you home," one of the women said.

They stayed for a few more minutes, chatting about the weather and next week's football game, aches and ailments and grand-children. The warm conversation wrapped around me. In DC you had to be guarded when you talked to people. This chitchat had no agenda except the easy exchange of information. When their lipstick-stained coffee cups were empty, they bustled around, picking up coats and purses. They passed out good-bye hugs, then trotted off toward the front door until only Mrs. Fisher remained.

I picked up the book bag I'd dropped by the door when I came in. The yearbooks peeked through the top. I turned to Mrs. Fisher. "Did Dad and Mr. Stone used to be friends?"

"Inseparable, if I recall," Mrs. Fisher said.

"What happened?"

"Nothing, really. Your father left for college and didn't look back. I don't think he wanted to be the small-town football hero his entire life. And maybe a small part of Bo Stone did."

"They seem to hate each other."

"They don't hate each other." Mrs. Fisher took a sip of coffee. "Your dad had everything Bo Stone has been chasing for the past thirty years. And Bo might say that your dad just threw it away."

149

"What do you mean?"

"Your dad was a hero here. Then he left. He had a family . . . that he never saw. He had a seat in Congress that he could inherit. He went out and got his own. At least that's the story Bo would tell. Your dad would paint a very different picture."

"What's his version?"

"Your dad wasn't cut out to be a big fish in a small pond. And all the expectations from your grandfather only trapped him."

"So this election is about more than winning the seat."

"It's about justifying all the choices they've made since high school."

I bit my lip. "That's a lot to lose."

chapter fifteen

I knew it was Election Day the minute I stepped into the kitchen. Dad was still weeks away from his special election, but any day devoted to politics was an opportunity. India, Mom, and Dad huddled around the coffeemaker going over a three-page schedule for the day. Staff wove in and out, cell phones in one hand and Styrofoam cups in the other. The table was piled with VOTE FOR HAMILTON yard signs. I escaped to school as quickly as possible.

My own campaign was going well. I could see the effects of my plan take shape almost immediately. I watched Ana walk by Hank in the parking lot. She stiffened automatically, but instead of his face breaking into that asinine snicker that made him look more like a weasel than normal, he turned his attention to his boots.

By lunchtime, there was a notable difference in how people treated Ana. People wanted to be nice to her. Her reputation was inching closer to what they saw. I excused myself from the table to get some ketchup and give Ana and Kyle some space.

I was picking though the box of ketchup and mustard packets when Hunter walked up. "I shouldn't have gotten so mad in Quincy's class yesterday."

"So you're saying you were wrong?"

"I'm saying I overreacted." He ran a hand through his hair.

"Having my mom back in town puts me on edge. Do you want to work together on the homework Quincy gave out, or split it like last time?"

I shook my head. "No way, we're doing it together. Last time we split the pages, and he couldn't even read your work."

"Funny, the way I remember it, I'm not the one who got two wrong."

"Fine, we use your answers and my handwriting." I glanced innocently over my shoulder at Kyle and Ana, hoping Hunter's gaze would follow.

"After school? Your house?"

"No. Election Day took over the house."

"The library?"

He was being willfully oblivious, so I nodded to the table where Kyle was talking to Ana. "How long are you going to ignore how brilliantly my plan is progressing?"

Ana said something and Kyle laughed, revealing a mouthful of enchilada surprise.

"It's only the first quarter, Hamilton." Hunter turned and walked off.

"Don't try to confuse me with football references," I called after him.

I was in no hurry to get home, so I stopped by the yearbook room after school. Ana helped me clear out a few more boxes, then sat on the counter in the darkroom while I fussed and fiddled with a series of test strips I'd developed. She wanted to watch me develop a photograph.

"So you just found Ms. Serrano's notes written across your pictures?" Ana said. "What did she write?"

" 'Muddy and predictable.' "

"What does that mean?"

"It means she didn't like them," I said.

"But they weren't for the yearbook?"

"She could have used the one of Kyle if she hadn't written 'mediocre effort' across it."

"Maybe she's trying to help."

I stuck a negative in a frame and positioned it under the enlarger. I hadn't told Ana about the picture of Dad. Ms. Serrano must have spotted it in the trash can, because it was taped together at the bottom of the stack with the words "somewhat interesting" scrawled across it. "I saw you and Kyle laughing at lunch today. Admit it, you had fun with him."

Ana could have been blushing. It was too dark to tell for sure. "It wasn't terrible. He has a kind of aura?"

"Glow." I wiped stray dust off a line of negatives.

"Yeah, where does that come from?"

"Confidence." It bordered on the edge of overconfidence, but that would average out Ana's underconfidence. "Okay, I'm ready," I said.

Ana rubbed her hands together. "Finally. What do we do?"

I lined up one of the sunset pictures I'd taken with Hunter. I exposed it for a few seconds, then dropped the paper in the tray of developer.

"That's it?" Ana said. "After all this work, I expected something more magical."

I checked the clock and leaned over the tray. "Watch."

Grays started to dissolve onto the paper. They darkened until you could see the outline of clouds across the top two-thirds of the photo and the muddy shape of a tree in the lower left corner. The liquid pulled the lines and shadows on the paper. After a few seconds, the image swam at its center.

"That was . . ." Ana's voice drifted off as she stared at the picture.

"I know," I said. "I never get tired of watching it. Some people put their images facedown to get a more even coverage of chemicals, but I wouldn't miss this part."

"Is this why you use film?"

"Partly. But mostly I love it because when you develop your own photos, messing up just gets you closer to a more perfect picture. Life isn't like that."

Ana leaned closer. "It looks like a good image."

I dropped it into the fixer. Ana was right. It was good, not great. The focus was sharp, everything was right, but it was just a picture of a sky. No soul. After the last rinse, I clipped it to the drying line next to the photo of the calves.

Ana looked at the calf picture. "Are you going to use this one in your portfolio?" she asked.

I shook my head. "It's boring. Predictable."

Ana kept looking at it. "Still, don't you think there's something really beautiful about it? Something raw. Look at the hay hanging on this one's eyelashes, and the lines where the coat is pressed down."

I took the picture down and studied it. She was right. There was something there. "I don't know how you find the best version of a picture like that. I've never been very good at it," I said.

"I just look."

We worked on the last few pictures. They weren't as bad as I'd thought they would be. I almost wished they were disasters. Then I could blame the landscape or the light, but there was something else missing. They skimmed the surface of beauty without cracking it.

"I have to go," Ana said at last. "Do you want a ride?"

I shook my head. "I already called Aunt Celia. She was hiding from the Election Day chaos too. She said she could pick me up on her way home from the feed store."

"Look at you, talking like a local."

I handed her a stack of pictures. "Can you take these out and hang them on the line?"

"No problem." Ana waved and slipped out the door. I spent a few minutes covering the chemicals and emptying the trays.

When I stepped outside the darkroom, I saw Hunter studying the drying pictures. Panic swelled inside me as I ran over and yanked them off the line. "What are you doing here?"

"Well, I waited in the library. Then I realized we never really decided where to meet."

"Meet?"

"To do the science homework."

I put my hand over my mouth. "I am so sorry."

Hunter grinned. "It's fine. I went to feed the calves and Celia asked if I could pick you up. She got called to a ranch a half hour away, and she didn't want you to have to wait all night."

"Let me just grab my stuff." I picked up my bag and slipped the pictures inside. "We'll go to the library and get this done."

"The library's closed. You really do lose track of time when you're working with photographs, don't you?"

I walked a half step in front of Hunter, but I could hear the steady thump of his boots on the floor. When we reached the truck, he followed me to the passenger side, stretched out his hand, and rested it on the handle.

"It's not like I know anything about photography," Hunter said.

"That's what I was thinking."

"But I liked the one with the blurry lines of white and the tree. That one was interesting." He pulled the door open and stepped out of the way so I could get in, then went around to his side.

"It was supposed to be the sky." He had seen me maneuvering to get recommendations for art school. Part of me wanted him to think it was worth it. "I know I didn't get the lighting right. The sky was this beautiful blue that should have turned a gray on the film, but it just went black. Some things don't translate well to black-and-white film. No more pictures of sky."

"That doesn't sound like you. If it was a cow birth, you'd stick with it."

He started the truck and pulled out of the parking lot. We drove in silence for a while, but instead of turning on the strip of gravel that would take us to my house, he kept following the road.

"Where are we going?"

"Celia said that your house is crazy. Fortunately, I have the perfect place for us to study."

"Where?"

"Don't worry. You'll like it. There won't be any campaign signs or election talk." Hunter turned off the paved road. The truck bumped along until it pulled to a stop.

"A water tower?" I looked up. The water tank hung thirty feet in the sky, supported by a crisscross of metal legs and supports. "This is where we're going to study?" Hunter got out of the car and started to climb a stretch of fence that surrounded the tower. "This is the dumbest idea you've had yet."

"I'm going up there, Hamilton." He stuffed our homework in his back pocket. "If you want to stay down here, I'll just tell Mr. Quincy that I did all the work on this."

I crossed my arms.

"I guess we can add climbing fences to the list of things that I can do better than you," Hunter said.

"Oh, that's mature."

"Birthing cows, being polite, science homework . . ."

"Okay, that's it." I got a firm grip on the links and scrambled to the top before I had time to think about it. Then I swung myself over and landed right next to Hunter.

"Not bad," Hunter said. "But jumping the fence is the easy part."

"This better not get me in trouble. My dad gets touchy about headlines that include my name and words like 'trespassing.'"

"Relax, Hamilton. Nothing's going to happen. Think of it as a thank-you for helping me out Saturday." He strolled over to a metal ladder that hung about seven feet from the ground.

"How do we get up there?" I asked.

"You can jump or let me give you a boost," he said.

I groaned.

"Admit it, now you're having fun," Hunter said as he grabbed me around the waist and held me up until I gripped the bottom rung; then he supported my feet while I scrambled up. The air cooled as I climbed higher. When I got to the top, I eased my way onto the narrow ledge running around the water tower and sat down, my heart pounding.

It took me a minute to get used to being so high off the ground. I gripped the bar and tried to steady my breath. Hunter slid next to me, his long legs dangling next to mine. The wind blew heavy gusts through my hair and pushed the chill in the air deep below my skin. I stretched the arms of my shirt over my hands.

"Are you cold?" Hunter slid out of his sweatshirt and handed it to me. It smelled like grass and soap with just a hint of the scent of horses. It was a nice gesture, something Parker would never do. For a second I imagined the kind of boyfriend Hunter would be—the kind who would do some traditional dates but still surprise a girl once in a while. He'd open the door and try to impress her parents. He'd make her laugh when she was sad, and back her up when things got tough. I slammed the door on those thoughts before they had time to gain a foothold in my mind.

The land stretched in front of us, crisscrossed with a few roads. Trees leaned forward, their trunks permanently bent by the relentless wind that pushed across the prairie. Clouds swept the horizon and piled up in heaps of white.

"What do you think?"

I ran my hand along the metal railing. Scribbles ran in lines and loops around it. More writing covered the tower itself.

"How many people come up here?"

"A lot."

"To do their science homework?" I asked.

Hunter grinned. "That's probably a smaller group."

"For all the trouble it took, I thought the answers might be written on this thing." I kept one hand on the rail but turned to study some of the writing. There were names—girls' names paired with boys' in front of 4EVER, names with football numbers, names with hearts. There were quotes: angst-ridden and optimistic. "Wait, here's the score of the game against Junction," I said, putting my finger on a set of lines written in Sharpie.

"Yeah, you'll find lots of those."

"Do you miss being on the football team?" I asked.

"Yeah, parts of it. But there were other parts that ate me up inside."

"Like what?" I glanced at Hunter's profile.

"The way everyone thought they had a right to a piece of you. The way everybody watched me during the season, constantly sizing me up. 'How's the arm, Price?' 'How's your timing with your receivers? You can't let that Junction defense get in your head.' I'd go back in a second if it was just a game again. But it was all wins or losses. I was either the town hero or I let everyone down. I couldn't live like that. Too much pressure. So I did what everyone expected. Ask anyone. You can't count on a Price."

"I hate to tell you this because you'll probably take it as a compliment, but you seem pretty reliable."

One side of Hunter's mouth lifted. "I'll try not to let your unbridled admiration go to my head."

"But I think I know what you mean about football. It's like politics. It's made up of people, but we turn those people into heroes and villains. You can't be anything in between."

Hunter looked into the distance. "Exactly."

"Is that why you don't live with your mom? Too much pressure?"

"I didn't leave her. She left me." His voice rumbled with the threat of anger.

"Right. I wasn't saying that. I guess I was thinking about my dad. Sometimes I wish I could just be his daughter, and I didn't have to worry about all the politics of it. I know he loves me, but that almost makes it harder."

"Because you can't just walk away."

"I guess." I spotted another set of names half scratched into the metal. " 'Tracy loves Trevor.' It's from seven years ago. Do you think they're still together?"

"Yep."

I looked at him. "So you are a little bit of a romantic."

Hunter leaned back and rested his arms behind his head. "No. Celia buys hay from Trevor. I know they're still together because I saw him last week."

I got up and ran my hands over the side of the tower. The worn metal had been scratched and sanded with dust. "We'd never have anything like this in DC. Things change too fast."

"Nothing changes here."

One cluster of thin, tight letters, two inches high in black marker, caught my eye. "This one says Ana is a slut," I said, scratching at it. Anger rumbled inside me. "People just get to write what they want up here."

"It's not necessarily true."

"Did you ever write anything up here?" I asked. "Any 'Hunter loves Missy'? Or 'Hunter and Gaye Lynn Forever'?"

Hunter pulled his science book from his backpack. "You can just ask me who I've dated."

"Okay. It has to be good. You were the quarterback. You're not bad looking. You can be a pretty nice guy when you're not being annoying."

"I wasn't naturally good at football. I had to work at it. Add to that one crazy mother, and I didn't have a lot of time to date."

"Seriously? No one? That just seems wrong."

"No matchmaking. I can find my own girl."

"I wouldn't dream of it." It was true. I had no desire to play matchmaker for Hunter.

"Besides, I don't come up here for the graffiti."

"What do you come up here for?"

Hunter nodded toward the horizon. "That."

I looked, and my breath caught in my throat. The sky had turned into a sea of pale light that melted into a pool of gold at the horizon. Short strokes of purple clouds swam across the blue.

I sat down again and punched his arm. "You didn't tell me to bring my camera. I left it in the car." I tilted my head and stared at the horizon. I would be able to capture only a fraction of the beauty and drama that filled the sky. "It doesn't matter. It would be a waste of film."

"It wasn't a waste of film when you first started taking pictures, and I'm sure those weren't as good as the ones you take now. People think you win games by putting points on the board, but you win by moving the ball forward play after play. Then the points take care of themselves."

"For someone who's not into photography, you act like you know a lot."

"I just think that if you love a game, you have to be willing to lose."

"Are we talking football?" I asked.

Hunter took a breath and looked out at the sky. "We're talking life."

I nodded as I took another look at the sunset.

chapter sixteen

Sitting with Kyle and his friends lost its appeal as the week progressed. On Monday I'd learned that the post was a kind of play and the spread was a kind of offense. On Tuesday they'd managed to shake themselves out of long stretches of silence to poke at each other about mistakes at practice. On Wednesday they ignored both Ana and me, too busy dissecting the Sugar Elm defense before Friday's game. By Thursday Kyle and his friends slumped on their stools, the heels of their sneakers tapping against the floor and their knees bouncing against the underside of the tables as they went over strategy.

So I wasn't that disappointed to find out that Ana was home sick on Friday. The timing was perfect, since it would give Kyle a chance to miss her. I went from my fourth period straight to the yearbook room, planning to finish the last two boxes of yearbooks, and maybe develop a roll of sunsets. But when I opened the door to the yearbook room, Ms. Serrano called me over immediately.

"Ana is sick, which means unless they develop a cure for the flu in the next six hours, I don't have a photographer for tonight's game."

"Do we need more pictures for the football page? There were dozens of good ones from last week."

Ms. Serrano sucked in a long breath. "No, we don't need more pictures. We got all the pictures we needed from the first game, so we can just ignore the rest of the season and hope no one notices."

"They would notice?"

She threw a pencil down on the desk. It bounced off and hit the trash can with a ping. "Half the people in this school think that newspapers and yearbooks exist to report game scores, and my staff just uses the remaining activities to fill in the space between. They would love an excuse to yank our funding, hire a professional photographer, and send me to monitor the delinquents in suspension."

"I just don't know if I can take game pictures as well as Ana," I said.

"You are not going to tell me you can't handle a few football pics when you came in here all high and mighty, Little Miss Too Good for Digital."

"You don't want me taking those pictures. You hate my pictures."

"You'll take the pictures, and you'll make sure they're great."

"Can I at least use my own camera?" I asked, biting my lower lip.

"You can use a grilled steak for all I care, but I better have those pictures Monday. Are we clear?"

"You'll have them. Even if they are muddy and predictable." I walked away.

"Kate," Ms. Serrano called. When I turned, she had her hand on her hip, but her eyes were soft. "What do you expect when you won't take any risks?"

"I take risks."

"You look for beauty, perfection." Ms. Serrano shook her head. "A picture is a piece of truth and life. That makes it as likely to be ugly as it is beautiful. And it's never perfect."

"But pictures can't ever tell the whole truth either, can they?" I thought of Parker's pictures.

"I don't want the whole truth. I want *your* truth. Photographs are reality and perception all in one image. You have the reality, but I have no idea what your perception is."

"Can't I just document what I see—like Brassaï or André Kertész?"

"That's not all those photographers did. They also documented their experience. You *see* great pictures, Kate. But you don't *feel* them. They don't hit you in the gut."

"Gut, huh." I tapped my fingers on the camera. "And if they hit you in the gut, I bet they would have some soul."

"One great image that says something." Ms. Serrano's soft eyes hardened. "But not tonight. Tonight I want high school football—action and sentiment. *Tomorrow*, find a picture with soul."

The bi-district game was forty-five minutes away in Crowe—a neutral field. Dad drove while Mom jotted notes on her calendar and India yelled at pollsters. "I don't care if you're having trouble getting a sample," she said. "I need those numbers." She clicked off her phone and threw it down next to her.

"How's the campaigning going?" I asked.

"Great," she said. "It's no problem getting people to trust a guy who showed up in town just as an election was starting."

"Have you tried campaigning outside Red Dirt?" I asked.

"The problem is Red Dirt is going to have a large turnout. Well over fifty percent because of the name recognition and volunteers," Dad said. "Turnout in the rest of the district will be low—a special election after a general election, this close to Thanksgiving and Christmas. We'll be lucky to get five or six percent."

"You know who's going to show up at the polls? No one. That's what our data tells us," India said.

"They need a reason to show up. Like a scandal or an issue," I said.

"Yeah, if you find one, let me know. I've been racking my brain." India frowned and turned back to her laptop.

I unzipped my camera bag and dug inside, making sure I had everything.

"Are you nervous?" Mom asked me as she pulled out her compact.

I thought about telling them what Ms. Serrano had said, but decided against it. My photography wasn't their favorite subject. "No. Why?"

Dad's eyes met mine in the rearview mirror, but he lowered them after a second. "You've checked that bag at least eight times since we left the house."

"I just don't want to screw up. Apparently the future of the yearbook program is on the line."

We pulled into the Crowe High parking lot. Dad stepped out of the car and walked toward Mom, who adjusted his collar. He patted me on the shoulder. "You're in a perfect position. The expectations are low, so you're sure to exceed them."

"Underpromise and overperform," India said.

Mom gave me a hug.

"Why are you guys being so supportive?" I asked.

"We're always supportive," Dad said.

"No. You're not."

"Well, we are now. Fresh start," Dad said. "We're getting back on track. In more ways than one."

The players' bus pulled in. I asked myself what Ana would do. Ana would start at the beginning of the story. If nothing else went right in this game, at least they would arrive with confidence. I walked in the direction of the bus.

I clicked a dozen frames as the players lumbered down the steps of the bus, stony expressions of determination on their faces, earbuds stuffed in their ears. Lines of parents and students cheered them to the field house. I knew I'd gotten at least one or two good shots.

Kyle came down the steps. I snapped a picture just as he spotted me. He strolled over, his helmet in his hand. "You're taking pictures tonight?"

"Yeah, Ana is sick."

His face fell. "That's too bad."

I tried to keep the excitement out of my eyes. His disappointment confirmed that he was just a light push away from falling for her. A few well-placed phrases, a couple of hints, and Kyle would be walking down the hall with Ana's hand in his (meaty, slightly sweaty) palm.

Kyle's spirits rallied. "I'm glad you're here. You can watch us beat these guys." He waved to me and followed the line of guys across the parking lot.

"You look worried." I turned to see Hunter, leaning against the chain-link fence that separated the parking lot from the bleachers.

"Why does everyone keep saying that?" I lifted my chin. "Ana's not here. I'm shooting the game tonight."

"You want some help?"

"Look, I know you think you're some kind of photography idiot savant now, but just because you—"

"Not with the photography. With the football. I'm pretty good at reading a field."

"What's your angle?"

"No angle, Hamilton." Hunter grinned, his dimples making a spectacular appearance.

"Fine." I fingered my camera strap. As easy as it is to talk people into helping, it's hard to accept it. "But stick to the football." I dug an extra press pass out of the yearbook camera bag and handed it to Hunter.

We walked down to the field to check out the lighting. I made a few adjustments to my camera, took some shots. A hint of warmth hung in the air, just behind the breath of cool blowing by my cheeks.

The Raiders kicked, jerseys ran down the field in formation, and the game started. The stadium lights made the colors more vivid. It was like the stadium had the same glow as Kyle. For me, being on the field ratcheted the intensity to another level. The Sugar Elm fans cheered with the loud brutality of underdogs. Kyle completed long passes that moved the team rapidly toward the goal line; then he would throw a short pass right into the hands of a Sugar Elm player. He was like a candidate who would pull ahead ten points in the polls, just to have another scandal leak out.

I had to admit, having Hunter there made my job easy. He watched as the players crouched over the line of scrimmage. Then he'd point to a Red Dirt player to follow or turn my shoulders until the camera framed a particular section of the field. He didn't always follow the ball. Sometimes he pointed to the white outline of the field or a receiver shooting out from the formation. I froze the players, their arms outstretched for a catch. I turned the camera on the crowd, who leaned forward, their elbows on their knees and their hands pressed together, prayerlike, at their lips. I got shots of the receivers fighting to stay in bounds, their bodies twisted, the ball clutched to their chests.

I blew through three rolls of film in the first quarter, so I retrieved the digital camera, switched the lens, and continued shooting. After that, I just stuck both cameras around my neck and moved back and forth between them. The digital gave me speed. The action would look sharp. The film camera gave me depth. I could play with light and shadows, bringing more meaning to the pictures when I developed them. I would give Ms. Serrano the sentimentality she needed along with the art.

Lost in the game, in the moment, I filled frame after frame.

Even though the pictures would be great, all the signs on and off the field indicated that the game wasn't going well. Red Dirt managed to score twice in the first half, but one score was a fumble return. The other was the result of a series of graceless passes and lucky catches. Kyle spent his seconds between plays shoving the shoulders of his linemen or yelling at his receivers.

I looked at the scoreboard and realized it was late in the fourth quarter. The Raiders had managed to claw ahead by seven points. I'd used up my last roll of film a long time ago, and I knew, deep in my photographer's bones, that Ms. Serrano would love the shots I got.

I turned to Hunter. "Have you ever had a Frito pie? They're amazing."

"Yeah, Hamilton."

"Come on. I owe you for this." I grabbed the sleeve of his jacket and pulled him toward the concession stand.

The woman sitting behind the cash register shook her head. "We're closing up."

"I just need two Frito pies."

"Sorry, honey." She reached for the metal curtain above the window.

Hunter tugged at my arm. "It's okay. You can owe me something else."

"You're the one who reminded me not to give up." I turned back to the woman and pointed to Hunter. "My friend has been helping me take pictures all night, and all he asked in return was one of your delicious Frito pies. What kind of person would I be if I didn't get him one?"

She dropped her shoulders and reached for a bag of Fritos. "Fine."

I smiled. "Two, please."

She grabbed another bag and turned toward the chili and cheese.

"Hamiton, you really know how to make yourself a pest," Hunter said as we strolled away, Frito pies in hand.

"I wasn't leaving without a Frito pie." I dug my plastic fork deep into the bag.

Hunter climbed to the top of a picnic table and helped me up beside him.

"What's your secret?" I asked.

"What secret?"

"How did you know where the ball was going? It's like you were seeing something even Kyle wasn't seeing."

"Kyle could see it if he looked," Hunter said.

"See what?"

"No way. I don't give away my secrets."

"Come on."

"You going to tell me how you get people to do everything you want?" He looked at the scoreboard. "Besides, I like when you have to ask me for help. It's good for you."

He winked and I melted inside. A guy with the confidence to pull off a wink was trouble.

By the time we finished our Frito pies, the game was over. Red Dirt had won. The team mixed with the fans, mothers hugging their sons' sweaty shoulder pads and fathers nodding their approval.

We walked by Bo and Kyle Stone. "Do you think that kind of football is going to take you to the state finals?" Bo said to Kyle.

"I can't help it if the receivers—"

"Don't tell me about the receivers."

The only thing that stopped that kind of lecture was an audience. Hunter must have seen something settle over my face. "Kate, don't get mixed up in it."

I took a step toward them. "Hi, Mr. Stone. Good game, Kyle. I think I got some great shots of that pass in the third quarter."

Bo's mouth struggled its way into a neutral expression while his chest continued to rise and fall. "Hi, Miss Hamilton. Are you headed home?"

I knew he wanted me to leave. Unfortunately for him, that just made me more determined to stay. "Not yet. I want to get some pictures of the celebration," I said to Bo.

Bo nodded, then frowned at Hunter. "What are you doing here?"

"I came to support the team," Hunter said.

Kyle crossed his arms. "Kate, there's a party later at the pit. You want to come?" he asked me. "I can take you." There was an edge to his voice, but I tried to ignore it. It was probably just left over from his anger at his dad.

"I don't know," I said.

"And you have an early morning at the shelter," Hunter said to me.

Kyle glared at him. The anger rolled off him in waves, and I didn't relish being near him. I was about to say no when he leaned closer and lowered his voice. "I want to talk to you about something."

I knew it. He wanted to talk about Ana. Bo's eyes had narrowed into slits.

I nodded at Kyle. "Okay. I'll see you back at school and we can go from there."

Hunter's eyes followed Kyle as he walked away. "Are you sure you know what you're doing?" ·

"Hey," I said, smiling. "I talked Tip into feeding and snagged us two Frito pies. Maybe you should learn to trust me."

chapter seventeen

"I don't trust that guy," India said when I told her about the conversation with Bo Stone and Kyle.

"Bo Stone? I don't either," I said. "I'm starting to think Dad *should* win."

"I'm not talking about Bo, and yes, if anyone asks, we are fully confident we can beat Congressman Hamilton's opponent. I'm talking about Kyle."

"Kyle?" I wrinkled my forehead. "I mean, sure, he's a little self-absorbed for a small-town jock, but he's harmless."

"He is a lot like his dad," India said.

"He's as much like his dad as I'm like mine."

"That's my point."

"You think I'm like Dad." I looked over to where my father stood, in the middle of a knot of jeans, boots, and hats.

"I think you and your dad both know what you want and go after it. I think you both like to win."

"And the Stones?"

"Bo and Kyle will do anything to avoid losing."

"What's the difference?"

"It makes them far more dangerous." She nodded to Bo Stone. He was talking to Principal Walker, but his eyes were focused on Dad. "If you want to win, you play by the rules."

173

Mom and Dad walked over. India said, "Kate is going to the victory party with Kyle Stone."

Dad's face hardened.

"I went last week," I said.

"Not with the Stone kid," Dad said.

"We're just friends."

"Of course you can go to the party with who you want, Kate. Just be home by curfew." Mom looked at Dad, pressing her lips together. "Right, Jeff?"

"Right." Dad turned to go.

We were all silent on the way back to the school. Once we parked, Dad recovered enough to shake a few hands and slap a few backs.

"Do you have your phone?" he asked me as the last player stepped off the bus.

"Yeah, but Kyle will bring me home."

Dad nodded.

"I just want you to be smart," he said.

"Okay."

"And careful."

"I got it."

Then, to my horror, Dad made his way over to where Kyle and Bo Stone were standing. Bo crossed his arms and widened his stance. "I was talking to some folks in San Angelo about your Farm Bill proposals," he said to Dad.

"Save it for the debate." Dad turned to Kyle. "She has a midnight curfew," he said without any formalities.

I was mortified. What if Kyle read this as some hint that I was interested in him? It could scare him away from Ana. I would have to negotiate this evening very carefully.

"It will be an early night. Remember Coach wants everyone home and in bed by midnight," Bo Stone said to his son.

"I know, Dad," Kyle said. He winked at me, but it wasn't the same as Hunter's wink. Hunter's was for me. Kyle's was for the audience around me. "We better get going. You ready?" Kyle put a hand on my back, then looked over his shoulder at his dad.

Dad turned and walked away. I handed my camera bag to Mom and followed Kyle through the crowd. He shook a few hands and signed an autograph for an eight-year-old. Men clapped him on the back. Kyle smiled and thanked them, but the tightness in his jaw intensified.

He got into his Jeep. I pulled at the handle, but the door was still locked. I knocked on the door, slightly irritated. I'd never admit it to Hunter, but I'd gotten used to him opening the door to his truck for me. Still, I was determined to make the best of this opportunity to get the scoop on Kyle's feelings about Ana. He unlocked it, and I climbed in.

Kyle leaned back in his seat and closed his eyes. "I hate that guy."

"The guy who was telling you what a great arm you have?"

He put the key in the ignition. "No, my dad."

The conversation was finally on familiar ground. "Ignore it. That's what I do. He's in the middle of a campaign."

"You're probably right." He put his hand on my knee. "I'm really glad you decided to come with me."

"Maybe the party's a bad idea." I turned toward the window,

shifting my leg away just as Kyle moved his hand back to the steering wheel.

"I think it's just what I need." He started the car and roared out of the parking lot.

After a few minutes of silence, I was beginning to feel grateful for Coach Watkins's midnight curfew. "It's too bad Ana was sick," I said.

"Yeah," Kyle said. He was staring at the road, a scowl on his face. Then his face brightened. "But it's nice to have you to myself." He pulled into the pit and parked the Jeep. "You want anything?"

"No, thanks."

When Kyle left, I pulled down the tailgate and texted Ana.

You feeling better?

> **Still sick. Did you get some good pictures?**

Yeah. Hunter was a lifesaver. I'm at the pit party
with Kyle. I think he wants to talk to me about
you. Maybe get advice on how to ask you out?

> **I don't know.**

You need to have more faith in yourself.

> **Right now, I need sleep.**

Okay, I'll call you tomorrow.

I put my phone back in my pocket, pulled the sleeves of my sweatshirt over my hands, and hugged my knees. The party went on in lazy circles around me, groups clustered in lawn chairs and on the backs of trucks. Country music blasted from open windows. Guys in jeans moved in slow orbits around girls with their long hair pulled back into ponytails. There were a few people stumbling, a few more loud voices, but most of it stuck with the steady, slow rhythm of the steel guitars and deep voices singing through the speakers.

I waited for Kyle to come back. At first I was relieved he wasn't around. After fifteen minutes, I was mad. Another ten minutes later, when I thought the party couldn't get any worse, Missy strolled by. When she saw me, she tossed her long blonde hair over her shoulder and said something to the sweaty jock following two steps behind her. He scurried off to do her bidding, and she hopped on the tailgate.

Missy flashed her white teeth at me. "This looks like Kyle's Jeep?"

"You know it is."

"Did you come here with Kyle?"

"Yep."

Her bottom lip stuck out a little. "Did he leave you here all by yourself?"

"I'm fine." *I'm going to kill Kyle.*

Her sweetness melted away and a threatening cool replaced it. "Don't fall too hard for Kyle Stone. He's probably just taking his shot at the new girl."

"I'm not interested in Kyle," I said.

Missy laughed. "Everyone's interested in Kyle."

"Look, I appreciate your advice," I said. "But I don't like Kyle, I'm not falling for anyone anytime soon, and I don't let other girls intimidate me."

Missy huffed her way off the tailgate and walked away.

Another five minutes slipped by before I called Tasha.

"I'm at a party with Kyle, and he just walked off and left me."

"Where'd he go?"

"Wait, I see him. He's over by the keg." I squinted in the darkness.

"And you're waiting by the car? I bet that feels familiar."

"What?" I watched Kyle stumble over to a group of guys and high-five them.

"I just remember all the time we spent waiting for Parker."

"He was always late, but this isn't the same. Kyle is not Parker."

"Driving Parker's drunk butt home."

I swallowed. "It's not the same."

"Making excuses for Parker."

I took a deep breath. "Okay, it's kind of the same. What was I thinking? I almost set Ana up with this guy."

"At least you found out in time," Tasha said.

"I'm getting my ride home." I hung up, marched over to Kyle, and tugged him away from the group. "I'm ready to go," I said.

"I'm not." His words were stretched and slightly muddy. He reached out for my hand, but I jerked it back.

"I've been sitting around all night, and I have to work at the shelter tomorrow."

"With Hunter? How do you stand that guy?"

"He's not so bad."

"Well, if you want to get out of here, let's go." He grinned at another guy before swinging his arm over me. The smell of beer filled my nostrils. He moved with a heaviness that he hadn't had before, and his eyelids slid a little lower on his eyes. When we'd left the warm glow of the headlights, he dropped his keys. He stumbled forward to pick them up, but I snatched them from the ground in front of his feet.

"Maybe we should find someone to drive us," I said.

"A chaperone? That's not the plan," Kyle said.

"Believe me. Plans change," I said, walking a half step ahead of him.

"Are you just mad 'cause I've been ignoring you?"

"No. I'm mad because you're drunk, and I'm going to have to find us a way home." I looked around at the party. I was ready to go. "I'll just drive us."

"Fine with me," Kyle said, following me around to the driver's side.

"Just get in the—"

Before I could finish, Kyle pulled me behind the Jeep and pushed his body against me. The party continued ten feet away, but we were out of sight in the shadows. "What are you doing?" I said, pressing my hands as hard as I could against his chest. His lips headed for mine. I turned my head and they landed somewhere in my hair. With that shock over, I could register hands creeping down my back toward my butt. "Get off me," I said, giving him one more push. I moved so that he couldn't pin me against the truck again. My hands made tight fists, the keys digging into my palm.

He took a step closer.

"Try it again and I'll break your face open," I said, holding up a hand with keys sticking out between each finger.

He stumbled back. "Relax, Kate. Come on. You've been flirting with me since you set foot in Red Dirt."

I took a breath. "You like Ana, remember."

"Ana," Kyle said, taking a step back. "No offense, but I don't do charity."

The disgust in his voice made my stomach turn. I almost wished he would make another move so I'd have a good reason to punch him. Whatever he had been drinking, it had wiped away the thin layer of charm that he usually wore. "Then why did you defend her with Hank?"

"I defended *you*. I thought you'd go for the whole white-knight act."

"But you liked the picture of you and Ana."

"I liked the picture you took," he said, trying to put his hand on my shoulder.

I shoved it away. "And when you said you liked girls who were original, unique—"

Kyle leaned back. His face was starting to harden. "I meant you."

I put my head in my hands. "This is terrible."

"She'll get over it." He moved closer.

For a moment, I felt a little bad. "I don't like you, Kyle. Not like that."

"Look, I know you're looking out for your friend," he said. He reached out and touched the ends of my hair, but all I saw was the calculating expression in his eyes.

"*Nothing* is going to happen."

"Think about it. This would drive my dad nuts. Your dad too. That alone would be worth it."

"You're using me."

"Don't act like you don't get something too. I'm QB1." Kyle's eyes got mean. "You can't be that picky. You've been drooling over Hunter since you got here. I'm offering you an upgrade."

"Is that what you think?" My blood boiled inside of me. "He was right about you."

He took a step back. "Oh, really? Well, you know what people say about you. You and Ana are joined at the hip. Everyone knows she's a slut. Makes sense you are too."

I'd heard enough. I pulled open the door and climbed into the driver's seat. Just as I was about to slam the door, a hand held it open.

"Where do you think you're going?" Kyle said, leaning into the cab.

"Home," I said, jerking at the door to close it.

Kyle kept a firm grip on the edge. "You don't come here with me and then run off. You can find your own ride home."

"I'll—leave—any—way—I—want," I said, pulling at the door with every word. Kyle's hand slipped slightly. He struggled to regain his grip, but the door slammed shut on his hand. He took two steps back, cursing. I gave the door one more pull and locked it. Kyle stood next to the truck, bent over his hand. My own hands were shaking, but I managed to get the key in the ignition.

This was what happened when people got away with everything they did. They got cocky. *I'll have to do a little damage control*, I thought as I started the truck and shifted into drive. I'd call Ana and warn her, then place my version of events with a few well-connected people. Maybe Missy's big mouth would come in handy. But for now, I just needed to get out of there.

I tried to calm my mind and go through the motions Hunter had taught me. People were gathering around the sides of the car, but no one was standing in front of it. I could still get out. I eased Kyle's Jeep forward and steered onto the ramp that led out of the pit. I pushed the gas gently. The Jeep crawled forward. I pushed harder. It moved a few feet more, then tipped at an odd angle and bounced to a stop.

When my heart stopped pounding, I pushed the gas again. The wheels whirled, but the Jeep didn't move. Pebbles ground against the undercarriage. I pushed harder on the gas, but the wheels only spun.

I crossed my arms. The headlights shone tiny circles in the dirt. More people gathered to stare.

"That's Kyle's Jeep."

"What was she doing?"

"Isn't that Ana's friend?"

"Her dad's in all those campaign ads."

I wanted to die, which I didn't have to worry about because Dad was going to kill me. Then I heard a tap on the window.

"Interesting parking job," a voice called. Hunter's face peered into the passenger window. "You need a ride?"

"What happened?"

"You ran the car off the ramp. It's going to be a long night for the people who parked in the pit. Lucky for you, I parked along the edge. Come on, Hamilton." He held out his hand. "Party's pretty much over."

I climbed out the passenger side and jumped out of the leaning door to see expressions that ranged from horror to shock. About ten feet away, Kyle was holding one hand in the other, surrounded by a group of football players.

I hesitated a second. Should I turn this around on Kyle? That might be tough at the moment, since I did technically steal his car.

"This is all a big misunderstanding," I said to Hunter. The crowd stared at me over their cups and cans. I grasped at the words that I needed, but they slipped through the desperation clawing through me.

"You broke my hand," Kyle shouted at me.

My breath squeezed out in tight gasps. "Broke his hand? That's impossible," I said, looking around as the crowd swelled and the glares sharpened.

Hunter took the keys gently out of my hands. "It's probably just swollen. Put some ice on it." He tossed the keys to Kyle. They landed at his feet.

"What about my Jeep?"

"Get it towed." Hunter led me to his truck at the edge of the circle. "You need to get out of here," he said to me in a low voice. "You just broke the quarterback's hand."

"I thought you said it was swollen." The panic that had ebbed with Hunter's confidence flooded over me again.

He opened the door. "Get in."

I jerked away from him. "I can't leave with you, people will think—"

"Kate, get in the truck," Hunter said. "You can't talk your way out of this one."

His movements were relaxed, but there was a darkness in his eyes that looked a little like fear. I climbed in and leaned back on the worn seat. Hunter let me stare out the window in silence as we drove back toward the lights of town.

chapter eighteen

I buried my head in my hands. "So I really am an idiot," I said. I'd just told him what happened with Kyle.

"You were trying to help," Hunter said.

"But you were right. Now Ana's going to be furious."

"She won't be furious."

"You think?"

"She might be hurt."

I collapsed against the back of the seat. "That's worse."

"Look on the bright side. She never actually had to date the guy."

"I don't think I get to take credit for that." I leaned my forehead against the window. "This involves you too, you know. Kyle thought I might have a thing for you. Ridiculous."

Hunter kneaded the wheel with his hand. "Can't fault the guy's imagination."

"You know what this means, right?" I said.

"You finally learned your lesson about getting involved with other people's business."

"No, it means I'm going to have to destroy Kyle." I lifted my head. "I wish I hadn't mashed his hand. Do you think it really is just swollen? It would help me play the victim."

"There's probably some ligament or tendon damage at least."

"Then I'll have to work another angle."

"Let it go."

"What is it with guys thinking they can just do what they want no matter who gets hurt?" I crossed my arms, my anger pulsing through me. "Actions have consequences. You maul a girl, she might break your hand. You post private pictures of someone, you lose your letter of recommendation."

"Are we still talking about Kyle?"

"Yes, we're talking about Kyle," I snapped.

Hunter raised a hand in surrender. "You could just let Kyle be an idiot. Those things tend to take care of themselves."

I looked at Hunter. "They *never* take care of themselves. What do you know about Kyle? Is there any dirt on him?"

"He's just your run-of-the-mill jerk," Hunter said. "Since you're so interested in politics, I'll tell you how they work around here. You do something. People talk about it. You move on."

"We can't all be above everything like you."

Hunter pulled into Aunt Celia's driveway. "I'm not above anything. I just accept things the way they are."

"If you do that, wrongs don't get righted. Nothing gets fixed."

"Have you noticed that things get pretty messy when you fix them?" Hunter asked. "Try to stay out of trouble, Hamilton."

"No promises." I slammed the door of the truck and stomped down the gravel driveway. I didn't know if I was angrier with myself for being so blind or with Kyle for being an idiot or with Hunter for being so . . . I didn't know what Hunter was being, but whatever it was, it burned under my skin.

I turned to walk up the steps to the porch. If I could get inside and in bed, I could figure out what to tell India tomorrow. That was when I heard it—a faint cry carried on the wind, a high-pitched bray. I listened. There was something familiar about it. I heard it again. It was one of the calves from Celia's shelter. I stepped out from the halo of light around the porch and headed toward the noise.

After stumbling around in the darkness for a minute, I pulled out my phone to provide some light. It illuminated a small circle of the grasses and brush at my feet.

The calf moaned again. It was such a sad, lost sound. "Keep calling," I said into the darkness. "I can't find you." I swept the light over the brush until I caught sight of Tip's black nose poking through the brown grass.

"There you are," I said, squatting down. "What are you doing out here?" I put my phone in my front pocket, let my eyes adjust to the darkness, and then reached down. My hands stopped at something sharp, and I jerked them back. I pulled out my phone again for light and pushed some of the grass aside.

A chill seeped into my gut. The tiny calf's leg was wrapped up in a scrap of barbed wire. There were spots of blood along her stomach and head. She'd clearly been out here for a while.

I called Aunt Celia, but got no answer. I knelt down. "Okay, Tip, we are going to unravel you and get you back to the shelter."

I started with the wire around the calf's foot. The barbs had sunk deep, so I steadied my breathing, held the sick feeling inside my stomach, and pulled. The wire tore off pieces of skin as the calf released a loud cry and kicked at the air. I didn't know if I was doing harm or good; I just knew that I had to do something.

As soon as I had her foot unraveled, Tip tried to stand. She stumbled for a second before falling onto her other side—onto more barbed wire.

The tears started to come. I was messing everything up again, only hurting Tip more, just like I'd messed everything up since I got here. I saw a light on in the veterinary trailer. "Come on," I said, rolling the calf into my arms. "Aunt Celia must be at the shelter."

I barely registered the scratches on my arms as I ran to the trailer. The calf continued to bray sadly. I didn't think I could stand much more, until she went silent. That's when I realized that the silence was worse.

I hurried into the trailer and put her down. Tip's injuries looked terrifying under the stark fluorescent lights. Bits of torn flesh trailed blood through the matted fur on her chest, which rose and sank with her sharp breaths. I rubbed my eyes and dropped to my knees.

The door opened. "Celia, thank God. I found—"

When I looked up, it wasn't Celia. It was Hunter.

"What happened?" he asked. "When I got here to do the feeding, the door was open."

I tripped and stumbled through the words. "Tip. She wandered up by the house and got caught in some barbed wire. I tried to help."

Hunter went to work, pushing aside the hair and dirt to get a look at Tip's wounds. He cursed under his breath and the muscles in his face tightened.

"You don't have to tell me. I know I probably made it worse. I didn't know what to do."

He pulled a couple of bottles and creams from the shelf and handed one to me. "Clean the scratches and put this on the smaller ones." His voice was hard. My hands were shaking, but I managed to treat a few lacerations. The cow was moaning again.

He rinsed and stitched the large wounds, then taped gauze over them. He finished with an injection. The cow closed her eyes.

"She's going to die, isn't she? I killed her." I collapsed into Celia's chair.

"I just gave her a tetanus shot. You've probably had one, but you should put something on your hands and arms," he said.

I looked down. My hands were more cut up than I'd realized. The tiny rips in my sweater were dotted with blood.

"Here," Hunter said, sitting in the chair across from me and taking my hand. He pulled open a drawer and fished out a first-aid kit. I leaned back.

"I'm okay," I said, my voice shaking.

"Kate . . ." He raised an eyebrow.

I let him reach over and pull my arm into his lap. He started dabbing the cuts with a cotton ball.

"I can't believe you knew what to do with that calf," I said.

"Celia has taught me a lot. I like animals because they aren't complicated."

"Speaking of animals, how are your mom and Lucy?"

"Speaking of complicated, Celia said Mom brought Lucy by for shots."

"Ah, so she is taking care of her."

"It looks like it."

"You're welcome," I said, hoping to hide the sob of failure and exhaustion behind my lame attempt at humor.

"I was working up to it."

His fingers were warm on my arm. He pulled out a tube and dabbed some cream on a few of my deeper cuts, then smoothed a

Band-Aid over the biggest ones. He shifted my arm from his lap to mine. "You're all fixed up." He pushed his chair back.

I stood. I brushed the tears away to find him looking at me worriedly. "Kate, you saved Tip. You know that, right?"

"You saved her. I just carried her here."

"You found her and found someone to fix her. If that's not saving something, I don't know what is."

I nodded. His words soothed me. I knew I should thank him for rescuing me from the party, for giving me a ride home, for patching me up. For saving me.

He watched me, a smile playing at his lips. "You're welcome," he said.

"I was working up to it," I said.

"I think we're even now." He stood up. "I'll walk you back."

"You can stay here. I'll be fine."

"You don't have to be so stubborn."

Tip's legs jerked.

"I'm not being stubborn. I'd rather you make sure that Tip is all right."

Hunter frowned, and I got ready to argue. I wasn't letting him leave Tip. But after a second, his face relaxed. "Watch out for snakes."

"You're just saying that to freak me out."

"True. After tonight, the snakes are watching out for you." Hunter pressed a flashlight in my hand. His touch lingered a second longer than necessary. "I'll see you tomorrow."

chapter nineteen

I trudged across the field to the house, the warmth of saving something humming inside me. This was what making a difference felt like. I wanted to tell someone about finding the calf and carrying her to the shelter. I wanted to describe what it was like to actually help. And I wanted to ignore the tingle that had spread through me when Hunter held my hand to bandage it. It was probably just part of the excitement from the rescue.

I walked up the porch stairs into the pool of light over the door. When I opened it, India, Mom, and Dad were sitting at the kitchen table with coffee in front of them.

"You won't believe what just happened," I said.

"I think I know this one. Someone wrecked a car and a campaign in one night," India said.

Her words snuffed out my excitement. I scanned their faces. Dad couldn't look me in the eye. Mom had a half-eaten cookie in front of her. It was one of the ones Caroline Fisher had brought over—full of butter, chocolate, sugar, and probably gluten.

Mom took a bite.

This was bad.

"It was hard to believe that the daughter of a respected congressman would steal the opponent's son's car," Dad said.

"I can explain—" I said.

"And then drive it without a license," Mom added.

"Into a ditch," India finished.

I was too blindsided to come up with a polished answer. "I wouldn't have had to do any of that if Kyle could keep his hands to himself."

Dad's jaw tightened. He glared at India. "This is exactly why I didn't want her involved," he said, his anger making the words snap.

My eyes burned with more tears, but I held them back. Dad was angry. He didn't get angry. Even when the picture of me glaring at him came out, he was disappointed but not angry. Not that I hadn't deserved his anger. Maybe I deserved it now.

India leaned toward me. "I would love nothing better than to have headlines all over Texas tomorrow saying that Bo Stone's kid got what he deserved. But if you wanted to play the victim, you should have acted like one."

"You should have heard what he said about Ana. About me." I studied the faces around the table. "He was just using me to get under his dad's skin." There was something they didn't want to tell me. "I'm not sorry that I did it. I'm glad his Jeep is in a ditch. I'm glad his hand is hurt. If you're expecting me to apologize to him—"

Dad pressed his lips together and looked at India. "We think it might be best if you went back to DC."

"What?"

"You can stay with Tasha," Mom offered.

It felt like a punch to the gut. "You can't send me away every time I do something you don't like." My throat tightened.

"We're just trying to protect you," Mom said.

"I can take care of myself."

"It's decided," Dad said.

"It gets you out from under the microscope," India said. "The media have moved on from the school incident in DC. They won't care about this story. You can lie low."

"While you do damage control for your delinquent daughter, and Kyle stays on his pedestal," I said to Dad.

"I don't think we'll use the word *delinquent*," India said.

"We thought you'd be happy," Dad said.

"It would be really convenient if I was happy, wouldn't it?" I snapped. "You pushed me out of the campaign and now you're pushing me out of town." Emotions flooded my face, my voice, every muscle, every pore. I took a breath and forced back my hurt enough to give me a few seconds before my voice broke and the tears fell. "I guess if you're trying to win an election, this is a great strategy. If you were trying to be some kind of real family, it sucks."

I shoved my chair back and ran to my room.

When I got there, I collapsed on the bed, buried my face in my pillow, and screamed with frustration. I had finally done it. I had freed myself from Hamilton family politics. This was what I had always wanted. I could go back to my old school, my old classes, Tasha. So why did it feel so horrible? Maybe that was the problem with being a politician's child: As much as I hated the fake, once you scraped it away, there wasn't much left.

The longer we stayed in Red Dirt, the deeper this sank in. Here, people owned who they were—they didn't apologize for being arrogant or ornery. Mrs. Fisher had her opinions. Aunt Celia had her principles. Hunter had his identity. You could rub

up against them or work around them. Even Kyle had his val-
ues—football, his reputation. They weren't noble, but they were
something.

I pulled my folder of pictures from the nightstand and studied
the early shots of our arrival in Red Dirt and a few attempts at
sunsets. Even my photographs were just pictures of what I thought
photography teachers and admissions committees would like. I
could see what Ms. Serrano saw: None of them held my truth.
I couldn't find any traces of what *I* wanted, what *I* had to say . . .
maybe because I wasn't sure what that was yet. I had been mouth-
ing other people's words for so long, mine had gone silent.

I came to the last picture in the pile. It was the one I'd taken
of Kyle my second day in Red Dirt, out by the fence that divided
our property and the Stones'. His smiling face mocked me. I
was about to rip it into a thousand pieces when something caught
my eye—the barbed wire. I'd seen it when we were catching the
cricket. Of course it was the Stones'.

My phone rang. It was Tasha. "I have more scoop," she said,
before I could say hi. "I was doing some early Spring Fling planning with Abby, and she said Rebecca told Lauren that Adam had
said Parker's grades were slipping."

"He doesn't get to use my notes anymore," I said, continuing
through the stack of photographs. I got to the picture of Dad that
Ms. Serrano had taped together. I studied it. She was right. It was
different from my other pictures. As Dad rubbed his hand through
his hair, he was lowering one mask—maybe the one he used with
donors or campaign employees, whoever he'd just walked away
from—and putting on another. I'd caught the split second when
he hadn't quite gotten the other mask in place. I knew that

moment. It was the same crack in the facade that had created the picture of me at the rally glaring at Dad. This was a picture only I could have taken.

"The rumor is with his SAT scores, he'll be lucky to get wait-listed anywhere without that recommendation."

Tasha's voice snapped me back to the present. "He has over a year. He'll probably just retake it until he gets a better score."

"It's still a win. He'll have to volunteer to keep up with you or study. Probably both. For once, Parker can't weasel his way out of something. I thought you'd be dancing by now."

"I don't know. . . . I'm starting to think I don't really care about the recommendation. I just didn't want Parker to have it," I said. "I'm not actually helping anyone or proving anything by taking it from him. Doing more harm than good is getting to be a thing lately." I told her about my evening, from Kyle's groping to Dad's dismissal.

"Kate, I'm so sorry. What Kyle did . . . It's not your fault."

"I know. But what it's going to do to Ana is."

Tasha was silent for a moment. "At least you're coming back to DC."

"Yeah." I picked up the picture of Dad again and pushed the rest of the photos aside.

"I'm going to try to not take the misery in your voice personally."

"It doesn't feel right leaving," I said. "I just made a mess of Ana's life. Aunt Celia needs me more than she realizes. Hunter will have to take care of the calves by himself. I've got yearbook pictures to shoot and Kyle Stone to put in his place." I rolled onto my back and studied the image of Dad. Somewhere in the hollowness I felt, one truth sparked to life. "But what I'd really like to do is get a great photograph. Something that shows what I see, not what I think other people want to see. Something so great that I don't even need that recommendation. Parker can have it."

"West Texas has really changed you," Tasha said.

chapter twenty

The next morning, when I looked out the window, a line of clouds lay low along the horizon. The sun brushed their underbellies with a golden fire and left the world in a still glow.

Mom and Dad didn't hesitate once they made a decision. If my flight back to DC wasn't booked already, it would be by the end of the day. I picked up my camera and headed out the front door. I didn't have time to fix everything I had broken, but I could take a few more pictures.

I froze in the doorway. Dad was pacing the yard, pulling up a dozen FOR SALE signs that broke the flat landscape. I turned to go back in the house. Then I noticed his face—the way his jaw was set, not angry but determined and a little sad. I raised my camera and snapped half a dozen pictures until his eyes met mine in the viewfinder.

"What's with the signs?" I said as I came down the porch steps.

"It's an old stunt that the town pulls."

"Are they telling us to leave?"

"Subtle, right?" He stopped and turned toward me. "I want to make something perfectly clear. I'm glad you slammed Kyle's hand in the door. And as far as I'm concerned, if a guy tries that with you again, you can wreck whatever you can get your hands on. I'll bring the sledgehammer." He yanked another sign out of the ground.

A mixture of relief and guilt churned inside me. "I'm not sorry about Kyle, but I am sorry about this," I said, gesturing to the signs. "And I'm sorry I messed up your campaign."

Dad passed the signs he held to me and continued plucking the last few from the ground. I followed him. "You know, this isn't the first time I've had to clean up *For Sale* signs. Did I ever tell you about the playoffs my junior year?"

I rolled my eyes.

"I'm going to take that as a no."

"You're good at reading people. Maybe you should go into politics."

"People say you're the funny one." Dad grinned. "It was the area game. We were down five to Singleton in the fourth quarter. It's fourth down and there are twelve seconds left on the clock. We're thirty yards from winning the game."

"Let me guess. You threw the game-winning pass and became the town hero."

"No. Coach gave me the perfect play—a bootleg right. The wide receiver runs a post on the backside of the formation. It works. His defender slips."

I groaned. "Dad, speak English," I said.

"The receiver is wide open. There's no one within fifteen yards. All I have to do is drop the ball in his hands and we win."

"So you did it, right?"

"I overthrew him by ten yards. I wasn't even close."

I'd seen Dad lose only once, this past fall, and that wasn't so much a loss as scorched earth. But that was a different Dad. I searched his face, but I couldn't find any trace of a mask. He was telling me something real. It dropped into all that emptiness that had consumed me last night and made me feel a little more solid.

"I spent years remembering that one game and forgetting all the other games I played and won."

I knew exactly what he meant. Somehow one loss could outweigh dozens of wins.

"I get it. You need to win. You should win. And you're worried I'll make you lose."

Dad shook his head. "This isn't about the election. It's about you." He rested a hand on my shoulder. "Listen, you're like me. You're good at winning. But you hang on to the losses. I'm worried that if I lose, you'll carry that loss. I can't risk that. I've made you think that winning matters more than family. It's not true, but . . ."

"Perception is reality."

Dad dropped his hand to his side. "What happens if I don't win? How will you feel?"

I took a good look at my dad. There were streaks of gray lining his temples and dark circles around his eyes. His expression was the same one in the picture at the pep rally—the wrinkled brow, the intense gaze. I could see what it was now—concern. Real concern. Not for what I would do or say, but for me.

This conversation felt so different from the directives I was used to. There was no strategy. There was no agenda. It was a little frightening, but also warm and real. "It wouldn't feel good. I appreciate that you're trying to protect me." I held my hand out for the other signs he'd pulled up. He passed them to me. "You're right. I don't have to win against the Stones or this town."

"I'll tell India to get you a ticket home. Mom has already called your school—"

"Dad, I don't need to win, but I can't quit. I want to stay in Red Dirt."

Dad pulled up the last sign. "You're not quitting. You're just taking a time out." He walked toward the house. When he reached it, he leaned the sign against the wall. I set mine down next to his.

I wanted to stay last night. Now I realized how much I *needed* to stay. I needed to find out what I had to say, and I didn't think I could do that in DC. I ran the last play I had. "The Singleton game. That was your junior year. What happened the next year?"

Dad rubbed his hand across his forehead. "I practiced that bootleg all summer, and it was the play that won State my senior year."

"What if Coach had never let you play again?"

"The empathy angle. Not bad."

"It's not an angle," I said.

He was quiet for a moment. "You're good. Dangerous but good."

"I just don't want you to give up on me."

Dad closed his eyes for a second. "I hate the idea of you within a thousand miles of that Kyle kid."

"I can handle Kyle."

"Think of the damage control India will have to do if I kill him."

"I think she would relish the challenge."

He sighed. "It's not going to be easy."

"I know that."

Dad looked around the yard, then back at me. "On Monday, hold your head high but not too high. Try to walk the line between sorry and guilty. If anyone asks, say you wish Kyle had backed away when you asked him to."

"Thanks, Dad." I hugged him. "You won't be sorry."

Dad squeezed me back.

The shelter was quiet, but the light was on, so I knew Aunt Celia was somewhere on the property. The pile of blankets where Tip had rested earlier had only a rumpled dip in it now. I spotted a piece of barbed wire on the desk against the wall, a couple of feet long and twisted into two loops. I went over and picked it up.

The door to the trailer opened. "I found that this morning," Aunt Celia said.

"Is that the piece of wire Tip got caught in?" I asked.

"Looks like it," she said, pulling some gauze and towels from a shelf. "You want to come see the calf?"

"Bo Stone should take that wire down," I said, following her down the steps and across the gravel to the barn.

"Bo is not going to care that one of my calves got caught in his wire." We found Tip, and Celia knelt beside her. "I heard about Kyle," she said as she started to clean and wrap Tip's leg.

"So everyone knows by now," I said.

"Just remember, news is like brush fires around here—quick to get out of control, but once there's nothing to burn, it dies out." She finished her work and patted the calf's head. "It was a little touch and go last night, but she didn't lose as much blood as she could have."

"You can thank Hunter for that."

"I heard you found her."

Aunt Celia stood. She picked up a piece of paper off the ancient printer in the corner and handed it to me. It listed my volunteer hours. "You think that will help you get that letter of recommendation you want?"

I scanned it. Thirty-two hours. Just seventy-five more and I would catch up with Parker. I nodded.

"And since I bet you're going to find a way to stay if you haven't already, I might as well tell you, I could use you as much as you want to show up. You'll have plenty of hours by the time you head back to DC."

"Thank you."

I didn't get a buzz of satisfaction from the hours like I would have a week ago, but I felt it a second later when Aunt Celia patted me on the shoulder. "Of course. Gotta help out family."

chapter twenty-one

I'd been taught how to navigate a hostile room. Dad would always stick by a powerful local figure who buffered him from the brunt of the anger. Mom would work her common ground as a wife and a mother. We also weren't above bringing along a kindergarten class or half a dozen puppies. If all that failed, we always, always had an exit strategy.

None of this helped when my hostile environment was high school.

The best I could do Monday morning was walk in with my head high. More than one shoulder slammed into me. Snickers and dirty looks followed me down the hall. Someone had Sharpied GO HOME across my locker. I was so intent on avoiding everyone's glares and whispers that I didn't notice Ana walking toward me until it was too late.

"Kate Hamilton," Ana said.

I stopped and turned to her. Of course she wanted to do this in public. After what I'd done to her, she'd earned this moment.

"I've been looking for you," she said.

"I wanted to call you this weekend. It's just . . . I didn't know what to say. I'm so sorry."

Ana crossed her arms. "You should be sorry."

"Go ahead." I turned away slightly.

She looked at me, creases between her eyebrows.

"Rip me apart." I looked around the crowded hallway. It was perfect. "I deserve it."

"I needed the game photos this morning. I came early to crop them so they'd be ready for captions."

"Photos?" For a moment I thought a miracle had saved me from the thresher of Red Dirt gossip. Then I remembered that made me the person who had to tell her. "You haven't heard?"

Ana smiled. "I heard that you tried to commit suicide because you have a stalkerlike obsession with Kyle Stone."

"What?" I said. My voice echoed off the walls of the hallway.

"Not everyone thinks that," Ana said. "Some people say you were stealing his car."

"Seriously?"

"Then there are all the rumors about you and Hunter."

I slammed my locker shut. "Yeah, Kyle let me know about those."

Ana glanced at the Sharpied words, then put a hand on my arm. "I just want you to be prepared for the stories."

We started walking down the hall. "So you're not mad?" I asked.

Confusion darkened Ana's features for a second before her usual brightness took over again. "Oh, because you were trying to set me up with him?"

"You didn't ever . . . like him, did you?" I pushed the words out. I didn't even want to bring it up if it would hurt her.

Ana shook her head. "Don't get me wrong, I like the *idea* of him. And I liked the way people treated me when he was talking to me. But I've known Kyle since we were in kindergarten.

I wasn't going to get too attached to the idea that he liked me. He mostly likes himself."

I threw my hands up. "Exactly. Why doesn't everyone else see that?"

"Like you did?"

"You have a point."

"We see it. We're just used to it." She sighed. "You were trying to help me. You really wanted him to be a good guy because it would fit into your plan so perfectly."

"You'll be happy to know that I am done helping." I looked up just in time to catch a group of girls whispering while they stared at me. "Are you going to escort me to and from every class?"

Ana's steps came to a halt a few feet from Mr. Quincy's door. "Whoa. You might not be the big news today after all."

My gaze followed hers. My heartbeat sped up. Kyle and Hunter were walking side by side.

And Hunter was wearing a Red Dirt Raiders football jersey.

A wave of betrayal and hurt washed over me, twisting my insides. It must have shown on my face, because Kyle looked up and saw me, and a sharp edge of satisfaction moved across his features. I glared back.

Mr. Quincy approached the door. "Miss Hamilton, Mr. Price, Mr. Stone. Would you like to join the rest of us?" I waved good-bye to Ana and went inside the room. The class had gathered around Quincy's desk, but their eyes were fixed on the three of us.

I hustled to the outskirts of the group. My thoughts raced, trying to figure out the game that Hunter was playing, but they kept running into one giant obstacle—Hunter didn't play games.

Along the bottom of the box on Mr. Quincy's desk, a web of caramel-colored ants wove back and forth. Mr. Quincy cleared his throat. "In the world of ants, these ants are special."

"They look like ordinary ants to me," one guy said.

Mr. Quincy smiled. "Ah, it's a good thing they can't hear you. They are kind of touchy about the fact that they're different. These are Argentine ants." He nudged one out of the box and put it in another tray with one of the black ants. "They come from the floodplains between two rivers in the northeastern corner of Argentina." The two ants met, each one tapping the other with its antennae. "Whenever it floods, all the ants' homes get destroyed and the ants have to battle over territory. This keeps them constantly at war. If they meet another ant that's not in their colony, they fight."

The brown ant started to attack the black ant. Its legs kicked and pulled.

"They don't live in West Texas—yet—but they are along the coast. I picked these up this weekend." The ants locked their small bodies together and continued their fight. The girl next to me gasped, and I had to admit, the violence was surprising in such tiny creatures.

We watched the ants battle for a few more seconds until the black ant was still. Mr. Quincy looked at us. "These ants have made it to every continent across the globe as stowaways on boats. They can travel across continents on trains. They are incredibly unified as a group. When they fight, they fight to the death. In the ant world, the only thing that can beat a colony of Argentine ants is another colony of Argentine ants."

"But why? What do they get from fighting?" I asked.

Mr. Quincy smiled. "Excellent question. What do you think? Mr. Stone?"

Kyle shrugged. "I don't know. Land? Little ant medals?" The class laughed.

"Peace. Inside the areas the Argentine ants control, it's peaceful." Mr. Quincy tipped the tray, and the Argentine ant slid into his box with the others. "I want you to do the same experiments on them that you did on your earlier ants and see if they behave differently."

While we returned to our seats, an office aide arrived and handed Mr. Quincy a note. Mr. Quincy frowned. "Mr. Stone, the trainer wants to take a look at your hand. Please remind him that you do not need to miss class."

"Sure thing, Mr. Quincy. It's just that everyone wants me back on the field as soon as possible," Kyle said. He swung his backpack onto his left shoulder and pushed toward the door. When he got to the threshold, he looked back at me and coughed the word "Traitor" into his hand. A chorus echoed around the room, followed by snickers. I lifted my head and stared at the front.

Hunter scanned the room with steady eyes and a tight jaw, and the coughing faded. Eventually, after the voices around us returned to a low buzz, he elbowed me. "You like my new look?" He had that infuriating smirk on his face.

"Is this some sort of joke?"

"Even my sense of humor has limits," Hunter said, raising an eyebrow. "And I heard you had a thing for sweaty jerseys. Guess you really can't believe everything you hear."

"Are you trying to get back at me for what I did to Ana?"

The smirk faded, replaced by worry. "Kate, you know I wouldn't do that."

"They just let you back on the team?"

"I live in the district. I'm passing all my classes. After a week of practice, I'm cleared to play." His face got serious. "I know you won't understand it, but I have to do this."

I tried to keep all my hurt below an icy facade. "I thought you didn't believe in all of this."

"His bruised tendon will keep him out for at least two games. I'm helping the team."

"Don't they have a backup quarterback?"

"Kyle was the backup quarterback last year. They have a sophomore, but he hasn't played a down this or last season. Believe me, they wouldn't use me if I wasn't our best shot at staying in the playoffs."

"I can't believe you are getting Kyle out of this mess."

The muscles along Hunter's jaw twitched. "I'm not getting Kyle out of anything. Wearing this jersey doesn't mean I like what Kyle did to you."

"It sure looks like it."

Hunter shook his head. "You of all people should know," he said, "things are not always what they seem."

chapter twenty-two

I made it through the rest of the day with just a few more bumps and bruises. It went better than I'd thought it would. Either Kyle wasn't the god he thought he was, or Hunter stepping in helped. And I owed him . . . again.

After school, I escaped to the darkroom. I pulled down the strips of negatives from the football game that I had hung to dry at the end of yearbook class. I put the first negative in the frame and started the enlarger. After three pictures, I fell into the rhythm of moving pictures from tray to tray. I had about ten or twelve pictures that I thought Ms. Serrano wouldn't hate, and two or three that might even make her smile, or at least stop frowning. I hated to admit it, but she was right. I'd made more mistakes, but I'd also stumbled onto some great shots. I could see pieces of me inside those photos—my eyes pointing the camera to a slice of truth.

I pulled a picture of Kyle. It was a great picture, though I almost wished it wasn't. I remembered the play. He had handed the ball off and was lining up to block a guy who was far outside the center of the action. His body stretched across two-thirds of the frame. He had just pushed off his back foot, so he looked like he was hanging in midair. There was an intensity to the shot that Ms. Serrano would love.

I couldn't see Kyle's face behind his face mask, but I could picture the smug expression he wore. He would do anything to win. I should have been the first person to recognize that. I'd fallen into the trap of seeing what Kyle wanted me to see. After all those years of watching Dad's campaigns struggle to control people's perceptions, you'd think I'd have known better.

I got out a magnifying glass and searched the edges for a blurred line or bad contrast. Nothing. It might be the best photo I had taken all night: perfect focus, perfect lighting. Kyle was close to the opposing sidelines, so I could see the opposing players' faces in the background. One Sugar Elm player caught my eye. In the negative, his face was a collection of shadows. But now, on print, I could see his expression. He was staring at Kyle, his eyes hard and flat, his lips pressed tight, one side curled slightly. It wasn't a look of defeat or anger. I looked closer. The guy was disgusted.

I hung the rest of the pictures, finished up the last few prints, and put them in the rinse before I went out into the main room, where Ms. Serrano clicked through pages on her computer screen. I set a stack of pictures on her desk.

"I hope they're good," she said.

"I think I got a few you can use," I said.

She flipped through the first three pictures. "Before you came, I'd almost forgotten how nice it is to hold real photographs."

I couldn't read her expression. She was just . . . looking. She picked through the pile and pulled out two—the one with Kyle and another I took at the bus after the game. Behind a trio of jumping preschool kids in mini-cheerleader uniforms stood the familiar cluster of men in boots and jeans with Bo Stone at the center. He had a lifted chin and a steely expression. The line of his jaw was in perfect focus. I had seen that ambition before, but never so close to the surface. When I clicked the shutter, I wasn't sure what expression I would get. A second before, Bo was talking to his neighbor. Two seconds later, he was waving his wife over. The picture wasn't of a student, but it caught the tone of the game on one man's face. She laid the photos on her desk, folded her hands, and looked at me.

"Your pictures are getting more complicated. There are sparks of life in them, not just lines and angles." Ms. Serrano slid the picture of Bo and the one of Kyle's tackle across the desk. "But I can't use these."

I rocked back. "Those are two of my best pictures. You don't think they have emotion?" If she couldn't use them, she couldn't use any of them.

"They are full of emotion. It's not the pictures. It's the story they tell. I can't put pictures in the yearbook that make the quarterback or the booster club president look bad."

"That's so . . ."

"Political?" She waved me away. "You should put them in that portfolio of yours."

I looked at them. "Really?"

Ms. Serrano raised her eyes and peered over her glasses at me. "They are perfectly framed and razor sharp. In addition to that, they are interesting. They tell a story. At least part of one, which for a picture is perfect."

I looked at the pictures again. "They don't really go with the rest of the photographs in my portfolio."

"Even better. They'll show that you have range. I used to love to see that when I was on the admissions committee at NYU."

All the assumptions I'd built around Ms. Serrano crumbled. She leaned back in her chair, amusement creeping across her face. "The question your blown mind is trying to form is what I am doing in this one-horse town."

I nodded.

"I grew up here. I didn't know it for a long time, but I love it here."

"What made you realize you loved it?"

"Perspective? Maturity? I'm not sure. Things just look different from a little distance. It is fine to be an artist, but I wanted to change lives, give people hope and a future. I wanted to do something meaningful."

"Art is meaningful."

"Of course it is. So what better way to spend your life than shaping a few more artists?"

"That's so . . . noble."

Ms. Serrano shrugged. "That doesn't do me much good. What would do some good is for you to figure out how to point the camera at some heroic moments. Keep the art for your portfolio."

As I left school, my phone buzzed in my pocket. I pulled it out to see Tasha's name blinking on the screen.

"When are you coming back? I'm in crisis," she said.

"I might be here a little longer."

"I thought you were on the next flight back to DC. How many hands do you have to break to get a ticket home?"

"I didn't break his hand. It's just a bruised tendon."

"Well, I don't want to freak you out, but after a week of ignoring Secret Crush, I smiled and said 'Hi,'" Tasha said.

"And?"

"And nothing. He said 'Hi,' then went back to reading. The plan isn't working."

I pushed through the front doors of the school. "I can help you more if you tell me who it is."

"What if I just told you what he likes?"

"Sure."

"He's really into animal rights. He's a vegan. He started the animal rights club last year."

"Robert Weaver? You have a crush on Robert Weaver!" Robert was a quiet, thoughtful guy. I didn't know him that well. I don't know if anyone did. He might be the last person I would expect Tasha to notice, much less pursue, unless she just wanted a challenge.

But Tasha normally went for the low-hanging fruit when it came to boys. Robert was tricky. He was cool and calm. He read books that weren't assigned. He debated with teachers. He was smart and aloof and a terrible match for Tasha.

"This never happens when you're here. I need you back in DC. What should I do?"

"Move on to another guy?"

There was silence on the other end. "Kate, I really like him."

"But why? He's not going shoe shopping with you. He wouldn't be caught dead at one of those sappy movies you like. Tasha, I wish I could help, but I can't imagine what you see in him."

"He's different."

"Different?"

"Yeah, I like him because he's different. The same thing I like about you."

I sat down on the curb. "Okay, so you just have to convince him that he wants something different too." I pulled out the picture of Kyle and studied it. That was it. I'd been so focused on the differences between me and Kyle—the fact that he was the star quarterback and golden boy of Red Dirt—I'd forgotten that those same differences might work to my advantage outside Red Dirt. "Wait, Tasha. You're brilliant. Got to go."

Ms. Serrano was locking up the yearbook room when I got there.

"Can I borrow a few of Ana's pictures from earlier in the season? To see what I can learn?"

"No problem. It's not like I need photographs. I'm just trying to spackle together a yearbook." She held open the door.

"I'll bring them back tomorrow, I promise."

I flipped through the files where we kept printouts of picture options from every event. I pulled a few, slipped them into my bag, and dialed India's number. I was finally sure about something.

"I know how to beat Bo Stone," I said.

"Kate, I told you to stay out of it." I could hear India tapping on her computer.

"You aren't even going to listen?" I asked.

"Fine, tell me."

"First, I need a ride home."

Five minutes later, India's rented bright red sports car screeched into the front parking lot. "This better be good. I still have to confirm three appointments for tomorrow and overnight the ad contracts."

"Do you know about Argentine ants?"

"Some new type of data mining system?"

"No, they are these ants that fight any outside ants to the death. The only thing that can beat an Argentine ant is another Argentine ant from a different colony." I handed her the picture I had taken of Kyle. "What do you see?"

"Kyle Stone on the football field. Red Dirt's hero."

"Now look at the player in the background," I said.

"So he's mad. Kyle is probably scoring another touchdown."

I held the picture up. "Can you see the disgust?" I put Ana's pictures of Kyle on the armrest one by one. "Red Dirt versus Singleton. Red Dirt versus Junction. Red Dirt versus Barnsdale. All games against towns in the congressional district. All the same disgust. What did you say the polling was again?"

India studied the pictures. Her eyes narrowed. "We are pushing forward, getting our message out there. We've got some momentum."

I looked at her. "The truth."

"We're fifteen points behind and the election is in two weeks. Bo Stone is in first. Your dad is polling in a weak second. If we could keep Bo from getting fifty percent, we'd have the runoff to make up ground. But voter turnout is going to be lower than low. It's desperate."

"This is what you need," I said. "The way Kyle acts on and off the field, that has to tick people off. He gets away with it in town, but people outside of Red Dirt must hate him."

India rubbed her forehead.

"This district is a web of rivalries. Rivalries are zero sum. If your opponent wins, you lose. If you win, your opponent loses. You know I'm right."

"People will vote against someone as often as they vote for someone," India said.

"You're running around trying to remind people how much they like Dad. Instead, you need to remind them how much they hate Bo Stone. If we want to take him down, we have to go outside the colony."

"You think people are going to get up and go to the polls just because Kyle Stone is a jerk on the football field?"

"I don't think it. I know it. If there is one thing I've learned here, it's that you can't underestimate the power of football. And that's what I have to offer."

"What?"

I smiled. "I'm the girl who just smashed the jerk's hand."

chapter twenty-three

"No," Dad said, loud enough that his scheduling team cleared the room.

"But—" India started.

"No. We aren't using my daughter."

"Dad, you have to let me do this."

"You already talked me into letting you stay. Now you want to campaign. Why do you care so much?" he asked.

"I want you to win that seat. It's our family's seat."

He stared at me. He pressed his lips together until they became a thin line hovering over his chin. "You get involved and they can go after you."

"I'm your daughter. I want to do this. It will matter. It will help people." The truth doesn't always crisscross agendas in politics. When it does, it can be very persuasive. "Dad, I can handle it. I'm tougher than you think."

Dad's back straightened. He studied me another moment. "I know you are."

"And I don't have to win, but I do feel right. This district needs you."

He frowned. "Fine," he said to India. "She's all yours, but if they start attacking Kate, if they criticize so much as the gum she chews, we are pulling her. Agreed?"

India nodded, and Dad turned back toward his office. She clapped her hands silently before pulling her phone from her pocket. She typed rapidly. "Get some sleep," she said to me without looking up. "We start tomorrow morning."

When India shook me awake on Tuesday, I rolled over and looked at the clock. "It's five in the morning."

"Right. Russell McCoy eats breakfast at six. We need to get there before he has his two scrambled eggs with a side of link sausage and a biscuit delivered."

I crawled out of bed. "Who is Russell McCoy?"

"He is the mayor of Singleton and has a lot of clout in the area. Your dad has been courting him since the campaign started, but we can't get much more than a lukewarm handshake. Stone hasn't gotten his endorsement either. It's two weeks until the election, and he's just sitting back with a tide of voters stuck behind him."

"What do you want me to do?"

"Very little." She threw a pair of jeans and a Texas Tech sweatshirt onto the bed. "I don't know how people are going to react to you. I have a feeling, but I'm using him as a test. If we win him over, he brings people with him. If not, we're no worse off than we were before."

I hated diner visits—a bunch of people saying things that don't matter to people who don't care. It was a lot of big smiles and small talk. But if it brought down the Stones, I would eat biscuits and gravy in every diner from here to Brownwood.

Rivers of dark blue crossed the sky between streaks of gray clouds, their edges softening toward the horizon. India drove at breakneck speed through three small towns before a sign welcomed us to Singleton. She turned in to a cracked parking lot, puddles of uprooted concrete along its dry surface. India shut off the car, but instead of getting out, she kept her hands gripping the wheel.

"You having second thoughts?" I asked.

"Nope. I'm just trying to get the timing right."

She sat staring out the front window for another thirty seconds before she turned to me. "Ready?"

I nodded. A ball of nervousness tightened inside me.

"Smile," India said.

I pasted on the bright, toothy grin that Dad liked.

"Too much. Just a natural smile. Like you're about to eat the best biscuits and gravy you've ever had."

The corners of my lips rose automatically and my mouth started to water.

"Perfect," India said.

A truck rumbled in next to us. India rubbed her hands together and pushed her car door open.

I stepped out of the car. The man who had pulled up in the truck was staring at India, shaking his head, a guarded smile on his face.

"You are persistent, Miss Truss," he said. "I thought we had settled what I was willing to do last time we met."

"This isn't business, it's pleasure, Mr. McCoy," India said, shaking the man's hand. "I've been craving the biscuits here for two days."

Mr. McCoy nodded approvingly.

India pushed me forward. "This is Jeff's daughter, Kate."

He shook my hand. "I've heard a lot about you, Kate."

I swallowed and searched his freckled face for a hint of what to say. Behind the leathery skin and white eyebrows shooting from his forehead, in the lines and cracks of sun-weathered skin,

I thought I saw a whisper of amusement, even approval, so I took a risk.

"Yeah, taking out the quarterback for the rest of the season gets around," I said.

Mr. McCoy stared at me, his eyes a steely gray. My heart pounded. It was over. Then a grin broke across his face, and he clapped a thick hand on my shoulder. "Why don't I buy you breakfast, young lady? Then I can figure out what to make of you."

India cleared her throat. "I'm going to make a quick phone call." She gave me a wink and stepped away.

Mr. McCoy pulled open the screen door. A waitress moved methodically from table to table, refilling cups, while another stood by the window to the kitchen. Worn wooden tables, soft from decades of arms and elbows, lined the walls. When we walked in, a dozen faces turned. Mr. McCoy led us through the diner to a table at the back, stopping to shake a few of the men's hands along the way.

He eased into a booth as a waitress poured coffee. "What did they tell you to say to me? Let's get it out of the way so we can enjoy breakfast."

I fumbled with my napkin. "Actually, they didn't tell me what to say."

"Interesting. Then what do you have to say?"

"I just want you to know that the people in your town, in this district, would be lucky to have my dad in DC. He's been in Congress for over a decade. He has connections. He knows how things work."

"That might be the problem. He's an insider there and an outsider here."

"But he's not. That's the thing. He grew up here. He could live in DC the rest of his life. He would still call West Texas home. If you left tomorrow, how long would it take you to forget?"

"I wouldn't."

"Exactly."

"I don't care much for political maneuvering, Miss Hamilton." He took a gulp of coffee and leaned back.

"Do you care about protection for small farms on the next farm bill? Because Dad plans to start working on that the day after he's elected."

"The farm bill caused us a lot of trouble last time."

"Right, the delays."

"People couldn't plant their cotton."

"That won't happen with Dad."

"Why not?"

"You may not like political maneuvering, but Dad is really good at it. Don't you want someone like that looking out for you and Singleton in DC? Plus, Dad hangs on to losses too long to let them happen much. He still remembers the area game his junior year. I bet you do too."

Mr. McCoy smiled. "Are you sure no one coached you?"

I shook my head.

"You just say the perfect thing naturally."

"Almost never. Ask anyone."

He laughed, a laugh that rang from deep inside him. "Humility. Refreshing. I like your style."

I raised my head and smiled.

Breakfast was delivered by a waitress who mentioned the number of trains going behind her house. Mr. McCoy said he would look into it. A couple came over to ask if Singleton was training more volunteer firemen anytime soon. Mr. McCoy said he had the dates back in his office, and he'd give them a call. I liked the way he talked—his deep voice with gravelly undertones, the pauses before words that showed he was listening.

When the couple moved on to their table, Mr. McCoy turned his attention back to me. "I knew your grandfather, you know." He took a sip of coffee. "He would be impressed with you."

"Who wouldn't want a granddaughter who went around destroying playoff chances?"

"People like you and your grandfather step on a lot of toes. They don't win battles. But they do win wars." He took another sip. "I don't know if you destroyed Red Dirt's championship chances. That Price kid may not have the raw talent that Stone has, but he's the player I would want on the field. Stone will give you flashes of brilliance. Price will give you something every time. If he keeps the spot through the next two games, Red Dirt will have a real quarterback controversy on its hands." He leaned back and slung his arm over the back of the booth. "I heard you're staying with your aunt while you're here. How's she doing with all this?"

"I think she's pretty ready for us to leave."

"I wouldn't be so sure about that," he said.

"I volunteer at the shelter. She tolerates my presence."

"Your aunt is a proud woman. She's not easy to help."

"Tell me about it."

"She's not that different from the rest of us. We all need a little help, but we sure like to scream and holler when someone tries to give us a hand."

"That's what you do here in the diner," I said, realizing it as I spoke. "You help people. You don't come for the biscuits. You come here because it gives everyone a way to get to you."

"Sure. It's my job." He leaned forward. "The biscuits are a nice bonus."

I smiled. "I like your style too," I said.

India came back in. "We better get you to school. It was nice to see you, Mr. McCoy."

We had turned to go when he called across the room. "Kate. Have your daddy give me a call."

chapter twenty-four

"You did great. Better than I expected," India said as her car squealed onto the two-lane road that would take us back to Red Dirt. "You got him to trust you, which was exactly what we needed."

"Doesn't he trust Dad?"

"Your dad is a very good politician and a very bad campaigner."

"He campaigns constantly. He's been elected six times," I said.

"He was elected once. He was reelected the rest of the times. Why do you think his opponents dug up that idiot to run against him in Charlotte?" India tapped her fingers on the wheel. "Your dad likes to play up his experience, his accomplishments. He wants people to think they are making a smart decision."

"And you don't."

"Most people will do more to feel good than to be right. Your dad wants their minds. I want their hearts. You, my little hand-crusher, are going to weasel your way into every heart outside the Red Dirt city limits." India glanced at me. "Speaking of crushed hands, how did it go at school yesterday?"

"Great. People are thrilled that they don't have to worry about that pesky state championship anymore."

"So, the narrative is 'new girl ruins state championship hopes'?"

"That sounds about right," I said.

"Wouldn't it be great if you had some sort of training that could help you point the mangled finger where it belonged?"

I rolled my eyes.

"I'm just saying, you don't have to sit back and let Kyle win. Why don't you play the game a little? Convince people that he's the villain."

"Okay, oh mighty consultant. What would you suggest?"

India tapped her lips with her fingertips. "I'd start to chip away at Kyle's version of himself. Offer a different perspective."

I thought for a second. "There's the way he doesn't think the rules apply to him. And the way he expects the universe to move to accommodate him."

"All good material to work with."

"Or the fact that his confidence crosses the line into delusion."

"Many a campaign has been built on questions of sanity."

"But what I hate most is the way he just takes what he wants."

India nodded. "That's it. That's your story. It's even better because he might see it as a good thing. He'll stand there grinning while you destroy him."

"So what do I do? Just start pointing all this out?"

"You have plenty of natural ability and good instincts. Watch for an opportunity to use them."

After India dropped me off at school, I signed in at the office and walked down empty hallways in the final minutes of first period. I wanted to slip right into my second period class, avoiding the harshest glares that burned in the halls. Unfortunately, the bell rang just in time for a cluster of red T-shirts to push through Mr. Quincy's door with Hunter in the lead and Kyle a half step behind. I tried to turn, but Hunter broke away and fell in step beside me.

"Did you oversleep? I saved plenty of work for you."

"I'm sure you did," I said.

Another red shirt patted his shoulder. "Good to have you back," the guy said.

Hunter pulled me out of the way just before the Neanderthal smashed into me. "Thanks to me," I said to Hunter. "How can they love you and hate me?"

He raised his chin. "I told you I was charming," he said. "I have bad news. I had to spend most of the period studying the playbook for this week's game. I hope you don't mind."

"So, now that you're on the team, I have to do all the work." I tightened my grip on my bag to keep from smacking him. "Why do I have to babysit—"

Hunter held his hands up. "Relax, Hamilton. Man, you're easy to get riled up." He pulled a paper from his backpack. "Quincy had us start writing up our conclusions from the experiments." He handed the sheet to me. "I jotted down some ideas."

I read Hunter's small, dense print. "This is good," I said. "At least the parts I can read."

"You can add your ideas tonight. It's nice to see you still have a little fight in you. I was starting to worry."

"Price," Kyle called from down the hall. "Come over here a sec." When Hunter didn't move, Kyle's eyes narrowed.

"He walks around like he owns the place," I said. "I wish there was a way to expose him for the idiot he is."

"Kate, people know Kyle's a shallow jerk. But he's a shallow jerk who wins football games." He pulled another sheet out of his backpack. "This is the rest of the ant assignment. It's due next week."

I scanned the paper. It was a lot of work.

"I've got practice after school all week. I'll be playing Friday and watching tape Saturday. Do you want to meet Sunday and get this done?"

I looked up. "Sure."

Hunter turned to go.

"Thanks," I said. He turned back and tilted his head. "For not leaving me with all this to do."

A familiar smirk washed over Hunter's face. "Are you kidding? I've seen you break hands for less." He said it loud enough that it echoed down the hall. My face turned red and my heart started to pound. Then I noticed that Kyle's mouth was squeezed tight. Hunter didn't say it to irritate me; he said it to get under Kyle's skin. There was a wave of nervous laughter. Kyle's chest rose and fell.

"Are you actually playing politics?" I said to Hunter under my breath.

"I learned from the best."

"Yeah, Kate, we would hate for you to take out our second-string quarterback too," Kyle said.

The crowd swayed back toward Kyle. I shrugged. "If I slammed Hunter's hand in a door, I think he'd still be man enough to play."

Kyle went red. "You ruined our chances at State."

It was a familiar feeling—digging for the one cut, the one blow that would knock Kyle out no matter the cost. But like India said, if I wanted to take him down, I had to coax the real Kyle out into the open. I had to bring his dark side to life the way film developed, faded at first, until the outline was crisp and clean and the picture showed my perspective.

"Some people think I improved our chances," I said.

Kyle took two steps toward me. "I'm the one who got us to the playoffs."

I saw a few shoulders stiffen as the other players exchanged looks. I lowered my voice, but made sure it was loud enough that the people close by could hear. "If the championship hopes were all in your hands, maybe you should have kept them to yourself."

Hunter didn't even attempt to hide his grin. There were a few muffled gasps and snickers. Kyle was getting what he deserved, and plenty of people enjoyed seeing it.

chapter twenty-five

My confrontation with Kyle didn't start a revolution. People still whispered about me when the teachers were around and bumped against me in the hallways when they weren't. They narrowed their eyes and dropped realty brochures in my backpack, and someone left a pair of pom-poms on my desk—Junction colors.

But I did get a few looks that were not hostile. I hadn't proven Kyle was a villain, but I had earned enough space to get through the rest of the day.

Ana and I sat on the floor of the yearbook room, organizing the last of the yearbooks.

"I wish I'd seen you put Kyle in his place instead of just getting a thirdhand play-by-play during second period," Ana said.

"It was no big deal."

"Then Gaye Lynn must have seen someone else question Kyle's manhood, then suggest that the team was better off without him."

I ducked my head to hide a smile.

"Ms. Serrano gave me a couple of your photos from the game to work into the layout. They were amazing."

"Thanks. She helped me. And Hunter. Those aren't even the best ones." I reached into my backpack and pulled out the pictures of Bo Stone and Kyle. "Ms. Serrano said they told the wrong story."

Ana studied the photos. "For the yearbook? Yeah, I can see that. But they sure ring true to me. Do you think they have soul?"

"A little. Maybe." I squinted at them. "A mixture of truth and perspective. That's what Ms. Serrano said a great photograph is."

"People do have a habit of showing who they really are to a camera. Eventually. No matter how much they try to hide it." Ana handed the pictures back to me.

"Is that what you look for when you take pictures of people?"

"Pictures are ways to relive moments. I look for moments I want to relive," Ana said.

"That reminds me." I pulled a folder out of my backpack and gave it to Ana. "I started to collect some pictures for your portfolio."

Ana took the folder and looked through them. "Thanks, but I don't know if . . ."

I held up a hand. "I know, you don't think you can ever leave, but you've got way too much talent to stay here. At least you should try. I have something else for you." I pulled out my film camera and passed it to her. "To borrow. Just for a week or so. It will give your portfolio some depth."

"Kate, I can't. What will you use?"

"I'll use the digital."

"You hate the digital."

"Not as much as I thought I would."

She studied the camera, holding it to her eye. "You're sure."

"I can't wait to see the pictures you take. Bring in your first roll and I'll help you develop it."

*　*　*

When I got home after school on Wednesday, Mrs. Fisher was poking through the kitchen, picking up abandoned Styrofoam cups.

"Where is everyone?" I asked.

"Bo Stone drew a line in the dirt." She dropped the cups in the trash.

"What do you mean?"

She frowned and put a hand on her hip. "He said, 'You're either with me or against me. No more volunteering for both.'"

"So people are at his headquarters?" I said, my shoulders dropping.

"No, people don't know what to do. They're probably hunched over cups of coffee at the diner, trying to decide."

"And you're siding with Dad?"

"Sweetheart, the day Bo Stone gets to decide who I help is the day pigs fly and Junction gets a decent defensive line." She started wiping the counter. "I'll be here and at Bo's like normal."

I laughed and slid onto a stool.

"Besides, he's going to be kicking himself soon. Your dad has volunteers everywhere. Bo's come mostly from Red Dirt. He's never been very smart when things aren't going his way. It doesn't help that Hunter's in as quarterback for the next few games."

"So what do people think of Hunter as quarterback?"

"Ah, you're taking an interest in the playoffs. Good for you."

"Something like that," I said.

"Some are worried. He did quit the team last year, and that's something people have a hard time wrapping their heads around. But he's good. He doesn't have the arm Kyle does, but he has the highest football IQ I've ever seen. And he knows how to work with what he's got on the field." Mrs. Fisher rose and picked up her purse from the chair next to her. "Will I see you at the game?"

I shook my head. "I am on hiatus from all Red Dirt events related to the playoffs."

She narrowed her eyes. "You don't seem like the type to back down from a fight. Are you sure you don't want to be there?"

I gave her a quick smile. "Don't worry, Mrs. Fisher. I'm not backing down. But the next time I go up against one of the Stones, I want to be ready."

I spent the rest of the week having breakfast with various party leaders and keeping up with homework. On Friday night, while everyone else was at the area game, I lay on the pale brown carpet in my room with the yearbooks I'd collected. I'd found an old clock radio, and I tuned in to an AM station broadcasting the game. I could tell from the announcer's voice that Hunter was doing surprisingly well. I held my phone to my ear while I flipped through old yearbooks. "Tell me exactly what happened," I said to Tasha.

"I asked Jamie Carraway to ask Robert what he thought of me. And he said I didn't seem to have a lot to say."

"You just spent the past two weeks ignoring him. You guys are different, but you've got to have something in common to start the conversation. Figure that out and talk to him about it."

"I can't do this without you."

"Digging up conversation is like digging up dirt or getting gossip. Do you remember how you got to be class social chair?"

"You reminded everyone that Geoffrey Clifton ate paste through fifth grade."

"No, you connected with people. You talked to them about things they cared about. You're good at it; it's why people love you."

"Robert cares about important things."

"*You* care about important things too. That's why we're friends."

She was quiet for a moment. "Speaking of dirt, how's it going with Kyle?"

"I think I figured out a way to show people what a jerk he is. I'll get them to compare him to Hunter."

"That's great. Boy, Hunter is the solution to everything lately—he rescued you from pigs, pulled you out of that situation with Kyle. He's like your knight in shining armor."

"I definitely owe him."

"Owe him? How are you not swooning all over him by now?" A cheer erupted from the radio as the announcer reported another Red Dirt touchdown.

"That's just Hunter. If you need him, he's there," I said.

"Exactly. Swoon."

chapter twenty-six

I spent most of the weekend at the shelter. With Hunter practicing for playoffs, I think Aunt Celia was even a little glad to have me. On Sunday afternoon, Caroline Fisher and the other women showed up to make phone calls to potential voters.

"I thought you had to choose," I said.

"Oh, we're not here to volunteer. Your mom invited us over for coffee. But she got so busy with all this campaigning that we decided to call a few friends to talk about the election. It's the neighborly thing."

"Your idea?" I asked.

"I don't know what you're talking about," she said, offering me a snickerdoodle.

I kicked a couple of communications staff out of the kitchen and laid all my science notes on the table in preparation for studying with Hunter.

"Stick to the phone script, people," India said in the living room. "I want to know what they think of the candidates, not what happened at their eye doctor."

"How *is* Gladys?" someone called out.

"People, focus," India said.

I was snickering when Hunter opened the back door and surveyed my piles. "You don't play around."

"Not with my GPA."

"Let's get started. I'm supposed to watch another two hours of game tape by tomorrow morning."

India's voice rang through the kitchen again. "Please. If you aren't going to stick to the script, at least mention Congressman Hamilton's name."

"What's going on in there?" Hunter asked.

"Campaign calls. India has volunteers over all day."

A woman walked through the swinging doors to the kitchen. She stopped when she saw Hunter. "Hunter Price, in the flesh. Am I glad to see you! That was a beautiful pass in the third quarter Friday night. Do you know if Coach is going to work with the line this week? They didn't give you much time."

Hunter shifted his feet. "No, ma'am, I don't know."

"Rose! Rose, come in here."

Another woman came through the doors. "Well, Hunter Price, what are you doing here?"

"We're working on a science project," I said, gesturing to the neat stacks of paper on the table. I turned to Hunter. "We better get started since you need to watch those tapes."

Hunter flinched when I said it. I didn't realize why until a second later, when both women started talking excitedly over each other.

"Tapes. Those better be game tapes," Rose said.

"Yes, ma'am."

"You watch the line. You'll see what I mean. They need to give you more time," the other woman said.

"Yes, ma'am."

"And tell Coach that the left side has to be stronger against Murdock next week," Rose said.

"We really need to get this project done," I said.

"Sure, sure, but don't take too long. Wait, Mary Jean said something about the defense. Mary Jean," Rose called through the doors.

"We have to get out of here," Hunter said. He took the bag and started jamming my carefully stacked notes into the top.

"Wait, I got everything organized. I'm not packing up just because you can't handle a few suggestions. Let people say what they want, right?"

He groaned.

"You signed on for this." I pushed the chair toward him with my foot.

Hunter dropped the bag on the table and slouched into a chair.

India swung open the doors. "Oh, good, you haven't started studying. Kate, get in here. I need someone to explain how a phone script works." The doors closed behind her.

I grabbed the bag and handed it to Hunter. "Let's go."

Hunter half pushed me out the door.

"We can go to the library," I said as he started the truck.

He shook his head.

"Right, your adoring fans will probably be there too. There's that diner on the square."

"It's closed on Sunday. Don't worry. I know where we can go." Hunter turned down the road that led out of town. He drove in silence for a minute.

"You hate all the attention, don't you?" I said.

He had one hand on the wheel and an elbow resting out the window. "Yep."

"I hear you're good."

Hunter shook his head.

"What's wrong with taking credit for it?" I asked.

He glanced at me. "Like Kyle."

"You don't have to be a jerk about it."

Hunter went silent for a few minutes. "I don't want this town deciding who I am and what I'm good at."

"I think they've decided." I put my hand on his shoulder. "You have been sent from heaven to answer their prayers for a state championship," I said in my best West Texas accent.

He shrugged. "For now."

"Until you lose?"

Hunter nodded. "Until we lose." His mouth hardened, the muscles in his jaw tight.

"Where are we going?"

"There's only one option." The water tower loomed in the front windshield. He grinned, and since it was the first smile I'd seen that day, I decided not to argue.

Someone had knocked the gate down, so Hunter pulled the cab of his truck up to the ladder and we scrambled up.

"Did you bring the bag?" I asked.

Hunter passed it to me. When I unzipped it, the wind whipped a stack of papers across the desert.

I turned to Hunter, my mouth open in shock. He was leaning back and laughing.

I watched the papers tumble across the dust. "I'm glad you're enjoying yourself."

"We'll just talk. I'll write—"

"Type," I corrected.

"Type it out later."

I leaned against the cold steel. "We're supposed to form a conclusion from our experiments." I started to dig for a pen. Then the wind picked up again. I zipped my bag closed and stuffed it behind me. "Fine. We'll do this your way. I think the obvious conclusion is that the ants have to help each other out."

Hunter shook his head. "They don't *have* to. It benefits them to work as a team."

"You're saying that ants do what's in their own best interest."

"Which makes them pretty much like everyone else," Hunter said.

"People are way more complicated than ants."

"Are they? Take Kyle Stone. Let's say we did the experiments on him. What would we conclude?"

I thought about it a second. "That Kyle believes in one thing—my world, my rules," I said. "Kyle is just slightly more evolved than the single-cell organism you see in pond scum. What about Ana?"

"I'm not saying the same things benefit everyone. Ana still does everything she can to get what she wants. She just wants different things."

"Like peace, and meaning."

"Yep."

"This is pretty deep for a football player."

Hunter shrugged. "I think I know yours."

"You probably think it's something like 'I'm right, you're wrong, deal with it.'"

"Not exactly. More like 'Make it right.'"

I stared at the horizon, my mind easing into the realization that Hunter might understand me more than I thought. As well as Tasha. Maybe better. It felt good to be understood, like the sun on my shoulders, or a deep breath.

"What do you want?" I asked.

"I'm still trying to figure it out."

The chill grew, and I wrapped my arms around my waist. "You want people to be real. Simple, like animals," I said.

"Maybe not exactly like animals, but you're not far off," Hunter said.

A comfortable silence settled between us for a few minutes. I looked over the land. "It really is pretty here. In an unconventional way."

"Doesn't still look like a hairy toe?"

I laughed.

"Mom brought the dog by the shelter today."

"Is everything okay?" I asked.

"Yeah, she was just dropping off some banana bread to thank Celia for the shots. She asked about you."

"Really."

"You make an impression. She seems to think there's something going on between us."

"That stupid rumor," I said.

Hunter cleared his throat. "She doesn't pay much attention to rumors."

"So that's where you get your cool oblivion."

He laughed. "I'm not oblivious."

"I'm glad she likes taking care of Lucy. At least I helped someone."

"You help more than you think. I know Celia's glad to have you since I bailed on her until playoffs are over," Hunter said.

"She tolerates my help. Although she wouldn't let me confront Bo Stone about the barbed wire he put up. She could get it down. It's on the Hamilton property line."

Hunter paused. His cool features darkened for a second. "It's not Hamilton property anymore."

"What?"

He looked at me. "Celia had to sell the back acres to Bo Stone to keep the shelter going. She pays rent every month. I've seen it in the books when I enter feed receipts."

"I . . . I didn't know."

"She didn't want to. But it's not easy. The feed and hay cost more every year, and it's not like she makes any money."

"I wish there was something I could do."

"I know you do." He leaned back. "How are the sunset photos going?"

"It's impossible. The sky comes out too dark; the clouds are shapeless. It never looks the way it looks in the viewfinder. Apparently, football is my new subject. Ms. Serrano told me a couple of the ones I took at the game are good enough for my portfolio."

"Look at what you can do when you listen to me." He slapped his hand against his knee. "And for telling me I was right—"

"I don't remember saying you were right."

"I knew what you meant. Remember when you asked how I knew where the ball was going to go before the play started?"

"Yeah, you wouldn't tell me."

"Here it is. I don't try to control the game. I follow its lead. I push every advantage, and I hope for a miracle, but I don't control it."

I looked at the sky again. Long strings of clouds swept across it. These teetered on the edge of dark blue. Higher, they burned gray and silver while the horizon faded to a hollow black. It was stunning, and impossible to capture. "So if I just watch . . ."

"Let the picture come to you," he said.

We sat together, enjoying the silence.

"We better get back," Hunter said.

"Yeah." Neither one of us moved. All my awareness was focused on the spot where his shoulder pressed against mine, sending a tingly heat through me.

Hunter rose after a minute and reached down to help me up, his hand warm.

I looked at the graffiti on the water tower. My hand grazed the scribble of names until I came to a spot that was scrubbed clean. I looked at the notes around it. "Hunter."

He turned.

"Wasn't this where that stuff about Ana was?"

Hunter shrugged. "Maybe." He started down the ladder.

My heart began to pound. "Someone liked Ana enough to scrub off that message."

"Yeah, so?"

"Don't you get it? That's the person I need for my plan. That's the guy I need to match Ana with. He already cares about her. He'll defend her reputation. This is the real thing."

"I thought we realized this was a stupid plan."

"No, the plan was perfect. I just used the wrong guy."

chapter twenty-seven

It was the week of Thanksgiving, but more importantly, regionals against Murdock loomed on Friday. With only eight teams left in the entire state, the football intensity ratcheted up a level. Teachers took a break from classes to discuss the passing yardage and turnover statistics of the remaining teams—all the teachers except Mr. Quincy, who kept us focused on our presentations. Kyle missed every science class that week. Missy explained to another girl in yearbook, loud enough that we could all hear it from her, that his dad had been taking him to half a dozen doctors between here and Dallas. If that was true, maybe Bo Stone was too distracted to campaign. I had to admit, there would be some satisfaction if hurting Kyle's hand actually helped Dad.

A small part of me wanted Red Dirt to lose the game. I told myself this was just my desire to make things go back to normal. It wasn't because Hunter would have time to work at the shelter again.

Monday afternoon, Mom and Dad went to a fund-raiser in Midland, and I headed out to the shelter with my camera, looking for carvings of light and dark in the giant sky that hung over Red Dirt.

Aunt Celia was filling the blue plastic pools with fresh water. "Anything I can do?" I asked.

"Yeah, you can put some feed in the pigpen, then brush down Madison."

I got a bucket and filled it from the bag that sat at Aunt Celia's feet.

"How is the campaigning going?" she asked.

"Fine." I remembered what Mr. McCoy had said about Granddad. "Did you campaign? With your dad?"

Aunt Celia shook her head. "He would take your father, but I wasn't ever interested in it."

"Did you ever think of running for office?" I asked.

"I'm about as likely to win as that goat over there." She pointed to Herbert Hoover.

"I don't know," I said. "I think a lot of people would like your sincerity. Maybe you could get funding for shelters like yours. Or the land rights protected." I snapped a picture of a horse nosing at the pail of food. "Plus, if you told people what you did out here, they might support you."

"I do just fine on my own."

"It's a good story—'Woman Devotes Her Life to Rescuing Animals No One Else Cares About.' People love baby animals."

"Kate, I don't want this shelter involved in any politics."

"It's called help." I sighed. "You're just like Dad."

"What do you mean?"

"He doesn't understand help either. He thinks it's messy. It must be genetic."

"More like training. Your grandfather was a 'pick yourself up by your own bootstraps' kind of guy. I got his love of history. Your dad got his love of politics. And we all got his stubbornness."

"What about your love of animals? Was that my grandmother?"

"No, that's my own. That's my photography." Aunt Celia looked across the shelter, then back at me. "It isn't easy to buck expectations in this family."

I shook my head. Aunt Celia picked up the bag of feed and headed into the barn.

Once the pigs were fed, I got a horse brush and tracked down Madison, the miniature Clydesdale who wandered from barn to barn, nudging the pockets of anyone who crossed his path, looking for sugar cubes. I patted the white spot on the top of his head and started to brush the pale brown hair along his side.

Aunt Celia brought a bag of oats and started to shovel it into the buckets that lined the fence. "I've been wondering," I said. "Where did you get all these animals?"

"Lots of places."

"You may not feel very political, but you sure evade questions like a politician." I kept brushing. "How did you get Madison?"

"He was abandoned on a highway. A woman from Griffith found him and called." Madison huffed and looked over his shoulder at me as I started on his other side.

"What about the pigs?"

"A few of them are from a fire at a breeder's a couple of years ago. I get one or two FFA projects every year that don't go to auction. Others had owners who wanted to keep them but couldn't. Some get dropped off at the gate. Sometimes people call me when they have an animal lying around."

Thoughts started to churn inside my head, gathering around a shadow of an idea. "Those are great stories."

"Yeah, a lot of good it does me. If you haven't noticed, you can't feed pigs stories."

My idea wove itself into shape. I looked at the shelter, then my camera. "I'm going to take pictures of the animals. You mind?"

"Knock yourself out."

I took dozens of sugary-sweet pictures of the animals. They weren't beautiful, they weren't artistic, but they were irresistible—heads tilted, eyes big and aimed at the camera. I also trailed Aunt Celia around the shelter, coaxing as many stories about the animals from her as I could. Then I headed back to the house, plopped in front of my laptop, and called Tasha. "Have you figured out what to talk to Robert about?"

"No, but it's about time you got involved in this."

"I need you to get his help. I have a plan to save Aunt Celia's shelter." I explained my idea. If we put pictures of the animals on a website, people could sponsor the individual animals, and Aunt Celia could get the money she needed for food and support. "It's exactly what people like to do — help out without having to get their hands dirty."

"And we start with the animal rights club?" Tasha said.

"We start with Robert. He's got to have a ton of connections."

Tasha's voice rose with excitement, even hope. "This is brilliant. I get to talk to Robert and you get a thousand hours for putting all this together."

"I can't get any hours. Aunt Celia doesn't know that I'm doing this."

She was silent for a moment. "You know your genius plan to turn in a bunch of hours and beat out Parker for the recommendation?"

"Yeah."

"You're not the only one to think of it. A bunch of juniors have been turning in hours. I think someone tipped off Parker, and he turned in five this week. You're the closest, but if you don't get more hours, he'll pull out of reach."

I shook my head. "I'll get the hours after I finish this website."

"You could lose the letter."

"Don't worry. I have a plan."

But I didn't, and even more surprising, I didn't care.

chapter twenty-eight

The halls cleared quickly as students left for Thanksgiving break. In DC, Thanksgiving meant trips home to campaign or quick escapes to Europe. In Red Dirt, it meant more time to talk about the playoffs. When I got to the yearbook room late Tuesday afternoon, I was surprised to see Ana there.

"I thought you'd be home by now," I said.

"Ms. Serrano said she would show up at my home on Thanksgiving Day with a laptop and a frozen turkey dinner if I didn't get these layouts done before I left. What are you doing here?"

"I have an idea that might save Aunt Celia's shelter. Actually, I could use your help." I sat down beside her.

"What are you planning?"

I explained my idea and showed her the website I'd set up late the previous night.

Ana nodded. "I wish I could help, but I've got dozens of corrections to put in before I can leave. I'm already going to be here a couple of hours."

"What if I did the corrections and you cropped the pictures for the website? You're so much better at it. I've got the stories entered, so once they're cropped, we can post them."

"Sounds perfect." We swapped places.

"What's your yearbook log-in?" I asked.

Ana blushed. "Hank4."

My fingers froze over the keyboard.

"We created them freshman year, and I haven't had the guts to ask Ms. Serrano to change it."

I nodded. "You just have to spin the password. Change how you see it."

"What do you mean?"

"Hank 4-mer human being," I said.

She laughed. "Hank 4 times the idiot he seems."

I laughed too. "Maybe, Hank 4-tunately you don't have to date him anymore."

"Much better."

I started on the corrections while Ana cropped and posted the pictures.

"How does the site look?" I said after an hour of silence.

"Take a look. I'm on the last picture."

I peered over her shoulder. She had tiled the animals on the home page and linked each picture to a page with a close-up and a story. "You cropped them perfectly."

"It wasn't hard. You took great pictures." She posted an image of Teddy Roosevelt, a large potbellied pig. I smiled. Teddy was sniffing at the camera through the wire fencing, his front hooves spread slightly and the tip of his nose raised.

"Is that the last one?" I asked.

"Yep. Are you going to show your aunt?"

I winced. "Not yet."

"Hunter?"

"Can we just keep this a secret for now? I want to make sure it works before I show anyone."

"Thanks, Ana. Okay, I'm done here." I clicked print, and Ana went to the back of the yearbook room to collect the pages.

I picked up my phone and called Tasha.

"I was about to call you," she said. "Parker turned in another five hours. Someone should call the children's hospital to confirm it's really him. Do we want someone like him around the youth of this country?"

"Forget that. The pictures and stories are up on the website. I have a few more to post, but can you take a look?"

Tasha squealed. "I am getting my laptop."

"Did you get a chance to talk to Robert about it?"

"Yes." She clicked a few keys. "It's the most he's spoken to me in the past two weeks. He was really interested in the idea of the site. But he was not interested in the killer outfit I put together to impress him." I heard keys clicking. "She is so cute! I am sponsoring Jackie Kennedy."

"She is pretty fabulous." More keys clicked.

"Look at Aaron Burr," she said.

"He has a temper. He tried to bite me last time I fed him."

"You put a lot of work into this. Are you sure you can't get any hours?"

"It's fine. Just show it to Robby, okay?"

"He hates that name."

"Rob?"

"No. I think Robert fits him perfectly. It's serious, mature."

I turned off the computer and leaned back in my chair. "Tasha, I'm worried about this thing with Robert."

"What do you mean?"

I snuck a glance at Ana as she was packing up her bag. "You probably shouldn't listen to me. I've been a complete disaster as a matchmaker lately, but I wonder if you should give him more of a chance to know you."

"I have smiled and chatted until I'm blue in the face."

"Did you ever talk about you? Real things about you?"

"Shopping and hair products?"

"That's not who you really are. You're thoughtful and fun. You work hard to make things special for other people. Tell him about your little sister's piano recital, when she messed up and froze so you went up and sat by her so she could finish the piece. Show him the homemade birthday cards you make your friends. Tell him how you raced to my house with a carton of ice cream and a jar of peanut butter the minute you found out how good they tasted together so I could try it. "

Tasha was silent for a moment. "Do you think all that dust is actually making you smarter?"

"I think it's the butter and processed cheese."

"I'll call you tomorrow and tell you how it goes."

When I hung up, Ana was standing a few steps away, waiting. "That was good advice."

I stood and picked up my bag. "It's about time I gave some."

Ana shook her head. "It's not your fault that things didn't work out with Kyle. I think I'm doomed to be stuck in this town alone."

"You'll find someone. If Tasha can, you can. You wouldn't believe the number of guys she's burned through."

"I don't need to burn through guys. I just want one great guy."

Somewhere was the guy who'd scrubbed her name off the water tower. "He's probably right under your nose."

"I think I'm done with high school guys," Ana said. "What about you? What are you looking for?"

"I swore off guys after Parker." Hunter's lopsided grin flashed in my mind. I shook my head. "Besides, after that disaster with Kyle, I definitely won't be dating anyone while we're here."

"What do you mean while you're here?"

I swallowed. I couldn't believe I'd let that slip. "We might go back to DC after the election. That's where we lived when Dad represented his Charlotte district."

"Oh."

"I would really appreciate it if you would keep that a secret too."

Ana pulled on her backpack. "You have to keep a lot of secrets."

"For now. You can't keep secrets in politics. You just try to control them."

I turned to see Hunter standing in the doorway.

"Hey," he said, looking from me to Ana. He shifted his feet. "I thought you might still be here. I came by to see if you needed a ride."

"I'll take her home. It's no problem," Ana said.

Hunter just stood there. There was something guarded about the way he stared at me. "You look like you just found out someone injured the first-string quarterback and the entire town's hopes are on your shoulders," I said.

He looked at the toes of his boots. "I'm under a lot of pressure."

"I told you joining that team would suck your soul," I said.

"It's not like you care." He turned and left.

"What are you talking about?" I called after him, but he didn't look back. I turned to Ana. "What was that about?"

"Cut him some slack. He's right. Everyone's expecting a lot from him."

"What is so terrible about losing one football game?"

Ana shrugged. "You'll find out if we lose." She logged off the computer. "Okay. We just have to drop the football pages by Principal Walker's office on the way out."

"Why?"

"He approves all the yearbook pages before deadline." Ana grabbed the printed pages and stuck them in a manila folder.

Principal Walker was at his desk when we arrived. "Are those the yearbook pages?"

Ana nodded and passed him the folder. Then the door banged open and Bo Stone stomped in. "Good news!" he said. "Doc thinks Kyle will be cleared to play next week." He spotted me and Ana and frowned. "It's a good thing too. It's one thing to play in the regionals, but now we're heading into quarters."

Principal Walker cleared his throat.

"What is it?" Bo Stone asked. "Don't tell me Coach is going to use Price."

The principal shook his head. "We have a different problem." He pulled another folder from his desk and handed it to Bo.

Bo opened the folder and frowned. "You're kidding me."

Principal Walker looked at me and Ana. "I'll take a look at these pages later."

I looked from Mr. Stone to Principal Walker. They wanted us to leave, which made me want to stay. "Actually, Ms. Serrano is upstairs waiting for them now."

Ana's eyebrow rose for a second, but then she flattened her expression.

"I'm sorry to ask, but we're on a tight deadline," I said. "We can wait outside if you and Mr. Stone need to talk."

Principal Walker started to say something; then he picked up the folder and flipped through the pages. "These look good. Approved."

Ana nodded and we slipped out the door to the main office. I put my hand on her arm as she started toward the hallway. "We need to see what's in that folder," I said.

"That's why you lied about Ms. Serrano." She stood next to me, facing Principal Walker's closed door. "How?"

We stared at the door for another second. I pressed my ear to it. Nothing. I took a step back as the door flew open.

"Who's going to tell? There's too much on the line," Bo Stone said into the office. He had cultivated the same smooth confidence most politicians use. "Besides, he deserves this, and you know it."

"I'll have hell to pay if we're caught," Principal Walker said.

"There's no way this blows back on you. You're a hero if we make it to State. You're doing the right thing." The printer whirred to life. I took two steps toward it before Bo Stone stepped out of the office. He pulled the page off the printer, slipped it in the folder Principal Walker had given him earlier, then spotted me and Ana.

His posture stiffened. People usually freeze when they're caught. They wait like chess pieces for the next move. The trick was to use my next move to make him believe what he wanted to believe, that he had gotten away with something. It would be even better if we could make him believe he'd won something.

"We almost forgot," I said, improvising. "We need a quote from you for the yearbook, Mr. Stone. And a picture by the trophy case."

"I'm a little busy right now."

"Ms. Serrano wants us to do a look back at other teams that made it to the state championships," Ana added.

"Can we do this on Monday?" he said.

I shrugged and turned to Ana. "I told you he wouldn't want to. We'll just get one from Dad."

Bo Stone's face twisted. "I guess I can give you ladies a minute."

"Mr. Walker? It might be nice to have you in the picture too," Ana said.

"I don't think——"

"Come on, Billy. I've said everything I need to say. The team's a shoo-in for the state finals, and these young ladies want to honor Red Dirt's football legacy. How can you say no?"

"All right." I watched from the doorway as Principal Walker returned to his office, slipped the folder into a drawer, locked it, and placed the key in his jacket pocket.

We led Principal Walker and Bo Stone down the hall. When we got to the trophy case, Ana placed the two men on either side of the large center trophy and knelt down to make them appear larger than life. It was going to be a great shot for the fake article.

"Do you think Principal Walker should take his jacket off? Since Mr. Stone doesn't have one?" I asked.

Ana studied the shot. "We could try it."

"Let's just get this over with." Principal Walker sighed and wiggled out of his jacket. He passed it to me.

"Perfect." While Ana took pictures, I slipped the key out of the jacket and into my own pocket before I folded it over the arm of a bench.

"Now for the interview." I patted my pockets. "Oh, shoot, I think I left my phone in the yearbook room. I was going to record . . . I'll just run back and get it."

"We'll come with you," Principal Walker said, reaching for his jacket.

I looked at Ana, my eyes pleading.

Ana flipped through the pictures. "I'm getting a glare off the case. Let me take a few more."

"We'll meet you there," Bo said.

Inside the office, I headed straight for Principal Walker's desk. I pulled the key out of my pocket, opened the drawer, and took out the folder. Inside were two identical lists, both with about a dozen names. But the second list had one name added—Kyle Stone. I grabbed my phone and took a picture of both pages.

I replaced the list and locked the drawer. When I heard voices in the hall, I tossed the key on the floor and sat on the bench in the outer office just in time for Mr. Stone and Principal Walker to swing open the door.

"Okay, I think I got a couple of good shots. Thanks for your time," Ana said.

"Didn't you want a quote?" Bo said.

"Of course." I stood, pressed record on my phone, and held it out toward him. "What was it like being on a state championship team?"

His head lifted. "Like I could do anything. It's the first time I remember feeling greatness."

I asked a few more questions, then put my phone away. "Thanks, Mr. Stone," Ana said.

We got to Ana's car, and I slid into the passenger seat. Ana put the key in the ignition. "That was exciting."

"You were amazing. Thank you. You didn't have to help me."

"What are friends for?" She smiled. "What did you find out?"

I pulled up the pictures and passed the phone to Ana. "It's just two lists of names. Kyle's name was added to the second list."

"So we don't know what it is."

"We know it's about football. We know Bo needed the principal to do whatever he wants done. And, most important, we know he's hiding something."

chapter twenty-nine

"Bo Stone and Principal Walker have a list of names that they're keeping secret," I announced to Dad, Mom, and India when I got home.

India slammed her laptop closed. Dad cleared his throat. Mom swept some crumbs from the table.

"What? What did I do?"

"Nothing," Dad said, his voice firm.

"Something happened," I said.

India rubbed her face. "Stone put out a new ad."

"It can't be that bad. What did he attack? Your residency? Your voting record?"

India opened the laptop and turned it to face me. Bo Stone's picture appeared on the screen. The early seconds looked like a standard campaign ad. Bo Stone was in front of an American flag with his wife, a thin woman with blond hair, standing beside him. I'd seen Kyle's mom at the football games, sitting quietly next to Bo, her legs under a red-and-black blanket and a vague smile on her face. Mom could more than hold her own against her. This was what campaign ads did. They pitted image against image. I looked at Dad and shrugged.

"Just wait."

A picture of Bo with his arm around Kyle hit the screen. They stood shoulder to shoulder, their smiles bright. Then an image of Dad at a Charlotte rally hit the screen. The camera zoomed over Mom and Dad's smiling faces to me standing behind him, glaring. It was the picture Parker had put up on the website.

The ad ended with a picture of the Stone family, pressed tightly together, smiling. Kyle looked like the perfect son.

"They made it look like Bo is Father of the Year and your daughter hates you." I looked at Dad. "You know that's not true."

Dad flashed a weak smile. "I know. But . . . perception."

"Is reality," I finished. "How did they get that picture?"

"It's tough to get rid of pictures once they're out there," Dad said.

"Bo's nervous. He's worried we're catching up, and Kate's the reason," India said. "She's been charming half the party members in the district while he's stuck in Red Dirt and a few of the big cities. On top of that, Kyle can't do what she's doing. Bo's starting to realize that he may lose the election by winning Red Dirt."

"It's a pretty low blow. Won't there be backlash?" I said.

"He played it safe. Technically, he doesn't say anything about you."

"Why would he release an ad like this?"

"He probably wants an outright win next Tuesday, no runoff. If you gain one more inch of ground, you take that away from him." India glanced at the laptop for a second. "I'll find out where the Stone campaign bought ad time and how much. We can counter with our own ad."

"We don't have an answer to that," Dad said.

"We could work something up—"

"Wait." I stared at the picture. "I don't think we have to. We have an answer." I looked at Dad. "We could campaign together."

"Absolutely not," Dad said. "You hate campaigning."

"I've already been campaigning in the small towns for a week. I can just start campaigning in some of the bigger markets where this ad will show. Besides, I don't hate campaigning."

Dad gestured to the computer screen. "Pictures don't lie."

"No, but they do tell only part of the story."

Mom put her hand on his arm. "Hear her out."

"Think about it. If India gets a few solid pictures of us together and those run online, across social media, in newspapers, all the free press we can get—"

India picked up her phone. "This is good. I'd just need to make a few phone calls. We'll stay away from controversy and go with photogenic—nursing homes, parades, goat roping . . ."

"—it undoes every ad that he puts up," I said. "Did you say goat roping?"

India pulled up a schedule. "I've got you booked for the rest of the week, Jeff. The 4-H club in Firthy wanted to know if you can judge a competition Friday, and you're serving Thanksgiving dinner to firefighters, nurses, and the elderly on Thursday."

"You can shift some of that to my schedule," Mom said.

"You're going to judge 4-H?" Dad asked.

Mom shrugged. "Just pitching in."

Dad got up from the table. He turned and faced me. "Are you sure you want to do this? You don't have to. That picture wasn't your fault."

"I know. It's not about the picture. You're the better candidate. You should win. I want to help."

"Thanks, Kate." Dad patted my shoulder.

When Mom and Dad left the kitchen, India pulled her laptop toward her. "Now, what are we going to do about Bo Stone?"

"I thought we already decided that," I said.

"This is just a warning shot. If he's going to play dirty, I don't want to be left without any dirt to fling."

"That's what I was trying to tell you. Bo Stone was up to something at school—there was a secret meeting and a list." I pulled out my phone. "Look—one without Kyle's name and one with."

India studied the list. "It could be anything." She shook her head. "I can't use it until we know more."

"I'll do some research and see what I can figure out." I slid my phone back into my pocket. "At my old school Kyle wouldn't be anything special. Here, he's untouchable."

"He is Red Dirt. Whatever people think of him, they know who he is and what he is going to do. There is a lot of comfort in that."

"What if this was something different? Something they haven't seen him do before? People don't like surprises."

"Nope, but they do react to them." She put a pencil to her lips.

"Do you think Bo Stone has a few more surprises planned?"

India twisted her hair off her neck and stuck the pencil into it to hold it in place. "It wouldn't be much fun if he didn't."

India had me and Dad sticking close to home on Wednesday. Mom met with larger groups in Midland and Lubbock. Dad and I packed up Thanksgiving dinners at a food bank while photographers and television cameras watched.

"Kate, you look like a natural on the campaign trail. What do you think of the political life?" one reporter asked.

In the past, I would have let my frustration with politics wash over my face without a thought, but today I was here to prove Bo Stone wrong. I brightened my smile and lifted my chin. "Well, today it's helping us put Thanksgiving dinners on hundreds of tables across the district, so I think it's pretty great."

"Are you thinking of following in your father's footsteps one day?"

My smile flickered. I didn't have a practiced answer for that. Dad closed the box in front of him and slung his arm over my shoulder. "Kate has plenty of time to plan her future," he said. "That's the great thing about our schools and teachers. They prepare kids for a number of opportunities . . ."

Just like that, he launched into the education section of his stump speech.

After the food bank, India shuffled us through two community meetings, a second food bank, then a church dinner. By the time we left the church, my cheeks ached and my head was numb from giving the same answers over and over again. India slid into the backseat and started making phone calls, leaving me next to Dad in the front.

We drove through the darkness in silence. West Texas is vast in the dark. Headlights fade into the night before they hit anything solid, only brushing against a few blades of grass or a patch of pavement now and then.

"You know, no one expects you to go into politics," Dad said.

"I just have trouble seeing the point."

"The point is to help people. To give them a voice in government."

"But that's not what politicians spend most of their time doing. You were great today, but in four weeks, if you win, you'll go back to DC. You'll come down for a few fund-raisers, but you'll probably put your offices in Midland, and you'll never see these people again. How are you really going to represent them?"

Dad blinked a couple of times and pressed his lips together.

"The thing is, I think you actually care. I'm not saying you don't. But really, what difference can you make?" I asked.

"Yeah, but Kate, you can't—"

"—tell that to a reporter. I know, Dad."

"No, that's not what I was going to say." He gripped the wheel. "There's a game to politics, and I'm well aware of your distaste for it, but have you ever considered what would happen if the Bo Stones of the world were the only ones who played it?"

I leaned my head against the window and stared into the darkness. He was right. In order to win, he had to play the game.

The next morning at six thirty, we gathered around the kitchen counter to look at the schedule India had set up for the day. "Is she joking?" I asked. "Do we have to visit every nursing home and fire station in the district?"

Mom sat her cup of coffee down. "It's ambitious."

India stormed into the room. She tossed her phone on the counter. "The photographer backed out."

"Why?" Dad asked.

"I don't know. Something about a family commitment."

"Like Thanksgiving?" I suggested.

"We are five days away from the election," India said, "and we have to get images of you three as a family. Now I don't have a photographer to capture those images."

"Wait. This is perfect," I said. "Ana can take the pictures."

"Is she good?"

"Amazing. Better than me," I admitted. "Her pictures have soul."

"Soul is good," India said.

"So I hear."

"Call her," India said.

"She might not be awake."

India picked up the schedule and slammed it in front of me, locking eyes. "Tell her to be here in five minutes."

I called Ana. The phone rang twice. "Kate? Is everything okay?" she said.

"Are you actually up?"

"I've been at my *abuela*'s house since four thirty this morning, cooking."

"Do you want to come on the campaign trail with us? We lost our photographer. I'm sorry to ask. I know it's Thanksgiving, but it could be your first professional photo credit. We'll pay you, and it would look great in a portfolio."

"Are you kidding? My grandmother has me chopping onions for the next two hours. I was considering knocking myself out with a meat cleaver when you called." A voice yelled in Spanish in the background, and Ana answered back.

"Can you get here in five minutes?"

"On my way," she said.

Ana's truck rumbled into the driveway a few minutes later. India got into the passenger seat and told Mom and Dad to follow. "I'll fill you in on the way," she said to Ana. Maybe it was the large family or the years of taking pictures of athletes with an overinflated sense of importance, but Ana didn't flinch.

Five hours later, at our third nursing home, I visited with table after table of overly perfumed women with billowy white hair and thick lipstick stains on the rims of their glasses of tea. When India slipped out of the room, I went over to Ana in a corner, looking at her camera screen. "Block me while I rub some feeling back into my cheeks," I muttered to her. "Did you get a chance to look at that list of names I sent you?"

"Yeah, but I can't see how they're connected," Ana said.

"It's got to be something Bo wants for Kyle. Athlete of the week?"

"Not all of them play sports. Some are in band, some in theater. Some don't do any activities. One kid just transferred." She shrugged. "He barely speaks English."

"Keep thinking." I looked at a tray of dessert plates littered with pie-crust crumbs and smeared forks. "Is it too much to ask to get one slice of pie on Thanksgiving?"

"It's not as good as it looks," Ana said.

"You had some?"

"Yeah, your mom got a slice for me twenty minutes ago. I don't know why you're always griping. This campaigning isn't half bad." Ana passed me the camera. "My grandmother just called. I have to go. I think I got some good photos."

I flipped through the pictures on the screen. "Maybe if we show India the pictures, she'll cut the schedule short and I can go home with you and eat tamales. "

"Not a chance," India said, joining us suddenly. She clicked through a few pictures herself. "Not bad. There are definitely some I can send around to the media outlets."

"I told you. Soul." I nudged Ana, who beamed. "And they'll use Ana's name for the credit, right?"

"Of course," India said.

"I better go. My family only yells louder when they get hungry." Ana waved and disappeared through the doorway.

"We have to go too," India said. She pushed the camera into my hand and headed toward the table where Dad was seated across from a woman who'd spread pictures of her six grandchildren out between them. I smiled and took a picture. It was hard to imagine Bo Stone paying such close attention to her.

On the way through the lobby, I got a text from Ana. "I smell pie. Diner across the street."

"I'll meet you at the car," I called after India.

Outside, I put the camera strap around my neck and rubbed my hands together to smother the chill from the air. Smells of butter and sugar drifted out the blue door of a tiny diner. If I hurried, I could have a slice to eat on the way to Midkiff, where India had us scheduled for an interview before we took a turkey to a fire station.

A cowbell clanged when I pushed open the door, and a woman in a denim skirt and plaid shirt stood wiping a counter. "Can I help you?"

"Do you sell slices of pie? To go?"

"We sure do, honey. Aren't you with that guy running for office?"

I pasted on my campaign smile one last time. "Congressman Hamilton. That's my dad."

"I saw you go in earlier. What kind of pie do you want? I have a pecan pie that I'm about to take out of the oven."

I slid onto a stool. "That sounds great."

My phone rang. "Where are you? We're at the car," India asked.

"I'm at the diner across the street. Getting pie."

"Kate, we don't have time for pie," India said.

"Pie?" I heard Dad echo.

"I'll be at the car in a minute," I said.

There was a jumble of voices. India sighed. "It seems we're coming to you."

The cowbell clanged again. Dad's figure filled the doorway. He sucked in a deep breath. "What is that? Pecan?" He strolled over to the stool next to me.

"It should be ready in a minute."

"It smells wonderful," Mom said, sitting on the other side of me.

"So, how's business?" Dad asked the waitress.

Dad had a gift for getting people to talk. I had to sprinkle questions until I hit a soft spot. He could get to the heart of what people cared about in one shot.

"It's good," the woman said. "Could be better, but I can't complain."

"It's nice of you to open up on Thanksgiving. You must own the place to be the one here on a holiday. Lucille, I assume?" More staff filed into the diner.

"In the flesh. You know your small businesses. I'm going to get that pie."

India's heels clicked behind us. "We still have four more events."

"Relax. We're having Thanksgiving. Hey, why don't you take some pictures?" Dad said to me.

"For the campaign? You'll have plenty of pictures from Ana."

"No, for your portfolio. You can't just send them pictures of sky, right? And you're in your element. They'll be great."

My mouth dropped open for a second. "How do you know about my portfolio?"

"I'm not an idiot. You carry around a camera like I carry around talking points and a friendly smile. So go ahead, get some shots."

"I took one of you when you were talking to the woman with the pictures."

Dad slid onto the stool. "Mrs. Bunting." I showed him the photograph. Dad smiled. "Can I have a copy?"

"It's not a great photo. The alignment isn't quite right, and the background lighting doesn't have the best contrast."

"Looks pretty perfect to me. Best I've ever seen you take." He looked at the picture again.

"Really?"

"Yeah, it seems so real."

I looked over his shoulder, trying to see what he saw. "Since when are you interested in my photos?"

"Since now. Is it too late?"

The warmth in his smile washed over me. "No."

The woman brought three slices of pie and set them in front of us. When I took a bite, the sticky warmth settled deep inside me.

"This is amazing," Mom said. Lucille passed out slices to the rest of the staff, and the diner filled with chatter.

"I hate to ask, but what happens if you don't win?" I asked Dad.

He chewed for a moment. "I guess we go back to DC."

"Or Charlotte," Mom added.

"What will you do?" I asked.

Dad folded his hands. "I could join a law firm. Or go on the speakers' circuit."

"You think you could give up politics?" I asked.

"I won't have a choice. If I'm benched, I'm benched."

"What about the house?"

"Celia can stay here as long as she wants."

"But will we come back to visit?" I asked.

Dad looked at me. "You like this place?"

"More than I thought I would."

He clapped his hands together. "We still have another quarter to play. What are the most important minutes of a game, Kate?"

"The last ones."

Dad took his last bite of pie. Lucille came over to take his plate. He ordered another round.

"They should have you cater at the nursing home," Dad said to Lucille.

"You think?" she asked. "I . . . I never thought of it."

"Absolutely," he said, taking a bite off Mom's plate. She shooed his fork away.

Lucille headed to the back. "I thought you said helping was messy," I said to Dad.

"It is. A little messy isn't always bad. I help Lucille, I get more pie. Win-win, right?"

I laughed. "Something like that." I snapped a few pictures of Lucille, then caught India typing an email on her phone. I took one of Dad's staff arguing over time slots for ads. It felt good. I knew where to point the camera, and the pictures came to me. And . . . I could feel them. Maybe not exactly in my gut, but somewhere in the vicinity.

"We've got to get to the interview," India said.

"Call them, tell them to meet us here," Dad said.

"In a diner? I thought we agreed that the city hall would be a nice backdrop."

"Kate, what draws media to your event?" he asked me.

"Something controversial, something photogenic, or something unexpected."

"Exactly. Tell them there's pie for anyone who comes." He turned to Lucille. "You don't mind the free publicity, right?"

Dad circled the room, taking pie orders and chatting with staffers. I watched him for a minute, then turned to Mom. "Dad's different, right?"

Mom smiled. A real smile. "Home does funny things to people."

The reporters, hungry for news and pie, jammed Lucille's tiny diner. They took footage and stacks of pie boxes home. Lucille hugged all of us as we left.

chapter thirty

The next morning, I was surprised to wake up when the sun was high in the sky. I went downstairs to the hub of the Hamilton campaign machine, expecting to find Dad fine-tuning a speech or India pushing everyone out the door.

Instead, India was perched at the kitchen table flipping through emails. "Those pictures are a hit. Thank goodness for slow news days."

"Are you giving Ana credit?"

"Like I promised. Why are you so interested in her name getting in the papers?"

"It's not the name, it's for the photographs. I want her to be able to put them in a portfolio if she wants to apply to art school." I pulled up a stool next to her. "Where are Mom and Dad?"

"They're in Snyder. Bo's ads didn't play there, so I thought I'd give you a break."

I picked at a plaid napkin. "Thanks. What about everyone else?"

"I sent the communication guys to do some final edits on the last round of media buys. Everyone else is on the streets trying to get out the vote for Tuesday." India looked up. "Ha! You've caught it, haven't you? The political bug. Here you are with an empty morning, and you don't know what to do with yourself."

"I have plenty to do," I said, looking around the kitchen.

"But what you'd rather do is race from one chamber of commerce meeting to another."

"That's ridiculous. I'm just at loose ends. The school's not open and I can't use the darkroom."

"You could go out to the shelter. Aren't you trying to get as many hours as you can for that letter of recommendation?"

"How did you know?"

"Nonstop community service. It was a little suspicious. Either you had a huge crush on Hunter or you were trying to get something. I just did a little research and found out about the policy change at your DC school."

"Impressive. And creepy. But Aunt Celia said she would be on calls all day."

India clicked through her emails.

"You spend a lot of time on me," I said. "More than any of Dad's other campaign managers. Did he put you up to it?"

India looked up. She put her chin on her hand. "No."

"Mom?"

"No. You may not ever be a congresswoman or senator, Kate. You may go off to some art school, become a famous photographer, and never get within a mile of a polling location. But you have potential. Not potential as a politician; potential as a person. I like potential." India picked up her phone. "Oh, wait, it looks like they need you in San Angelo after all."

I sat up straighter, my skin starting to tingle. "What do I need to wear?"

A grin crept onto India's face.

"You're messing with me, aren't you? I don't think you're supposed to do that when someone has an addiction."

"The first step is admitting your problem," India said, returning her attention to her laptop.

"I don't think it's just the campaigning. I really want Dad to win."

"We all do," India said.

"No, I think before I just wanted Bo Stone to lose. But now I'm starting to see that Dad actually cares about people."

"He has a lot of integrity. It would be easier if he didn't."

"What do you mean?"

India picked up her coffee. "He won't let me release anything that attacks Bo."

"Dad doesn't like dirt. He says politicians who throw dirt get dirty."

"We don't have any dirt to throw. I just want to be more aggressive."

"How do you know when it's time to go negative?" I asked.

India folded her hands. "You go negative when you're behind and you can prove the information beyond a shadow of a doubt. Otherwise, it's not worth it."

I pulled over a doughnut box and fished out a cold, half-eaten bear claw. "What if you're not sure what the information is?"

"Is this about that list?"

I took a bite of the pastry. "I'm just curious about the process."

India raised an eyebrow.

"Fine, it's about the list."

"You can cast it out in the water. See if the other sharks smell blood."

"Leak it?" I licked my fingers.

India handed me a flowered napkin. "Yeah, but be careful. You don't want your own hands to get dirty. Or you can put enough pressure on Kyle, and he might tell you himself." Her phone buzzed, and she looked at the message. "Look at that. There is some politicking for you to do after all."

I stood up. "Are we going to Lubbock?"

"Nope. Higher stakes. A Red Dirt playoff pep rally."

"The key is to keep smiling," India said as we walked toward the gym. "The last thing we need is a photographer to catch you yawning or scowling at the mascot."

"Got it. Nothing but smiles."

The whole town packed into the gym bleachers. I slid in next to Dad, who put his arm over my shoulder. It even felt natural. I could sense Ana taking aim at us with her camera. India was on my other side. The team marched down the line of folding chairs on the floor and took their seats. Hunter sat off to the side. He leaned forward, his elbows on his thighs and his hands clasped. He could have been sitting at the back of science waiting for Quincy to tell us what page to turn to, except his eyes were sharp, alert. He watched and waited. It was the way he looked at people when he talked to them, with the same intensity he had when he was at the shelter. I don't know why I didn't see it before. He didn't take football seriously because it was football. He took it seriously because behind all his jokes and the easy way he wore his skin, he took everything seriously.

After a few cheers, the coach thanked everyone for coming, then passed the microphone to Missy, the head cheerleader.

"Are you ready for a dance-off?" she shouted to the crowd, who responded with a deafening cheer. I saw Dad nodding his head, so I brightened my smile and cheered with everyone else.

Several of the football players rose. Kyle raised his hand to his ear, demanding more cheers from his adoring fans. I noticed that Hunter stayed in his seat, leaned back, and put his arm over the chair next to him.

The band began a drum-thumping, fast-paced number, and the varsity cheerleaders scattered, pulling moms, grandmothers, two-year-old girls in red-and-black cheerleading outfits to the stage. I watched in horror as Missy grabbed Ana from the wings.

"She's up to something," I muttered.

"I don't care if she starts an animal sacrifice," India said on my other side. "You keep smiling."

Missy paired Ana up with Kyle. He stood there for a second, then put his hands up, pointed to his hurt hand, turned, and sat back down. Ana's face reddened.

Fury coursed through my every pore.

India must have been watching me. "I don't have time to clean up any more messes," she whispered, nodding to where Bo stood by a man with a large video camera perched on his shoulder.

Ana was trapped in the middle of the stage, alone. I was trapped in the audience, my face fixed in a benign smile. Ana's head dropped and her posture shrank. She looked like a cornered animal.

The last of my self-control drained away. I stood up and started forward, but India grabbed my arm. I glared at the stage. "I don't care if you have to clean it up. I have to fix this."

India pulled me back with one hand and pointed to the corner of the gym. "It's already fixed."

Hunter appeared next to Ana onstage. He swept her into a galloping two-step across the gym floor, then cotton-eye-Joed her to the pounding bass of the pop song playing. Ana danced along. The crowd cheered louder. Then he gave Ana a big hug and escorted her back to the sidelines. By the end of the song, everyone had forgotten that it was supposed to be Kyle up there—except for Kyle, who leaned forward in his folding chair and glowered.

I'd never been prouder of Hunter.

When the pep rally ended, I raced to catch up with Hunter, who was slipping out a side door to the parking lot. I reached him as he was pulling open the door to his truck. "Hey."

He stopped. "Hey."

Sudden nervousness bloomed in my stomach. It took me a second to remember what I wanted to say. "You never told me about your dance skills. You were great."

Hunter grinned. "I keep a few surprises in my back pocket."

"You really saved Ana. Thank you."

"Kyle's an idiot. I'm not saying you were right to set them up, but he would have been smart to take advantage of it and not act like a jerk to her."

"I'll take that as a very small compliment." We stood there for a moment. "I haven't seen you at the shelter."

"I've been at practice a lot. And I spent some of the break with my mom. I'm helping her train Lucy." He brushed something off his sleeve, then squinted at the horizon. "You coming to the game?"

"Dad doesn't think it's a good idea. He says to give it one more week. But I've been listening on the radio, and I would love to see you play."

One side of Hunter's mouth lifted. "I think we'll make it through this round." His eyes found mine. "Unless you're leaving town before the next game."

"I'm not leaving."

"But eventually you'll go back to DC, right?" He stuck his hands in his pockets.

Part of me wanted to say that we wouldn't go back. Another part of me wanted to say anything to stand there longer with Hunter. Instead, I told the truth. "Maybe. Probably. I don't know."

"Too bad." Hunter climbed into his truck. When he drove off, it was like there was a hole where he used to be.

chapter thirty-one

That weekend, while everyone else was at the game, I studied the two lists from Principal Walker's office. Mrs. Fisher had loaned me the last four years of yearbooks, and I looked up every name, their activities, their friends. But I couldn't find a pattern Kyle would fit other than the fact that they were all students.

Luckily, Tasha and Hunter had given me a plan B. Nothing makes people see what a jerk someone is like a comparison. A face-to-face competition. A duel.

By Monday, I was ready. I went to the yearbook room. Ana sat at the computer working on layouts. "Are you going to develop pictures?" she asked me.

"Yeah," I said, the lie rolling easily off my tongue. "I think I have a few that might be good."

"Good enough for your portfolio?"

"Maybe." I sat in the chair next to her. "How's *your* portfolio going?"

"I looked over the pictures you chose. I'm just not sure they are my best."

"You're too modest. They'll blow the admissions committee away. Do you want me to make a contact sheet for you?"

Ana pulled a roll of film out of her backpack and handed it to me. "That would be great. I'm headed to the basketball game."

"By yourself?" I leaned back and studied Ana. She sat straighter. Her chin lifted a fraction farther from her chest.

"Yeah, I decided that I'd let Hank control me for too long."

"Good for you."

"Hunter stood up for me. You stood up for me. Even Kyle stood up for me. I've decided I need to stand up for myself." Ana picked up her camera.

"You look ready."

"I hope so," she said.

I snuck to the door and watched her disappear down the hall. Then before I could think about it too much, I moved to the computer and logged on with Ana's name and Hank4. Ana's log-in gave me access to all the pages I needed—the football pages.

Most of the pictures were from earlier in the season and showed Kyle in all his glory. I deleted every picture of Kyle on one spread and replaced them with Ana's pictures of Hunter from the last two games—Hunter launching a pass, Hunter in the huddle with everyone's eyes glued to him, Hunter on the sidelines listening to the coach, a screaming crowd behind him. When Kyle saw this, it would mess with his head enough to pay him back for what he did to Ana. As a bonus, he'd probably self-destruct. I'd have to get to school early tomorrow to make sure I didn't miss it.

I studied the spread. There was something off. I deleted one of the pictures of Hunter and replaced it with a picture of Kyle, his arm around an opposing team's cheerleader and that obnoxious look of self-satisfaction on his face. It was just enough to point out the difference. Best-case scenario: He would show the page to half a dozen people to try to find out who planted it. Worst case, he would still have that story in his head—Hunter as the hero and Kyle as the villain. It's not easy to live with being cast as the villain. I'd push him off the edge and let his pride take care of the fall.

I printed the pages, then closed the screen without saving. All I had to do was drop the spread in his locker and enjoy the show. It should give me enough leverage to keep Kyle in check for the rest of our stay.

I headed into the darkroom. An hour later, I was laying down negatives for a contact sheet. Ana's pictures were a series of portraits, mostly the women in her family. Even the small shots on the contact sheet held power—her grandmother helping one of her cousins roll dough, her mother kneeling in front of an open fire. I couldn't wait to see them cropped and enlarged.

I'd just left the darkroom when Ana burst through the door. Her head was tipped lower than I'd ever seen it, a curtain of hair hiding most of her face. She slammed down the camera.

I flipped the altered layouts facedown beside the computer. "What happened? What did Hank say?"

"Just some stuff. He said he heard Kyle was hanging out with me for one reason."

"He's probably just making that up."

"But that's the thing. If he's telling me, he's telling everyone. I'm so tired of this. I let everyone else say who I am. I think I need one of those . . . you know."

"New images?"

Ana nodded.

"I don't think you need to change into something you're not."

"Why not? No one knows who I really am anyway."

"Okay. We'll figure this out." I picked up the layouts and started to fold them up. I'd have to deal with them tomorrow. Right now, Ana needed me, and some fudge ice cream.

"What are those?" she said, pointing to the pages.

"Nothing. Just some proofs."

"They look like yearbook pages." She grabbed them. I held my breath.

"This is so—" Ana flipped through the pages.

"I know. I'm so sorry. But after what he did to you at the pep rally, I just wanted to—"

"Brilliant."

"—teach Kyle . . . wait . . . what?"

"Forget the new image, this is better." Her head was lifted, her eyes bright. She had a glow. "Revenge. Like you're getting on that guy you dated."

"Yeah?"

"Sure. Like you said, yearbook is powerful." Ana handed the pages back to me. "You're going to put these everywhere, right?"

"I was just going to put one in Kyle's locker. You know, to mess with his head."

"You should do more than mess with his head. You should mess with his reputation. That's what he deserves." Ana's chin lifted a little more.

I found myself nodding. What Ana was saying felt true, real. "Okay, let's do it."

Ana went to the computer. "We'll just print a couple hundred more."

"We'll have to make copies of this one. I didn't save the pages."

"No problem. We'll go to the teacher's lounge. I know Ms. Serrano's code."

Ana and I worked quickly, shoving copies in lockers on either side of the main hall. My stomach twisted a little. This was more public than I'd intended, but I wanted revenge.

"You feel better?" I asked Ana on the way home.

"I will when I see Kyle's face tomorrow."

"I almost forgot." I handed her the contact sheet. "Circle the ones you want me to print."

"Thanks. You're a good friend, Kate."

She wasn't lying, but I wasn't sure it was the truth either.

chapter thirty-two

The next day—Election Day—Mom and Dad left early for an appearance at a polling location in Singleton. Aunt Celia drove me to school.

"You comin' to the shelter after school? I could use help with the feedings." She eased the truck to a stop in front of the high school.

"Yeah, sure." I studied the clusters of students. Everything looked normal.

"What's with you? You haven't said a word this whole drive. Not that I'm complaining."

"Nothing. Do you need me to come by the shelter after school?" Aunt Celia studied me, exasperation and maybe even a little worry in her eyes. I realized my mistake. "Sorry. I know. You just said. I'll be there." I got out and started to shut the door.

"Kate. You're not letting that Stone kid get to you?"

I shook my head and tried to smile. "I just haven't woken up yet."

"Chin up. You're a Hamilton," Aunt Celia said.

"Thanks for the advice." I shut the door of the truck and watched her drive away.

When I got to science, Kyle was standing outside the door, his meaty hands in fists at his side. The other students stood in clusters, passing something from person to person. He followed me into the room and slammed the page on my table.

"You did this."

I looked at the paper. Like Aunt Celia said, chin up. "I don't do, layout design, but Missy does. Maybe you should talk to her. She's probably over that whole breakup thing from last summer. Girls let go of that stuff pretty quickly."

Kyle glared at me.

"And Ana does the pictures, but she wouldn't hold a grudge just because you embarrassed her at the pep rally," I continued.

His face reddened.

"But, really, why worry? You don't think people might start to believe that Hunter is better than you?"

A few students glanced in Kyle's direction and whispered. I didn't know what I had been worried about. This was definitely better than just sticking the page in his locker.

The bell rang and Hunter sat down next to me.

"Mr. Stone, why don't you take your seat," Mr. Quincy called.

Anger folded into the lines between Kyle's brows. "You won't get away with this," he said to me.

Hunter's eyes followed Kyle to his seat before he turned to me. "Please tell me you didn't have anything to do with that spread."

I realized what I had been nervous about. This moment. When Hunter found out. "It could have been anyone," I said.

His eyes seemed to drill into me.

"I was just going to mess with his head a little."

"You did that. You messed with everyone's head. And you messed with me."

There it was. The problem with the plan. "I didn't mean . . . That's not what I intended."

"Never is." Hunter rubbed his forehead. "Isn't this exactly what that loser you're still hung up on did to you?"

I leaned back. "No . . . I am not still hung up on—"

"Destroy your image by posting pictures to the school website?"

"But this is dif—" The tears started to sting.

"Pictures that were chosen to make you look bad."

I wiped my eyes. "Come on. Kyle got what he deserved," I said. "He hurts people."

Hunter's face was hard. He was holding back emotion. Anger. Disappointment. "You're far more dangerous than Kyle. Kyle uses matches; you use lighter fluid."

I opened my mouth, but my next argument stuck in my throat. "I . . . I'll fix it," I said.

Hunter's voice softened. "Don't bother. You're going back to DC anyway. The rest of us have to deal with this mess."

More tears gathered, but Hunter didn't see them. He pushed back his stool and moved to another table.

When I got to the yearbook room, Ana was at the computer. I sat down next to her. "That didn't feel as good as I thought it would," she said.

"I should have stopped you," I said.

"I don't think you could have." She handed the contact sheet to me with a few pictures circled in red wax.

The classroom phone rang. Ms. Serrano picked it up. "I sent them to the publisher yesterday," she said to the person on the line. "Yes, I understand the importance. I don't know how they got them." She hung up the phone. "Ana, print the finals of the pages we're sending this deadline. Principal Walker wants to see them."

"We took them up before Thanksgiving," Ana said.

"He is taking a real interest in our work for some reason. Print them again."

Ana opened the pages and clicked print. The yearbook printer whirred to life and printed the twelve pages devoted to football.

Ms. Serrano picked up the pages. Her mouth dropped open and her face went white. "Who did this?" She held up the spread with the photos of Hunter in place of Kyle.

Missy came over. "I told you to let me do the football spreads."

I forced myself to take slow, steady breaths. "I didn't save it," I said to Ana. I was sure about that.

"It autosaves," Ana said. "I should have remembered."

Ms. Serrano pushed herself through the maze of desks. She tapped a few keys. A history of edits appeared on the screen with Ana's name next to them. "Are you responsible for this?" she said to her.

Ana nodded.

"Did you use my code to make the copies?"

She nodded again.

The phone rang. Ms. Serrano picked it up like it was teeming with virus. The yearbook room was silent. "Yes . . . I'll get there by the end of the day . . . Well, we're having a few technical difficulties . . . Yes, I'll be right down." She hung up the phone and put her hand to her head. Then she took a breath and left the room.

I struggled to breathe. I had meant to cause a ripple and had ended up with a tsunami. I pulled Ana into a corner by the bookcases. "Why did you tell Ms. Serrano you did this?"

"I did."

"Not all of it. I made the layout."

She looked down. "I copied the pages."

"We both put them in the lockers. I'm just as guilty as you are."

Mutterings and stares filled the yearbook room. "You must really have it bad for Hunter," Missy said to Ana.

Ana's eyes were frozen between shock and tears. She hung her head as she walked away. I reached for her arm, but she shook me off and continued out the door.

"It's not how it looks," I said to everyone else.

"It looks like she has a new obsession with our substitute QB," Missy said.

Ms. Serrano came back ten minutes later, her broom skirt swirling around her. "Did you guys finish the rest of the yearbook while I was downstairs? Or at least get those football pages fixed? If not, get back to work." I went to her desk, ready to make a full confession. "Apparently, we are a pocket of malcontents, a hive of troublemakers out to stir up mockery of the football program," she said to me. "Ana is suspended from yearbook until further notice. She'll be down in the office filing during class starting immediately. You're taking pictures at the games from now on."

I shook my head. "I don't think Ana should be punished for—"

Ms. Serrano held up her hand. "This is over my head. Apparently, there is a concern that Ana will take bad pictures of Kyle Stone on purpose."

"If anyone is going to take bad pictures of Kyle, it's going to be me."

"Yes, it was pointed out that I seem to have an affinity for photographers who are determined to create bad press for the football team. But it was Ana's log-in."

My stomach twisted and turned, trying to smother the guilt inside me, but it only churned up disappointment and despair.

I kept my hands at my side. "I need to tell you something."

She looked up. "You made the layout of Kyle and Hunter."

"You knew?"

"It looked like your work. You always go for the most obvious part of the picture."

Ouch. "So you shouldn't ban Ana."

"It wasn't my choice," Ms. Serrano said, dropping into her seat.

"It's not fair."

"It's not fair that I can only recruit two photographers. It's not fair that I will get calls if I don't have a photographer at every event where there is a scoreboard. Bo Stone is pacing the floor in Principal Walker's office, probably debating the possibility of stapling a bunch of football programs together and calling it a yearbook, so I'd appreciate it if you would just take the pictures." She shuffled the papers on her desk. "You know what, you're right."

"I am?"

"You should face some consequences for your part in the layout debacle." She pursed her lips and sighed. "You're banned from the darkroom."

"Banned? How will I finish my portfolio?"

"You'll figure out something."

I started to walk away. I took two steps, then turned around. "Can I just have one hour? Today? Not for my pictures."

"Why?"

I looked at the floor. "I owe someone a favor."

"Fine. Put the key on my desk by five today."

I went into the darkroom. I opened the notebook that held the negatives I'd developed and flipped past all of mine to Ana's. I stared at the red wax circles she'd made around half a dozen pictures on the contact sheet; then I pulled out the chemicals and started to pour them into trays. I would develop Ana's pictures. It was the least I could do.

The yearbook pages floated around the school the rest of the week, folded into the front pockets of backpacks and jackets. They didn't have the reach online pictures have, but you couldn't just take them down. I should have gotten a lot of satisfaction from the raised eyebrows and whispers that flowed in Kyle's wake. But all I could see was Ana's dipped head and stooped shoulders.

chapter thirty-three

Election Day campaigning is a simple numbers game: Smile and shake as many hands as you can. I moved like a zombie from place to place—a smiling, polite zombie. Mom and Dad exchanged a few looks, but didn't say anything. India didn't notice. She was too busy checking the exit polls every ten minutes.

We watched the election results at home. Dad didn't win, but he did get enough votes to come in second and keep Bo Stone from a majority. That meant Dad and Bo Stone would go head-to-head in a runoff election in two weeks. When the news anchors delivered the final tally, Mrs. Fisher and her cluster of women erupted in cheers.

"They do know we didn't win? We didn't even come in first," India said, rubbing her forehead.

"I think they have it confused with the playoffs. People are celebrating that we're moving on to the next round," I said.

I grabbed a plate and headed for the kitchen. Mrs. Fisher had wrested control of the night's food from Mom, who was too tired to put up much of a fight. Women bustled around, sliding between each other to reach towels or plates or glasses.

"Did you get something to eat, honey?" Mrs. Fisher asked me.

I held up my plate piled with mini-quiches and something Mrs. Fisher called pigs in a blanket.

"I sure am happy for your dad," she said.

"Are you going to Bo Stone's house later?" I asked.

She pushed a plate of brownies toward me. "I already stopped by. He has catered food," she said, wrinkling her nose.

The living room was covered with men grouped in tight conversations. I slipped into Dad's office and sat on the couch. I closed the door, but I could still hear the hum of voices.

A few minutes later, Mom slid through the door. Her face had that long-suffering look she got when someone brought in another tray of lemon bars or crammed cream casseroles into the fridge. She jumped when she saw me, then smiled. "Oh, good. For a minute I thought you were a volunteer." She kicked off her heels and folded her legs underneath her. "If I have to hear more about Travis's defense or your father's brilliant pass in the final seconds of the semifinals against Hargrove, I'm going to put myself in a sugar coma with those brownies they're pushing on people."

I lifted my plate. "Way ahead of you."

Mom grabbed a brownie, took a bite, closed her eyes, and leaned back into the sofa. "These are amazing. What do you think is in them?"

I swallowed a spoonful of banana pudding. "Carbs?"

The door opened, and Mom and I automatically sat up straight. "So this is where you guys went. I was coming to find you," Dad said.

Mom pointed a fork at him. "Liar. You were escaping just like us."

He collapsed into the overstuffed chair across from us and put his feet on the coffee table.

"What's on your schedule for tomorrow?" Mom asked.

Dad waved his hand. "A few interviews, some fund-raising calls. India has me scheduled with you in the morning and then I'm going to a luncheon in Midland and a school or nursing home after that."

India threw open the door. "Both. You're going to both." She scanned the room. "What are you all doing in here?"

"Family meeting," Dad said.

"Walker Casey just ran to his house to get VCR tapes of all your playoff games."

Dad rubbed his face. "We don't have a VCR."

"Caroline is pretty sure you do. She's rummaging through some closets in the back."

The back door slammed and Celia's voice rang through the house. "I have to get up at the crack of dawn tomorrow. I'm glad you all enjoyed yourselves, and I think you know the way out."

India winced. "I'll try to smooth it over."

"But don't stop them from leaving," Mom said, her mouth full of another bite of brownie.

India opened the door and Aunt Celia stormed in. "Jeff, I think I've been pretty understanding about all this."

"Is that a congratulations?"

"When is this runoff?" she asked.

"You're wondering when we get out of your hair?"

Aunt Celia widened her stance and stuck her hands in her back pockets. "That . . . and I might want to make sure I find time to vote."

"I appreciate your support."

"I didn't say who I was voting for."

Dad winced. Then the lines around Aunt Celia's eyes softened and her mouth twitched with the smile that was trying to surface.

Dad smiled. "You can vote for me two weeks from today. You can vote for my opponent the day after that."

Aunt Celia sat on the couch beside me. "I don't know how you stand it. All those people around day after day."

"At least they bring brownies." I held out my plate.

India came back. "Everyone is leaving. It's almost safe to come out."

"Good news," Dad said. "Celia is thinking of voting Hamilton for Congress."

"Only about six hundred more votes to go," India said.

Everyone was silent.

"How many does Bo need to get the majority?" Mom asked.

"Two hundred," India said.

"People are fatigued. It's a good thing the campaign didn't get any nastier. Turnout might have been lower," Dad said.

"Can he get those votes here in Red Dirt?" Mom asked.

India slumped in a chair. "If he does a good job of getting his voters to the polls."

I rubbed my forehead. "It's my fault. If I hadn't slammed Kyle's hand—"

"He would have gotten the votes anyway. You're probably the reason we're still in this. You and that Hunter kid," Dad said.

"What do you mean?"

"He's pulling them through the playoffs. People aren't mad. People can vote against me as easily as they can vote for me."

"And when you win, you'll go back to DC?" Aunt Celia asked.

"*If* we win, we'll decide together." Dad flashed her a small smile. "Don't pretend you'll miss us."

"It hasn't been bad having you around." Aunt Celia rubbed the back of her neck.

"What is it going to take to win?" Mom asked.

Dad shook his head. "A smooth playoff, good weather, and about six hundred more votes."

chapter thirty-four

The next day, Ana sat in a chair in the back corner of the year-book room, a textbook across her lap. I dropped the pictures onto the book.

"I thought you were banned from the darkroom."

"Seriously? People know that?"

"It's a small school."

"It's barely news." I sat down beside her. "Ms. Serrano let me develop those before she took the key."

Ana picked them up, holding them lightly. The top one was the picture of her mother, her long hair pulled back in a ponytail and the light from the fire dancing over the angles of her face. She shuffled through a few more until she got to my favorite. The camera centered on her grandmother's hands as they kneaded dough. The veins popped, and the muscles of her thin arms were hard, but her face was soft and focused.

"They're . . ."

"They're beautiful," I said.

Ana closed her eyes, then looked at the picture again. "What did you do to make the people come to life like this?"

"Nothing. You did it." I tapped the picture. "You don't ever have to worry about rumors. This is who you are." I took a breath. "I am so sorry for everything, Ana. You don't need a new image or a new boyfriend. That's what I should have said when you wanted to pass out the pages."

Ms. Serrano came in and pulled some papers out of her box.

"I better get to class."

Ana nodded. "Thank you."

"No problem." I slipped out the door.

Ms. Serrano caught up with me in the hall. "Those were the pictures you needed to print."

I nodded.

"That was a nice thing to do." She walked beside me a few seconds in silence. "I never know what to make of you. I saw the set of sunset pictures that you had hanging in the back."

"You don't have to tell me how terrible they are."

"You said it yourself. You're trying too hard to fix the photograph in the darkroom. And the effort shows. Everything is right in your pictures, but nothing is great. To find greatness, you need meaning." She put her hand on my arm and pulled me to a stop. "Why do you want to take these sunset pictures?"

"That's all there is here. Sky. It's hard to ignore. It is everywhere."

She brought a hand to her hip. "There's dust everywhere too, but you're not taking pictures of that."

I reached inside for the words. It took a moment. I had to dig deeper than usual. "There is something vulnerable about being under such a big sky. It's like everything is stripped away."

"It makes you feel small?"

"It makes me feel small in a giant universe. And sometimes that's terrifying, like the way I feel when I can't fix something.

And sometimes it's beautiful." I thought about sitting on the water tower next to Hunter, watching a sunset.

"Then that is what your pictures need to show. That has to be the soul of your images. And you can't plan it, and you can't force it. You're just going to have to catch it when it happens."

"When did photography get so complicated?"

"When you started caring." She fished in her pocket, brought out the darkroom key, and held it out to me. "For what you did for Ana. But don't think you're off the hook. You'll be cleaning out the photo files from the last five years. And taking names at all the group photo sessions. And I need you to—"

I held up my hands. "I get it. I'm your yearbook slave."

"I'm glad we finally understand each other," Ms. Serrano said, her heels clicking down the hallway.

As Dad loaded us all in the car for the game against Travis on Friday, he made an announcement. "We're taking tonight off to enjoy the quarterfinals."

Mom raised an eyebrow and put a hand on Dad's arm.

"No campaigning, no phone calls about the campaign, no talking about the campaign," Dad said. "The players deserve our undivided attention."

"Fine," I said.

"The runoff is in eleven days. This is crazy," India said.

"How far behind are we?" I asked.

"Eight or nine points. We're gaining ground, but the clock is ticking."

"It's not crazy. It's good strategy," Dad said. "We're out of the district and the only voters we have within reach are probably voting for Stone anyway, so I say we don't talk about the campaign at all."

I scooted back in my seat and stared out the window. "I think we better practice not talking about politics if we want to pull this off at the game," I said.

"Fine, starting now, no talk about politics," Mom said.

India opened her laptop.

The car fell silent for a few miles.

"So, if we don't talk about politics, what do we talk about?" I asked.

"Kate, how is school?" Mom asked in her Junior League–luncheon voice.

"Good."

"You seem to get a lot of opportunities on the yearbook staff," Dad said. "Your teacher must see what a talented photographer you are."

I swallowed. "That might be overstating it." We were silent again.

"Okay, someone else try a conversation," Mom said.

"We can talk football," I offered.

Mom groaned.

"What do you know about Travis's team?" I asked Dad.

"I know quite a bit. They have one of the best defensive lines in the state," Dad said. "That means that you should keep your camera focused on the ball. I'm guessing there'll be a lot of screens and hitches to neutralize their strength. The whole game will be won or lost within three yards of the line of scrimmage."

I clicked the lens cover on and off and adjusted the shutter speed for the third time.

"Number seventy-four should get you some good shots. He's made a hundred and forty-two tackles. He also has a knack for stripping the ball. But if you really want a good picture, point it at your friend Hunter."

"Does he make big plays?"

"No, but it's not always what something is that's impressive. It's what it might become," Dad said.

"I think Ms. Serrano is looking for something more obvious for the yearbook."

"Well, take a few pictures for me. He is fun to watch—precise, deliberate. There's a player who knows he isn't bigger than the game."

"I heard that the Stone kid might be playing tonight," India said.

"I didn't hear that," Dad said.

"They're keeping it quiet. He's cleared, but they don't want the Travis defense changing their game plan."

"How did you find out?" Mom asked.

"I can't tell you. No political talk, remember?"

"I never found out what Bo Stone and the principal were doing with that list," I said.

"Me either, and I bet I've been looking harder than you have," India said. "There are two other football players, but they are juniors. I checked the yearbook pictures; they're usually on the sidelines. Other than that, no one is in the same grade or sport or even sports in general. I can't figure out any reason Bo Stone would want Kyle on that list."

"If it's a secret, it will come out, but probably not until after the the runoff," Dad said.

I watched a tumbleweed roll along the fence line. "Because you can't keep secrets in politics."

"You can only control them," India said.

Dad's advice helped. I took shots of the defensive line as they crashed into Travis's offense. I aimed the camera at the receivers as they tucked Hunter's short passes under their arms. I even took a couple of shots of Hunter. It was my first time seeing him play, and Dad was right. He executed economical, precise moves, almost elegant in their simplicity. He threw short, exact passes that got the ball into the end zone. Unfortunately, Travis answered with its own longer carries. By the end of the first quarter, they were one touchdown ahead. The Red Dirt offensive players crashed into Travis's royal-blue jerseys like waves breaking before they got to shore. Hunter squeezed pass after pass through narrow alleys between players, but the crowd was getting restless. After a season of Kyle Stone's long, arcing throws over the goal line, Hunter's plodding, determined game felt too slow and awkward for the quarterfinals.

Even though Hunter worked the ball over the goal line a second time, a handful of boosters started to frown. I could see Bo Stone at the center of a knot of men in belt buckles at the fifty-yard line. By the end of the first half, he was yelling, "Put Kyle in, Coach. It's the playoffs. What are you waiting for?"

I zoomed the camera in on the coach's profile, a landscape of fury and determination lined with cracks of anger. Then I shifted it to the bench where Kyle sat, his white uniform shining under the lights. His elbows rested on his knees. His head was barely lifted, just enough to catch a glimpse of the game through narrowed eyes. It felt like a story, but it was hard to tell if it was the beginning or the end.

Hunter started the second half, but the coach had Kyle warming up on the sidelines. Hunter worked the ball down the field for another touchdown that was answered almost immediately. The crowd rumbled, hungry for a comfortable lead.

The next play, Kyle stepped on the field. He raised his hands in a premature victory celebration, and the crowd clapped under their blankets and exchanged worried looks. Bo Stone and his knot of men nodded their approval. Kyle was not as consistent as Hunter, so the plays went back and forth. Luckily the Travis defense was tiring.

The Red Dirt team didn't move the same way with Kyle. When Hunter was on the field, the movements felt in sync. Kyle seemed a half step ahead of or behind the rhythms. After weeks of watching ants, I was getting good at seeing the whole, the system instead of the individual. Hunter was focused on pushing forward step by step. Kyle hungered for the next point, and he didn't care how he got it. I remembered what India had said about Bo Stone and Dad—Dad wanted to win, while Bo Stone was desperate to avoid failure.

Failure. I scanned the sidelines, looking for the other football players on Bo Stone's list. There were two juniors who were also on last year's varsity team. I knew their numbers. I'd learned them to check the yearbook pictures. Neither jersey was anywhere in sight.

Kyle wasn't put on a list. He was taken off one. That's what the list was—people who were academically ineligible for activities. No pass, no play. And it should have had Kyle's name on it.

I charged up to the stands where India sat tapping on her phone. I squeezed onto the cold metal bleacher between her and Dad. "I know what the list is."

India's fingers stopped. Dad looked at me.

"It's the failure list," I said.

India started typing again.

"You don't get it. I think Kyle is ineligible. He didn't complete the work he missed, probably in Mr. Quincy's class the week he was gone. If Coach puts him in and someone finds out, Red Dirt will have to forfeit the game. They'll be out of the playoffs. And it will be all Kyle's fault."

"There's only one problem," India said. "We're not running against Kyle."

A man in the stands yelled for "the Price kid" to be put back in. Another man two rows up shouted for the coach to keep Stone. "But Bo orchestrated it. You know he did," I said.

Dad looked up at the two men, still arguing. Other voices joined in. "You don't mess with the kids," he said. "There's too much backlash."

"Are you kidding me? After the way Bo Stone has used me to get to you?"

"It was low, but you're tough," Dad said.

Kyle completed a pass, and a cheer swelled through the stands, people shifting to his side. I scanned the faces of the Red Dirt fans. Their eyes were wide. The women's hands pressed together on their lips. The men leaned forward and fixed their eyes on the field. The kids clutched their plastic footballs.

"If you leaked the information, you would take all this away," I said.

"Right," Dad said.

"Don't you want to win?"

"Yeah, but it wouldn't be much of a victory. Not at that price."

I knew what I had to do. I had to let Kyle take this one.

I returned to the field in time to snap a picture of him laid out by a defensive lineman.

chapter thirty-five

Hunter's steady progress and Kyle's long passes won the game, and the Red Dirt fans gathered at the visitors' field house to congratulate the players, their sweaty uniforms circling through the crowd. Much of Kyle's swagger returned. He slapped high fives and rolled past people on a wave of admiration. But evidence of discomfort weighted his movements, like he'd put back on the QB role, but it itched.

I took a few pictures when the players returned from the locker room. When I lowered the camera, Hunter was standing next to me. "Looks like I get to hang up my cleats again," he said.

"You're not going to play in the semifinals?"

Hunter shook his head. "Naw. They don't need me."

"I don't know. I think there are a lot of fans who will be disappointed." He stood there silently for a few moments. I swallowed while I searched for something to say, something that would keep him next to me. "Me, for one. I was impressed. You play a smart game," I said at last.

Hunter cocked his head to the side. "Wait, was that a compliment?"

"I mean, the game is barbaric, and the pace of it is excruciatingly slow considering how much gratuitous violence is packed in, but you play it well."

"Well, I guess you'll have some good stories to tell people when you get back to DC."

"Yeah, I guess." I took a deep breath. Standing close to Hunter threw me off balance. "I talked to Ana. Apologized."

Hunter shifted to face me. Those intense eyes.

"You were right. I shouldn't have changed the layouts. And I definitely shouldn't have gotten Ana involved." I fiddled with the buttons on the camera. I looked up. "Friends?"

It took one beat. Two. "Friends," he finally said.

A rush of breath. I didn't realize I'd been holding it.

Kyle walked over. "You did a nice job filling in," he said to Hunter. "I'll take it from here."

"If you think you can do better," Hunter said.

"You should never have been on that field," Kyle said.

"Come on, Kyle. Hunter's not the one who didn't belong on the field," I fired back.

Kyle took a step back. "What are you saying?"

Speaking before thinking was becoming more and more of a habit for me, and a bad one. Bo stepped in the space that had widened between me and Kyle. "Yes, Miss Hamilton. Just what are you accusing my son of?"

"Nothing. We're just talking." I looked for an exit, but before I could slip away, Dad strolled over and nodded at Kyle.

"Did you send your daughter to threaten my son?" Bo demanded.

"No one threatened anyone," I said. I looked at Dad. "I didn't say anything."

Bo pointed a finger at me. "You walked into town yesterday, and you think you can tell us how to do things." He turned toward Hunter. "And you. You can't even stick to quitting."

My whole body tensed.

"It's not worth it," Hunter mumbled—to me, to himself; I wasn't sure.

"Dad." I looked at him. "I didn't say *anything*. Not this time."

Dad nodded. "Bo, we don't know what you're talking about."

"I made this town, this team, this season," Bo said. "This was my win."

The people around Bo started to whisper.

"Then enjoy the win," Dad said. "Let's leave our history and the politics out of it for once."

"Our history? Our history ended the day you turned your back on this town and everyone in it." Bo shook his head. "First you walk into my town. Then your daughter breaks my son's hand! Then this kid"—he jerked a thumb at Hunter—"walks onto my field."

The crowd's attention was shifting toward us. I nudged Dad as two cameras closed in.

Dad held Bo's eyes. "Don't say something you'll regret, Bo."

Bo moved in close. "I don't need you telling me what I can and can't say. You may have been the big man in high school, but that was decades ago. Kyle's the only one who could get us all the way to the championship. If he needed to be on that field, I was going to make damn sure he was on that field. I don't care what some two-bit science teacher says."

Kyle's face froze, his mouth open. He stared at his father like he didn't recognize him. Kyle didn't know about his grades. My throat tightened, and my mind reached for something that would undo the words that Bo Stone had just launched into the world.

But it was too late. Men and women turned to their neighbors and a rumble passed through the crowd. The hostility swelled.

Dad felt it. He took a step back, grabbed my hand, and started to pull me away.

"Yeah, you get out of here. Just like last time," Bo shouted. "This town's not good enough for you."

"It's too good for you," Dad said.

It happened too fast for anyone to stop it. In a flash, Bo's fist slammed into Dad's face. Dad stumbled back and stared at Bo.

"Don't do it, Dad," I said, nodding toward the cameras.

But Dad didn't look at the cameras. He looked at me and at Mom while Bo stood panting next to him. "It's no big deal. He never could throw a decent punch. Maybe Kate should give him a few pointers."

There was a huff of laughter, but it wasn't friendly. In its echo, the cameras moved in.

"Mr. Stone," said one of the reporters. "What exactly did you do to get Kyle on the field tonight?"

"What led to you punching your opponent just now?" another asked.

"Are you saying you changed his science grade?"

"Do you think the strain of campaigning is affecting your judgment?"

The coach pushed his way into the circle that had widened around the men. "Bo, I need to see you. Now."

We drove down the stretch of dark road leading back to Red Dirt in silence.

"What's going to happen next?" India asked.

"Either they'll drag out the investigation, or Coach will get to the bottom of it tonight," Dad said. "But if Bo messed with those grades or had someone else mess with them, Red Dirt will have to forfeit tonight's game, and the season's over."

"So just to make sure I understand this," India said, "Bo Stone would be solely responsible for the forfeit?"

"That's what it's looking like," Dad said.

"Do you think the cameras got footage of him punching you?" I asked.

"I'd be surprised if they didn't."

"That will run everywhere." India leaned back in her seat, smiling.

"This is going to have a pretty big effect in the polls, right?" I asked.

"The news will pick up the forfeit. From there, it will depend on how he handles it."

"What are the chances that he manages scandal well?" I asked.

"Low," Dad said.

India closed her eyes. "It's like Christmas came early."

"Why would he do it? Change the grades?" I asked. "It seems like he has everything to lose."

"Don't know." Dad rubbed his jaw. "He broke the first rule of politics."

"Nothing is over until it's over?" India said.

"Don't talk down to the voter?" Mom tried.

"Always assume there's a camera?" I added.

Dad shook his head. "Do good without doing harm."

chapter thirty-six

The coach didn't drag out the investigation. By Sunday morning, Red Dirt had forfeited, Coach Watkins had wished Travis luck in the playoffs, and the name Stone was cursed over coffee and lemonade after every church service in Red Dirt.

When I walked toward the shelter on Monday morning, the black outlines of dozens of FOR SALE signs broke the orange at the horizon, filling the Stone yard. Kyle stumbled through a narrow path between them, pulling them up one by one.

I lifted my camera and took a shot. Stripped of the pads and loose jersey, he looked small in a gray shirt and jeans.

Kyle didn't know how to lose. He tried to argue and shout his way through the first few days at school. He moped his way through the rest of the week. The entire time, he didn't say the one thing that would have explained everything—that it was his dad's fault. He was more loyal than I'd given him credit for.

Ana was still exiled to the office during yearbook. Hunter was barely speaking to me in Mr. Quincy's class. He wasn't mad, just distant. I caught only glimpses of his truck at the shelter early in the morning, and with our ant presentation done, I didn't have many excuses to force him to talk to me.

On Friday, Kyle stood in class, giving the ant report that had forced Red Dirt to forfeit their playoff spot.

"So your question was about how ants react to being injured," Mr. Quincy said.

Kyle nodded, shifting from one boot-clad foot to the other.

"What were the results?" Mr. Quincy asked.

"Maybe they had their dad forge a grade and lost the playoffs," a guy in front of me muttered.

Mr. Quincy frowned and turned to the class. "How animals behave when they are hurt is actually a fascinating question and can tell you a lot about a species. Who has an observation?"

"My dog hobbles around like he's not hurt," one guy said.

Mr. Quincy nodded. "Exactly. He doesn't want to show weakness."

"Sometimes they attack," another guy said.

"Or hide," his neighbor added.

Mr. Quincy turned to Kyle. "What do ants do?"

There was silence for a moment. "They send out signals. With chemicals," Kyle said. "Then the other ants come to their rescue."

"Precisely. They broadcast to their fellow ants that they are hurt, and their fellow ants pick them up and take them back to the nest," Mr. Quincy said.

The bell rang. I found myself walking behind Kyle. One of the Neanderthals bumped Kyle's shoulder as he passed, hard.

He looked like an injured animal.

I caught up with Kyle in the cafeteria. He was staring into the web of students and cliques. I took a breath and stepped into the space next to him. "You can't do that, you know. Show weakness. You have to pretend you're not hurt."

"I'm fine." He started to walk away.

I followed. "You're not fine. You're in the middle of a scandal. And you could probably use my help."

He spun to face me. "Leave me alone."

"See, you don't get to do that either. You don't get to curl up and lick your wounds."

The word "Loser" was coughed behind Kyle.

I elbowed him. "Hold your head up," I said. "Literally."

Kyle's posture straightened, but the brooding glare stayed fixed to his features.

"Next we need a Kim Jong Il." I looked around the cafeteria.

"A what?"

I spotted Ana at a table in the corner. "Follow me."

I walked him to the table where Ana sat. Kyle hesitated.

"It's not a date," I said. "It's strategic. Ana is the nicest person in the school. You could use the credibility. Believe me, she doesn't want to see you either."

I laid my tray in front of the seat across from Ana but didn't sit. "Now, we just need . . ."

I saw Hunter and waved him over.

Kyle shook his head. "This is a terrible idea."

"No, it's not. You need to win back some trust. People trust Hunter. And he's a team player."

"I get it. I'm not nice; I'm not trustworthy; I'm not a team player. This is starting to seem like an opportunity to bash me," Kyle said.

"Help feels like that sometimes," I said.

Hunter didn't look any happier when he arrived at our table. "What are you up to?"

"I'm just fixing something. All you have to do is have lunch with me and Ana. Kyle is going to sit here quietly."

"I don't know. People might think Kyle is interested in me," Ana said.

Kyle's shoulders slumped and he took a bite of his burger.

"You deserve that," I said, sliding into the seat next to him. "Don't smile, but don't scowl. You should seem confident in your choices, but sorry that they hurt people."

"What is this? Pity?" Kyle asked.

"This is the friendliest conversation you'll get today," I said.

Hunter sat down beside Ana. "I thought you said he wouldn't talk."

"You know what else helps a scandal?" I said. "An apology."

"I'm not apologizing to anyone," Kyle said.

"Well, then maybe you deserve all the flack you're getting," Hunter said.

Kyle glared at him. "Maybe you should mind— "

"Boys," I snapped.

"I'm sorry," Ana said.

"What?" I looked at her. "Not you. Why are you apologizing?"

"I'm sorry about the layouts. I never should have passed them out." Ana looked at her lap.

Kyle looked at his tray. I looked from him to Ana to Hunter. All of them avoided eye contact.

"Me too," I said in a low voice.

Kyle looked from her to me, his brow wrinkled. "Is that supposed to make all this better?"

Ana got up and rushed out of the cafeteria. Hunter stood up. "Happy, Kate? Is that what you wanted?" He stomped toward the door.

I followed him. "I'm just trying to do the right thing."

"You're redeeming Kyle now. Is he your new project? Is this how you get rid of your guilt? I thought you'd learned your lesson."

"No. I would never. It's just . . . We're not that different—Kyle and me. We understand each other."

Hunter shook his head. "I'm glad someone understands you."

"Come back to lunch," I said.

"I lost my appetite," Hunter said. "I'm going to find Ana."

As I watched his back disappear down the hall toward the office, I realized something. Hunter liked Ana. He always came by the yearbook room when she was there. He saved her at the pep rally dance-off. He was probably the one who cleaned her name off the water tower. That's why he didn't want me setting her up with Kyle. All I had to do to fix this was nudge Hunter and Ana together.

But the thought wrenched my stomach. Why didn't I want to set them up?

And then I finally admitted it. *I* liked Hunter. I liked the way he smirked at me when I was being slightly ridiculous. I liked his iron-clad morals. I liked the way he relaxed until it was time to act and then his eyes became focused and sharp. I liked the way he laughed at the world, but not in a mean way. And I liked the warmth of him when he leaned toward me or his shoulder brushed against mine.

The realization was surprising, unsettling. For once, I wanted something that I couldn't see a way to get.

I stumbled through the rest of the day. I called Mom and arranged for her to pick me up. When I got home, I headed to the animal shelter. I needed to catch up on a few hours. At least, that's what I told myself. I wanted to see Hunter.

He wasn't there, but Aunt Celia was in the trailer at her desk.

"You look like someone spit on your boots and said it was raining," Aunt Celia said.

"Rough day." I collapsed into a metal folding chair.

"Polling numbers aren't going up? I told your dad that it's hard to predict how people will react after a scandal."

"No, Mom said the polling looked great. Bo is seven points behind and still losing ground."

Aunt Celia's face froze. "Oh."

"Looks like he'll pull this off," I said.

She fiddled with her belt loops. "Good. Guess you can all head back to DC after this. You'll have your hours and your recommendation. Your dad will have his seat in Congress. Everyone got what they came here for."

"I guess," I said. "Do you need any help?"

She typed a few keys on the computer. "I don't have anything for you today. I'm just going over the budget. I don't know how I'm going to buy feed this month, but that's not your problem."

"Actually, I have something that might help." I'd finished the website over Thanksgiving, and Tasha and Robert had been getting animals adopted left and right. Maybe now was the right time to show Celia what I'd done. I reached over and pulled up the website on her computer.

"What is this?" she asked with less delight than I'd hoped for.

I pushed a smile over my worry. "Your website."

Aunt Celia frowned at the screen. "Is this for those hours of yours?"

I shook my head. "It's not for hours."

"I didn't authorize this."

"I was just trying to help." I clicked to the sponsorship page. "See, people can sponsor an animal. They help pay for their food."

"I don't need help taking care of my animals." Aunt Celia rose and faced me. "You can't just sweep in here and take over my shelter. And I definitely don't need you trying to fix things that have been working just fine without you."

"I . . . I . . ." My track record for helping was taking a real beating.

"This shelter survived without you for twenty years, so I think I can figure out how to pay for the feed this month. The truth is, you and your family are gone in, what? Three, four weeks? Forgive me if I don't start relying on your help now."

Aunt Celia slammed the door to the trailer. The lights flickered off for a second, just long enough to let the tears fall.

chapter thirty-seven

When the door swung open again, Hunter stood there.

He took a step back, a classic move for someone looking for an exit. It stung almost as much as Aunt Celia's anger. "What are you doing here?" I said.

"I was going to make a run to the feed store, and I wanted to see if she needed anything. About lunch . . ."

"It's fine. I understand," I said. "I shouldn't have done that to Ana."

"You were trying to help. I get what you're saying about you and Kyle. You do have a lot in common." He rubbed his hand through his hair. "I feel like we spend half our time fighting and the other half apologizing."

I got up my courage. "Can I drive to the feed store?"

"If you want to." The lights flickered again. "I guess she didn't get the wiring in this place fixed yet," he said.

"She's been busy. I don't think she had much time after you joined the football team."

"Yeah, well, that won't be a problem now."

As I climbed into the driver's seat, I spotted a can of paint remover and a wire brush in the back of his truck. It only confirmed what I already suspected. Hunter had cleaned Ana's name off the water tower.

"You okay?" Hunter asked.

"Yeah. Great." I didn't want to ruin the little time I had with him explaining how I screwed up again with the website.

"Hamilton, you're the worst liar I've ever seen. How do you manage in DC?"

"I don't have to lie. I just spin," I said.

"I'll take the story without the spin," Hunter said.

"Aunt Celia's mad at me." I started the truck and shifted into reverse.

"She's always tense when she's dealing with the budget."

"How did you know she was working on the budget?"

He rolled the window down and leaned his elbow out. Cool air whipped through the cab. "That's the only reason she ever turns on the computer. And the lighting starts to flicker when the computer is plugged in."

"I don't think she's mad about money."

"What do you think she's mad about?" Hunter asked.

I took a deep breath. "I took pictures of the animals and set up a website where people could sponsor them. I was trying to raise money to help Aunt Celia. Dad is probably taking us all back to DC or Charlotte, and I didn't want her to lose the shelter."

"Oh." The word dropped between us.

"But Aunt Celia doesn't want my help. She said I should mind my own business."

Silence. After a few minutes, I couldn't stand it. "I know, I know. I made another mess."

I felt Hunter's eyes on me. "You didn't make a mess. It's a great idea. She's needed something like that for a long time."

"Really?"

"Really. She'll come around."

I pulled into the feed store and waited while Hunter loaded the bags into the back of the truck. He got into the passenger seat.

"Maybe Celia isn't mad about the site. Maybe she's mad you're leaving." I tried to catch a glimpse of his profile, but he was turned toward the window.

"She'll probably celebrate when we leave. She'll have some peace."

"I think she's gotten used to having you around. Even if she doesn't always show it."

I started the truck and pulled out of the parking lot. We were a few miles down the road when I spoke again. "Part of me wants to stay."

"Why would you want to do that?"

"We have family here. Ms. Serrano is the best photography teacher I've ever had. Ana." *You.* I almost said it, but I didn't want to ruin any friendship I might be able to salvage out of all my mistakes. "Keeping an eye on Kyle," I joked, smiling at him.

Hunter looked down at his hands. "Do you think you'll stay?"

"It's up to my dad. We always lived in DC and commuted to the Charlotte district, but there are plenty of congressmen who live in their districts and commute to DC."

I don't know why I thought Hunter might want me to stay too, but he just stared out the window. We drove back to the shelter in silence.

When I pulled down the gravel drive that led to the trailer, Hunter gave me a small smile. "Well, I don't think you'll have any trouble passing your driver's test wherever you end up. Now, are you going to show me this website?"

We sat down at the laptop, which was still on Aunt Celia's desk. I opened it and the website flickered onto the screen. Hunter clicked through it, reading a few of the pages. "How many sponsors did you get?"

"A little over fifty. My friend Tasha convinced the animal rights club at my old school to participate. It's a bunch of politician's kids. They're very persuasive. We've got about twenty animals fully sponsored. Another twenty partially."

He stared at the screen with that intense focus of his. "That's amazing."

"So far. A couple more come in every day. People can help an animal without having to really help. It's exactly the kind of thing people love in DC."

He clicked through more pages. "Kate, this is great."

"Really?"

Hunter closed the laptop and spun to face me. "Really." The beam of his gaze was on me now, and I could feel myself leaning toward it. His hand brushed against mine as he stood. I blinked, putting a hand on Aunt Celia's desk for support. "I better get that feed unloaded while there's still light," he said.

I stood. "Yeah, I need to get back to the house."

Hunter held the door open for me. When I was a dozen steps down the driveway, I heard his long strides crunch beside me. "Kate, I know I give you a hard time sometimes."

I kept my eyes on the distance. "Sometimes I deserve it."

He took a deep breath. Something was making him nervous. Then I knew, like a punch to the gut, he was going to ask me about Ana.

"I know how you like to fix things, and I need something fixed. After lunch today—"

My heart sank. I was right. "You should ask someone else."

Hunter leaned back. "I think you're the girl to help me."

I put my face in my hands. "I'm not. I'm not the girl to help you. I don't want to help you." It came out before I could stop it. I wanted Hunter to be happy, and I could try to pretend that my knees didn't melt when he looked at me, but I didn't think I could help him ask Ana out. He was on his own.

Hunter's eyes were pools of hurt.

"I'm sorry," I said.

"No, I get it."

He walked away without saying good-bye.

I went back to the house under a gold and purple sky. My stomach twisting and my eyes blurry with tears, I did what I'd always done when faced with a loss—I looked for a win. It was more habit than hope that it would make a dent in the hurt.

I decided to take one more stab at the sunsets. I went into the house and got my camera, then started to fiddle with the settings. Then I remembered what Ms. Serrano had told me. It wasn't about getting it right—it was about making it great, something that transcends right. Something that pulls at people and makes them see more than what is on the paper.

I looked across this landscape that I'd grown to love. The shades of brown that seemed flat when I first arrived now teemed with tones and contrast. Tumbleweeds collected at the foot of trees bent by the winds. The sky stretched over all of it. I pointed my camera into the distance, but when I looked through the viewfinder, there was nothing there. Looking at it, I just saw sky and ground.

It dawned on me. It needed contrast. If I wanted to show how big the sky was, how it smothered everything in its vastness, I had to find something small. I shifted the camera toward the shelter. In the distance, Hunter moved back and forth from the truck, unloading bags of feed.

It wasn't easy, waiting for a picture to come to me. But it did have a bit of magic to it, the same magic I loved about the dark-room. When Hunter finished, he put his hands in his pockets and stared at the horizon for a moment. I snapped a quick series of photographs of his black truck and the silhouette of his figure under an endless sky. I didn't know what the picture would look like, or if people would understand it, but I could already feel how much it would mean to me.

chapter thirty-eight

India swept us through a frenzy of events leading up to the runoff on Tuesday. I was grateful for every diner, every VFW hall, every call list, every interview. Hunter had given up on even the smallest conversation. Kyle followed me around at school like a lost puppy.

Ana was avoiding me. Or Kyle. Or both. It was hard to tell. I did find the time to develop the pictures of Hunter. They were beautiful, everything I had hoped they would be. I left them on Ms. Serrano's desk.

The next day she called me over. She continued to flip through the images while I stood there, biting my lip and trying to read her face. After an eternity she looked up, my favorite on the desk in front of her. "This picture will get you into any school."

I let out the breath I'd been holding. "You think?"

She nodded. "But I'll throw in a recommendation just in case the idiots on some admissions committee can't see art when it drops in their laps."

"That would be amazing! Thank you." I'd gotten a recommendation without beating Parker. And it still felt good.

Dad won in a landslide, but the victory party was subdued. He read the mood of the town and knew that no one felt like there was much to celebrate. Red Dirt was out of the playoffs, and the cuts were too fresh and too deep to start talking about the next football season.

As I wove through the paper plates and gentle chatter at the party, I spotted Ana with a camera in her hands. "You're taking pictures," I said to her.

"I was. I think I've got what I need." She pulled the camera off her neck. "India hired me. I could use the money. Especially since I sent off an application to a photography program a couple of weeks ago, after you printed my photos. The school called yesterday. They were impressed with my pictures. Especially of the campaign." She handed over the camera.

I clicked through the pictures she'd taken. A few showed Dad listening to Mrs. Fisher. He leaned toward her, smiling. One showed a group of men huddled over a plate of cookies. Ana had caught a moment when they were all gesturing at once. "Where did you apply? Chicago? MassArt?"

"University of North Texas."

I froze the smile on my face. "Okay, that's a good start, but you're way better—"

"I'm not applying to an art program."

"What did you apply for?"

"Photojournalism."

I looked up from the pictures. "But Ana, you're so talented. Your pictures belong in museums. They're art."

Ana lifted her head. Her dark eyes were strong but soft, like her grandmother's hands in the photo. "I don't want to create art. I want to tell stories."

"Oh," I said. "So once again, I was just pushing you into something you didn't want to do."

She smiled. "I'll miss you when you go back to DC."

"I'll miss you too," I said. We hugged.

I needed a break. I followed Ana out and watched her disappear around the side where her car was parked. I stayed on the back porch and stared at the sky. Stars poked through the tent of clouds that had hung in the sky all day.

Hunter walked up the steps and joined me. "What are you doing here?" I asked.

"I heard there was a celebration," he said.

I leaned forward against the wooden railing. "Yep, Dad pulled it off."

"Never bet against a Hamilton, right?" Hunter gripped the railing for a second.

I had thought a lot about it during the past few days of silence, and I knew I had two choices. I could refuse to help Hunter, and lose him. It's not like he needed my help to get Ana. Who wouldn't want to date him? Or I could agree, and at least keep my friend. I was about to bury my heart behind my best campaign smile and tell Hunter that I would be happy to help him ask Ana out when a movement at the edge of the porch light caught my eye.

Bo Stone walked toward the house, trailed by Kyle. He frowned at Hunter and me as he passed. Kyle shook his head. "I tried to stop him," he said to us.

Bo stumbled on the last step before righting himself and jerking open the back door. Kyle stayed close behind him.

"We should probably . . . ," I started.

"Yeah," Hunter said. We followed them inside.

"I thought I would deliver the concession in person," Bo said, his slurred words booming through the room. A rustle moved through the people at the back. Kyle tugged at his arm, but Bo jerked away and took a few more steps forward. All eyes shifted to him, which must have been what he was waiting for.

"I hope you're happy, Jeff Hamilton," he called out.

Dad stepped forward and crossed his arms. "If that's your speech, it needs work."

"That seat was mine," Bo said.

I winced. People's looks of surprise hardened into disdain. Mrs. Fisher's eyes stayed soft, but she shook her head.

Kyle slipped beside his father. "So sorry, he's just . . . just . . ." His shoulders hunched as he shuffled from one foot to another.

"He's dehydrated and exhausted from the campaign. It happens all the time. Right, Dad?" I said.

Bo Stone leveled his eyes at me. "I don't need your help," he spat.

Dad pushed between the two of us. "I've had enough of you attacking my daughter. It was low, even during the campaign. Campaign's over. You're not the opponent anymore, just an arrogant bastard who doesn't know when to stop."

"Dad, it's okay." Dad was standing up for me. It felt good, but it increased the animosity throughout the room.

Two men came over to Bo, one taking him by the arm. "Go home, Bo," one said. "You don't belong here."

He shook the man off. "I don't belong here? Me?" He turned to Dad. "What about him? He's the one who doesn't belong here!"

Voices swelled around me as the room rumbled with anger and resentment. I realized how I'd grown to love the gentle hum of friendly banter, the good-natured poking and prodding that goes on in a small town. Now everyone's voices were tight and angry.

Hunter had turned his back on all of them. This was why he stayed out of things. He was staring out the window that looked over the backyard to the shelter. "Kate," he said suddenly. "Does that look like Teddy to you?"

I squinted at a shadow racing toward the house. "Maybe Aunt Celia forgot to lock up the barn." A faint glow swelled in the distance. "Do you see that? What is it?"

"Fire!" Hunter pushed through the back door.

I scanned the room for Celia but didn't see her, so I turned to Dad. He was face-to-face with Bo, who was flanked by the two men who had tried to get him to leave. Kyle stood at his dad's elbow, gently tugging on it. "Listen to your son and go home," Dad said.

"I'll leave when I'm ready to leave," Bo slurred.

"Dad!" I said.

"You're only embarrassing yourself. Always did have trouble knowing when to quit."

"Dad, listen! The shelter. It's on fire!"

Faces turned to me. It took another second of silence for them to digest what I was saying. "I'll call the fire department," Mrs. Fisher said.

Aunt Celia appeared from the back of the house. "Oh, God. The animals," she said. She ran out the door.

Bo and Dad looked at each other. Dad pointed a finger at him. "Was this you?"

"You can't just accuse me of—"

"I was with him the whole way over here," Kyle said.

"The wiring in the trailer has been acting up for weeks, Dad. Hunter has been warning her about it," I said.

Dad's face stayed hard.

Celia came back in the house. Hunter followed close behind. "From here it looks like most of the animals are out, but they are loose in the fields. It's not safe to get close. That place can go up in seconds. We need to coax them toward the house and round them up."

"Do you have a list we could use?" Hunter asked.

Aunt Celia rubbed her face. "In the shelter, but that won't do us a lot of good."

"You could use the website," I said. "It lists all the animals."

She stared at me.

"I'll pull it up," India said, grabbing her laptop.

"The fire department is on their way, but they're held up at an accident on the highway," Mrs. Fisher said. "We need a plan."

"Hunter can get the cows and horses and tie them to the mesquite tree in the front yard," Aunt Celia said.

Kyle stepped forward. "I can help."

Hunter hesitated for a split second. "Follow me."

"Good. The rest of us will get the smaller animals—pigs, chickens, dogs, cats," India said.

"Bring all the animals to the back porch, and Aunt Celia will check them in," I said.

"We need to run as much water as we can in the house in case the fire gets that far. Clear the brush if we can," Dad said, looking around the room. "Half stay here, half go to Bo's house."

Bo eyed him suspiciously. "Save your energy. You may be everyone else's hero, but you're not mine."

Dad's eyes grew hard again. "Don't be an idiot, Bo. Do you want your house to burn down? I sure as hell don't."

Bo's posture stiffened. For a moment, he looked like someone who might let everything burn.

"If it does, they'll probably have a parade in Junction," Dad said.

Leave it to Dad to find the whiff of common ground deep below the rivalry. Bo grunted reluctant agreement.

People scattered to the two houses and the field between. At our house, they filled the bathtubs and sinks with water, sprayed down the vegetation, and cleared what they could in the pasture between the shelter and the house. I could see people moving around the Stone house in the same pattern. Animals wandered in the empty yards. People made trips to the shelter to get animals, opening fences, clearing lean-tos, their faces covered with bandannas and their clothes heavy with the smell of burning wood and ash.

The smoke continued to drift between the houses, and we could see the shelter blazing in the distance. The flames had swallowed the trailer completely by the time the fire truck arrived, and threads of smoke rose from the larger barn and two of the lean-tos. People had done what they could and stood watching the firemen pump water from the tanker truck onto the structures around the burning barn.

The yard looked like a traveling zoo. Cows were strung along the side fence. Chickens darted between the horse and mule legs.

Aunt Celia was watching the fire from the porch. I went up to join her. "Why aren't they putting out the fire?" I asked.

"I told them to let it burn. They'll save what they can."

"But your shelter . . ."

"It's more important that they save the houses."

Hunter joined us. I saw that Aunt Celia had a printout of the website on a clipboard. "Did we get all the animals?" I asked.

Hunter exchanged a look with Aunt Celia. "Almost."

"Who's missing?"

"It's amazing that we got any of them," Aunt Celia said.

"Who is missing?" I repeated.

"That's quite a website," Aunt Celia said. She tapped her pen on the clipboard. I could see her thick check marks by the pictures. "Thank you . . . for the help." She turned and walked down into the scurry of people and animals below before I could reply. I'd had just enough time to glance at the list, and I knew who was missing.

I started walking toward the shelter.

"Where are you going?" Hunter called after me.

I heard his steps speed behind me. "I need to find Tip."

"Tip?" Hunter said. He cleared his throat.

"Please. I saw the list. And you're a terrible liar." I continued walking.

He grabbed my shoulders and looked into my eyes. "Stay here. Let the firemen find Tip. Those buildings could collapse."

I searched my mind for something to convince him, something logical, something persuasive. I couldn't find anything but a deep pain that was choking me. For all the helping I did, I was starting to realize how much harder caring was. "Hunter, I need to do . . . *something*. I did not stick my hands inside a cow and pull barbed wire out of Tip's leg for her to die on me now. She might be the one good thing I've done around here."

Hunter hesitated, looking over my shoulder at the shelter. "Fine, but if the firemen tell us to go back, we're going back."

We worked our way across the back acreage. By the time we reached the western boundary, the heels of my shoes were caked in mud, and my dress was dusted in ash and soot. All I could think about was finding Tip.

When we got within fifty yards of the trailer, a fireman approached us, blocking our way. "You need to head back to the house."

"We're looking for a calf."

He crossed his arms and widened his stance. "We haven't come across any animals."

"Is the fire out?" Hunter asked.

The fireman nodded. "As far as we can tell, but it's not safe. The wind could have planted sparks in some of the wood. Until we get everything sprayed down, the whole place is just a tinder-box. You can't go anywhere near it."

The thought of Tip in a tinderbox sent another wave of tears to my eyes. I scanned the shelter. Aunt Celia kept the calves in the barn on the southwest corner. Refusals are tricky to undo. Sometimes it's not worth trying. "Okay, we'll head back."

Hunter eyed me like I'd suddenly sprouted a second head.

I started walking back toward the house. Hunter followed me. "I thought I would have to fight you on this," he said.

"Nope."

I veered into the shadows, closer to the shelter, but out of the line of sight of the firemen. "I was sure you'd have some elaborate scheme to talk the firemen into letting you poke your nose into every deathtrap on this place."

I stopped. The shelter I wanted was to my left. I listened, and I thought I heard a quiet whining. The same whining I'd heard the night I found Tip wrapped in barbed wire. "I'm not trying to talk anyone into anything," I said.

"Refreshing," Hunter said.

I took off sprinting. Hunter called after me, but I ran to the barn and stepped inside. I passed the stall in the corner, then thought I heard a sound and went back. Tip cowered on her side, her eyes wide and filled with fear.

"I'm going to get you out of here," I said. But when I went to lift her, I realized her back leg was wedged under a fallen beam. She let out a long whine when I tried to free it.

Hunter's boots pounded through the barn floor. "Hunter! I found her!" I called out.

He pushed me aside and squatted down by Tip. "This is your worst plan yet." The wind picked up and the roof groaned above us.

"It was never really a plan. No time to argue."

Tip kicked at Hunter. "If we could dig under the beam, she might be able to move her leg enough to slide it out." He looked at me. "Or the roof might collapse." Hunter moved some of the dirt, but when he brushed against Tip's trapped hoof, she whined and kicked.

"If she keeps kicking, she's going to bring the place down on our heads," I said.

The air was filled with the smell of stale smoke, but a thread of fresh burning tickled inside my nose. I put a hand on the panel of wood beside me. They hadn't soaked this barn yet.

"We need to get out of here," Hunter said.

"Not yet. Not without Tip."

He rose. "You're going to have to do it."

"Me?" I took a step back. "You're the animal expert."

Hunter took both my shoulders and steered me in front of him. "Tip trusts you. You're the only one she'll let touch her right now."

I knelt down and looked into Tip's eyes. She raised her head. I took a breath and dug my fingers into the dirt, moving as much as I could. Tip whined a couple of times but lay still. When I had scooped a little more dirt out, the beam shifted, digging deeper into her leg. Tip let out a long whine.

"I'm hurting her more," I said, tears in my eyes.

"You can do this. But you have to hurry." He looked up. "This wood will catch fast."

I wiped the tears out of my eyes and looked at Tip's leg. If I dug a little in front, I could slide it out from under the beam.

"I think I see smoke. Start the water," a fireman called from the door. More boots moved in.

"Wait!" Hunter called. "We've got a calf in here."

"Someone in there?" A fireman stomped around the corner. "I told you to get out of here!" He grabbed Hunter's arm. Hunter stood between the fireman and me.

"I've almost got her," I said.

When I had made a deep enough hole, Tip slid forward on her belly and tried to get up. Her hoof was still stuck. "You smell that?

There's fresh burning in here! This whole place could collapse!" the fireman said.

"Kate, we have to go," Hunter said, putting his hand on my back.

I reached behind Tip, closed my eyes, and yanked on her leg. Tip yelped, then stumbled forward into me. I pulled her up just as the fireman wrapped his gloved hand around my arm, dragging me toward the door. Hunter shoved me the last few steps, the fireman behind us. As I crossed the threshold with Tip in my arms, a long groan began, followed by a crack. Dust flew into my eyes as we ran. After a few more seconds of running, I felt Hunter stop. I looked over my shoulder. The building's walls and ceiling had crumbled.

I stood, staring, Tip pressed tightly against me. Hunter put his arm around me and pulled me against his chest. His head bowed over mine. "Don't ever do anything like that again. Promise?" he said, his breath in my ear.

I nodded. He let me go, and we walked back toward the house in silence, Tip hobbling beside me, whining every few steps. I could feel her breathing against my leg.

When we were fifty feet from the house, Hunter stopped and ran a hand over her leg. She jerked it away the first time, but after a few tries, she held still. "I'm going to have to wrap this leg, but Tip will be fine." His tone had cooled.

There was only one thing I could do to make us even again. There was no win-win. I swallowed. "Hunter, you were going to ask me to help you with something earlier, and I said I wouldn't. I'm sorry. I'll help you with whatever you need."

Hunter stared at me.

"We're still friends, right?" I asked.

He looked down at his boots. "That's the thing. I don't want to be friends."

"Don't say that. I know I'm hard to be friends with, but—"

"Kate, I want to be more than your friend."

I shook my head. "But that's impossible. I . . . I've done nothing but screw up."

"You keep things entertaining." The corners of his eyes crinkled.

"Is that spin?"

His eyes slipped to that focused intensity. "It's not spin." He took a step closer. I could feel the warmth of him. "Ever since I had to move you out of the way to get those twins born, and you were sitting there with your arm up the cow's—"

I put my hand over his mouth. "Don't remind me."

He gently moved my hand away. "Kate, you are the most wonderfully stubborn, amazingly caring person I have ever met." He held my face and brushed his thumbs against my cheeks. I could smell the earth and wood scent that hung around him. It was so real. He leaned closer and brushed his lips at the corner of mine, then pulled back to study me. I smiled and tipped my head toward him, and we kissed, long, slow. It rumbled deep inside of me.

Tip stirred next to us. I leaned back just enough so I could see his face. "I . . . I thought you liked Ana."

He raised an eyebrow. "You might want to seriously reconsider your future as a matchmaker."

"I think I'll retire."

Hunter pulled me close and kissed me again.

* * *

Eventually, we took Tip to Aunt Celia. Hunter went to get supplies to bandage up her leg while Dad buffered the fireman's wrath with sympathetic nods and Mrs. Fisher's banana bread.

Some of Dad's friends had wrapped plastic fencing around stakes they'd hammered into the dirt. Kyle helped herd the pigs into the makeshift pens. After the animals were settled, Aunt Celia and Hunter visited the shelter to survey the damage. Inside the house, a party mood returned, laughter echoing from the corners. Mrs. Fisher found the old yearbooks I'd borrowed and gathered a group at the kitchen table to smile over them, Bo Stone trapped in the center. Some of the women even convinced Mom to try a bite of seven-layer dip. I could feel that unity that Dad would have sacrificed everything to protect.

"So what are you doing next?" I asked India.

"Don't know. There are phone calls to make and thank-yous to write, but it's all pretty much wrapped up."

"No, I mean long-term."

India grinned. "Your dad offered me a spot on his staff."

"That's great!" I said.

She nodded toward the scene. "Feels good, doesn't it?"

"Winning?" I shrugged.

"Being part of something."

"It does." I looked across the clusters of people. "Do you know where Dad is?"

I found him on the porch talking to Mom. I walked up and, without any maneuvering, said the one thing I realized I'd wanted to say for a long time. "We should stay here."

Dad looked at Mom. He tipped his chin to the right.

"Before you say no, hear me out. How are you going to know what the district needs for the Farm Bill, or anything for that matter, if you only spend a dozen weeks here a year, and most of those campaigning?"

"Kate—" Mom said.

"We just started talking to people. And I hate to bring this up at your victory party, but this win was mostly a fluke. I'm not going to be around to slam the quarterback's hand in a door in two years."

"Kate, I know—" Dad tried.

"You need to establish yourself here. Sure, you grew up here, but all the more reason . . ."

Dad put his hands on my shoulders. "Listen. We know. You're right."

The rest of the speech got trapped in my throat behind my surprise. "So we're staying?" I asked.

"Your mother and I want to. We were just going to ask you."

"Oh." Mom and Dad still seemed to be waiting. "You were going to ask me?"

Dad nodded.

I smiled. A real smile. "I think we should stay."

Dad put his arm over my shoulder in a classic Hamilton campaign move meant to show support and approval. But this time, it actually felt like support and approval. "It was a good speech."

"I've been trained by the best," I said.

chapter thirty-nine

Dad and I sat in our car, watching a man lock a glass door. The sky was clear, with only a few breaths of clouds. "We'll come back Monday," I said.

"I think we can talk him into it," Dad said.

"It isn't necessary. Let's just come back on Monday like regular people."

"Look, I didn't spend the last two weeks walking you through every nuance of the driver's ed book to back down now. We are getting this license."

"What do we say?"

"I could pull out the 'service to the community' line."

I shook my head. "I could try a filibuster until he caves."

"That's going to be tricky, since he's technically free to leave."

The man straightened a sign on the door, checked the handle to make sure it was locked, and wiped the glass with his shirtsleeve.

"Did you see that?" Dad asked.

I nodded. "Looks like he takes a lot of pride in his job." I hopped out of the car. "We can work with that."

"Absolutely," Dad said, following me.

As we approached, I gestured to the door and said loudly, "I told you the DMV would be closed."

Dad threw up his hands. "Well, you were right." He stuck his hand out to the man, who shook it, narrowing his eyes.

"Aren't you that quarterback?" he said. "The one who ran for office?"

Dad's smile brightened. "Congressman Jeff Hamilton. Nice to meet you. I didn't catch your name."

"Buddy," the man said. "We'll be open on Monday at eight."

I looked at Dad. "We'll just go to Junction," I said. "They're open on Saturday. One DMV is just the same as any other."

"I don't know." Dad rubbed his chin. "I bet Buddy's given more driver's tests than the average man."

Buddy stuck out his chest. "Been testing people for almost thirty years."

"See?" Dad said to me. "He has experience, and experience is valuable." He turned to Buddy. "Now, I know you're going home, but do you think you could squeeze in one last test?"

The man ran his hand through a gray shock of hair. "I remember that bootleg pass you threw in the fourth quarter of the state championship."

I started to roll my eyes, but Dad shot me a look. "Then you'll understand why I don't want my daughter issued a license in Junction. I want her to get it right here in Red Dirt."

"Then come back Monday at eight," Buddy said.

"I'll be back in DC," Dad said.

"Mom can take me," I said.

"And I miss my only child's driver's test?" He turned to Buddy. "Can't you help me out?"

Buddy sucked in a breath. "I hope you don't drive as fast as you talk. I'll get my clipboard." He unlocked the door and disappeared inside.

I held my hand out for the keys.

Dad frowned. "For the record, this license is a terrible idea. Do you know the kind of people on the roads these days?"

"Dad. We agreed."

"You and your mother ganged up on me. I had no choice."

"It's just a driver's license."

"You have the Hamilton name to think of. If people think Jeff Hamilton can't take care of his own daughter—"

"Let's get the license and go. I have liquor stores to rob."

He groaned and dropped the keys in my palm as Buddy reappeared. "Fine, go take your test."

I waved and got into the driver's seat. Thirty minutes and a few well-placed compliments later, I was a licensed driver in the state of Texas.

When we got home, it took just a little more pleading to get Dad to loan me the car for the night. He handed over the keys and I drove to the shelter.

Hunter was carrying a plank of wood when I got there. "How does the new barn look?" I asked.

"Bo sent over some surplus boards, so we should be able to finish it."

"Do you want a ride? I'm a licensed driver now."

Hunter grinned. "Sure." He put the plank down by a fence and got into the car, his long legs stretched beside me. "Where are we going?"

"I have the perfect place." I backed out and drove toward the streaks of purple-bellied clouds brushing the horizon. "So, what do you do around here when football season ends?"

Hunter rolled down the window and leaned his elbow out. "Plan for the next season. What do you do when an election is over?"

I shrugged. "We start planning the next one."

Hunter fixed me with one of his intense stares. "So what's *your* plan?"

"Honestly, I don't have a lot of plans."

Sitting in his gaze felt like sitting in the warm rays of the sun. "Me either."

When I pulled up to the water tower, Hunter raised an eyebrow. "I'm not the quarterback anymore. We could get in trouble."

"You scared?" I drove under the ladder, parked the car, and climbed on the hood.

Hunter laughed. "Terrified, but I can't let you show me up."

"I already drive better than you. I'm also kind of a local hero." I scrambled up the ladder.

"Are you?" Hunter said.

"I rescued a whole shelter of animals. People love animals."

"That's something," he called from from a few rungs below.

"Three generations of my family have represented this district."

"Impressive."

"So you're pretty much looking at the next congresswoman for Red Dirt," I said as I reached the top.

"I'll keep that in mind."

I sat down. Hunter sat next to me and put his arm over my shoulder. "When does Tasha get here?"

"In a couple of hours. She could have been here yesterday, but she was helping Robert with the fund-raiser for the shelter."

"How did it go?"

"Great! It gave Robert enough hours to get the third recommendation. Tasha went with the *Green Acres* theme. She got to wear the cowboy boots I sent her, and Robert got a vegan menu. Win-win." I shook my head. "The two of them together—it should never work."

Hunter tilted his head toward mine. "Wouldn't you say the same about us?"

"Exactly. Look at the pattern so far. We've spent most of our time fighting."

The darkness had deepened and stars poked through the sky. I could see Hunter's profile, the angle of his chin, the curve of his lips. He slipped his arm off my shoulder and laced his fingers through mine. "I'm not saying we're perfect, but I think we have potential."

"It could get complicated. You hate complicated."

"It could get amazing. And I think I would like that," Hunter said.

I rested my head against his chest, letting the thud of his heartbeat roll through me, and watched the last sliver of golden light fade into black.

acknowledgments

Writing is not simple or effortless for me. I am fortunate to have many extraordinary people who make it possible.

I work with the best people in publishing. Thank you, Cheryl Klein. You are a brilliant editor! You not only make my stories better, you make me a better writer and storyteller through your encouragement, patience, insights, and advice. You have my admiration, my respect, and my trust. I am also grateful to my agent, Rosemary Stimola. I think we both know that I would be lost in this industry without you. You smooth a path through publishing for me and my stories.

Thank you to Katie Cohen and Ana Rudnicki. You both help me see the potential in my worst writing. You, my precious friends, bring out the best, not only in my writing, but also in me. And to my dear friend and mentor Suzanne Frank: I don't know what you have taught me more about—writing or life. Thank you for all your help with both.

It has been such a gift to connect with fellow authors who I admire. I'm especially thankful for Victoria Scott—I love our writing sessions, especially the ones where we don't get any writing done.

I'm always inspired by the student and adult writers I work with at the Writers Path at SMU and Highland Park ISD. You remind me how much I have to learn.

I owe the most to my family. To my mom and dad—thank you for your unwavering faith in me and steadfast love. It helps me believe in myself. To my sister, Sarah—you have the uncanny ability to say exactly what I need to hear. Having a sister like you is one of life's greatest gifts. Finally, I owe a big thank-you to the people who put up with me every day. Jeb—thank you for your love, support, and patience (and answering a million questions about football). Jack, thank you for your enthusiasm. And Lily, thank you for your joy.

about the author

Kay Honeyman's roots in football and Texas run deep: Her grand-father coached high school and college teams in the sport, while Kay was born in Fort Worth, attended Baylor University in Waco, and now lives in Dallas with her husband and two children. Her first novel, *The Fire Horse Girl*, received a starred review from *Booklist* and was nominated for three state awards. Please visit Kay on the web at www.kayhoneyman.com and on Twitter at @kayhoneyman.

This book was edited by Cheryl Klein and designed by Yaffa Jaskoll. The production was supervised by Elizabeth Krych and Rebekah Wallin. The text was set in Perpetua, with display type set in Athletico. This book was printed and bound by R. R. Donnelley in Crawfordsville, Indiana. The manufacturing was supervised by Angelique Browne.